Salvador began his journey with all good intentions. He is forced to leave his homeland in Portugal and find a life for his family. This book will take you through many emotions. When Salvador's daughter is then dragged into a pool of pain. Her beautiful glowing light inside burns out like a candle in the wind.

Salvador's Daughter

Artist: Chad Randol

Melissa Seeback

authorHOUSE®

AuthorHouse™
1663 Liberty Drive
Bloomington, IN 47403
www.authorhouse.com
Phone: 1-800-839-8640

Certain characters in this work are historical figures, and certain
events portrayed did take place. However, this is a work of fiction.
All of the other characters, names, and events as well as all places,
incidents, organizations, and dialogue in this novel are either the
products of the author's imagination or are used fictitiously.

Published by AuthorHouse 11/19/2013

ISBN: 978-1-4918-2090-2 (sc)
ISBN: 978-1-4918-2087-2 (hc)
ISBN: 978-1-4918-2086-5 (e)

Library of Congress Control Number: 2013917278

I would like to dedicate this book to my grandfather and grandmother William and Mable Oros. With much love. May you rest in peace together forever. R.I.P. Wiliam Oros February 2007 R.I.P. Mable Oros August 2007

Eu vou sempre me lembrar de você para a sua grande força. Eu vou chegar para as borboletas em sua memória para sempre.*

Estou grato também ao meu pai, Tom Antoni e a mãe Shirley Randol/Antoni para todos o seu apoio através da escrita e publicação deste livro. Eu te amo tanto tanto. Graças também ao meu marido, Jeff adorando Seeback para todo o seu amor e paciência através da criação deste livro.**

---

* Translation: I will always remember you for your great strength. I will reach for the butterflies in your memory forever.

** Translation: I am also grateful to my father, Tom Antoni and mother Shirley Randol/Antoni for all your support through the writing and publication of this book. I love you both so much. Thanks also to my adoring husband, Jeff Seeback for all his love and patience through the creation of this book.

Table of Contents

Chapter 1

This story began in the early 1900's. Salvador Cardoza was a man who lived in Portugal in the Azores on one of the islands with his family. The Islands name was Terceira. His wife, Jessica Amelia Cardoza and their two young daughters where a very happy family. This family spoke the native Portuguese language, English and some Spanish. Many of the neighbors spoke Spanish as well. Portuguese was a sweetly romantic language. They had a very large family farm that had been passed down through many generations. The farm consisted of miles and miles of corn. Salvador worked very hard at the farm with the hired hands. He was generally out of bed at sunrise, working long hours at the farm and tending to the fields. He was a good looking, tall, slender and medium built man. He had very dark, thick, brown, wavy hair which was always very well groomed. His large, dark brown, almond shaped eyes were his best feature. He was a friendly man and cared for his family. The wife spent all her time at home with the children. She was a young twenty three year old with beautiful long, thick, dark brown hair. Her thick hair draped over her shoulders and ran all the way past the middle of her back. Her hair was always in a very long single french braid. She had a large red flower tucked into her hair, just over her right ear. She did that just for Salvador. She had large, dark brown eyes and full red lips. She was a slender woman and very petite. Her height was only about five feet. She had a glowing dark beige complexion and long dark black eyelashes. Hers was a natural beauty. The women of Portugal wore long, shapely, off the shoulder dresses in layers of very thin, bright fabrics. This enabled them to stay cool because Portugal got so humid. They always used beautiful beads in that country. Jessica adored her beads. She draped several layers of color in beaded necklaces around her neck.

At the crack of dawn, Jessica arose from her bed. After getting dressed, she fixed her beautiful hair, washed her face and headed for the kitchen. She would always take one last glance at herself in the mirror. She often wondered if Salvador noticed the pretty flower she placed in her hair just for him. Jessica loved her life. It was full with love and laughter. In the early mornings she approached her quiet, empty kitchen. Her daughters were already outside picking some fresh vegetables from the garden. They were also helping their father with any chores he had for them. Jessica was ready to begin her morning duties. Her kitchen was very old fashioned, set up in all red bricks and colorful stones around the cooking pot. She always made all of their meals fresh. She made tortillas daily, as that was the tradition in Portugal to have them with every meal.

They also had a lot of bacalhau, which is dry cod. She enjoyed preparing cultural meals for her family. Another delicacy called feijoada, a stew of beans with various types of meat. Jessica liked using beef, linguica and pork in that dish. She also had a maid named Theresa. She always assisted her in the kitchen and with the children's schooling. Everything was perfect as she started putting together all of her ingredients. She was very meticulous, wanting everything to be just right for her family. She decided to prepare morning crapes today, since this was a special day for Jessica Amelia and Salvador. They became husband and wife when she turned fifteen. They had been together for eight years. She was still very much in love with Salvador. Everything she did, was done with love. As she was finishing up her crapes, she called out for the girls to come in and help her set up the table. She opened the screen door and yelled out, "Louisa! Maria time to come in menina's (girls)!" As the girls were approaching, you could see the joy in Jessica's eyes. Her daughters were very pretty. Of course both of them inherited the beautiful long, dark brown hair. They had eyes as dark as Salvador's. Maria, at seven, was the oldest and Louisa was five. Maria was very good at watching over her sister. As the girls came in, they brought baskets with them. They showed Jessica their grand collection of chicken eggs and corn. Jessica patted Louisa on her head and said to her, "what a hard working set of young ladies I have here." Louisa smiled at her Mama, "Agradecimento Mãe (Thank you Mother)." The girls knew exactly what their morning tasks were. They immediately went for the dishes and cloths they used for napkins. Maria handed the cloths over to Louisa and showed her repeatedly how to fold them. Louisa had a very short attention span. It was quite difficult at times when she was trying to teach Louisa the tasks. Jessica stated to Maria, "It's a good thing you are so patient with your sister. Some day she will do better." Jessica turns to Louisa, "Muito bom trabalho Louisa (Very good job Louisa)."

Of course Louisa immediately noticed the grand crapes their Mama had prepared today. "Oh Mama! Yum! Yum! Is it a birthday today?" "No menina, it is your Mama and Pappa's celebration of togetherness." The girls were delighted for their parents. Maria had an idea. She quickly finished setting up the table, then called her little sister into the other room. "Louisa, we should do something special for Mama and Pappa." The girls sometimes referred to their parents as Mama and Pappa, or (Mae and Pai). Louisa became very excited. She always loved surprises, "What should we do?" Maria pondered for a moment. "I have an idea, c'mon Louisa, come outside." The girls ran out through the screen door. Jessica then yells to the girls while waving her hands in frustration, "Louisa, Maria where are you going? It's time for breakfast." Maria yells back, "I know Mama, we will be right back. I promise." Jessica shakes her head, but decides to continue working on the crape's. She pulls out the special china and starts placing each crape in each beautiful plate. She goes over to the wine selection in her cabinet, picking the perfect white wine for the special meal. It wasn't uncommon for families to have wine at every meal in this country. So while Jessica was finishing up her beautiful table display, Louisa and Maria were heading to a barn across from the house. Louisa was anxious to see what Maria's plan was. As they entered into the large barn, they ran through the many chickens that wandered in. Maria disregarded them as she ran through and both girls started laughing as the chickens balked at them. "I hid it over here, under the hay." Louisa's eyes grew bigger as she watched Maria pull out this fancy little basket. "Where did you get that Maria?" She grinned as she was pulling all the hay off and proudly displaying this hand crafted basket. It was so pretty and Louisa was very pleased with how nicely it was made, "I made it", Maria states proudly. "I just used the hay and started working with each strand individually. I was saving this basket for a very special occasion and this is pretty special to them. They can use this and Mama can make them a special picnic lunch, then they can go spend time alone together. They will always have this special basket to remember this day by." "I love it Maria", Louisa said with so much excitement, "they will love it too. Can it be from me also sissy?" "Of course, Louisa of course, let's go get some berries and put them in the basket."

Meanwhile Jessica was getting anxious to get things started. She stepped out on to their patio and hollered out for Salvador and the girls to return to the kitchen. Eventually Salvador came strolling towards the patio and he could smell the aromas of Jessica's great meal. The girls came running in and ran passed Salvador giggling with excitement. Everyone found there place at the table. Maria quickly stuffed the basket under the table so they wouldn't see. Jessica glanced over and saw there was something in Maria's hands. "What mischief are you girls up to now?" She pierced her eyes at her, with a small grin. Jessica knew her girls quite well and she could tell they were hiding something. "Well Mama me and Louisa want to give you and Pappa something special for your special day today." Salvador chuckled, "now, now, you girls didn't have to do that." Although Salvador did love surprises, just as much as the girls did. He clapped his hands together and looks over at Maria, "you got something cooked up for us over there little menina?" "Yes I do Pappa and Louisa does too." Louisa stood up in her chair smiling and proud to be a part of the surprise. So Maria reaches down under the table and pulls out the beautiful basket she made. Louisa stood up again proudly announcing, "I picked all the blueberries Pappa and a flower too." Jessica was smiling so proudly, "you girls are so maravilhoso (wonderful)." Pappa reaches over as Maria hands the basket to him. Salvador smiled and observed closely at all the berries in the basket. There was one flower in the middle of all the berries. It was a sunflower, but it looked so fitting with the basket and the berries. "What a handsome display and what a nice looking basket you have here. Did you make this all yourself little Maria?" She arched her back up in pride smiling wide at her Pappa, "yes Pappa." "Wow I'm so grateful to have such loving young ladies", exclaimed Salvador. "Thank you menina's, it's the best gift ever." The girls got out of their chairs and ran over to their Pappa and Mama hugging them. "Now let's start this great feast Mama has put together for us." Jessica admired her husband so much, he was such a gentle loving man. She felt so delighted and blessed with her family.

Jessica had a surprise for Salvador as well. A few months ago she was cleaning up and glanced over at her old chest of memories. Her Mother and Father had given this to her. She decided to take another glance at her contents inside. While she was rummaging through them she discovered a shirt that had belonged to her Father, with these very special buttons that her Mother had sewn on the shirt for him. These buttons were something Jessica always remembered. While her mother was sewing, she sang a beautiful song. She had the voice of angels. It was always so soothing to listen to her. Jessica was very fond of both her parents. They struggled for many years, but somehow always managed to make Jessica feel wealthy with love. These buttons were metal buttons, with an incised iridescent design. The color in them was so different. They were earth green and brown, with what looked like small leaves inside the buttons. She remembers her Mother having her hold them as she would string each one individually and very carefully so that they would stay strong and never break. She would rub one of the buttons and loved the way they felt on her fingers. Her Mother always said, "these are to represent the simple ways of life. These may look like simple buttons, but they are very special. I am placing each one with all my love for your father. We may be poor, but we are rich with love. Never forget that little miss Jessica Amelia." Jessica decided that she wanted to share these special buttons with Salvador. The shirt was old and worn, so she decided to do as her mother once did and put together a nice shirt. Sewing the very same buttons for him onto his shirt. She meticulously put together a bergundy fabric that would be perfect for Salvador and sewed each button in its place. It gave her peace thinking about her parents with such fondness while doing this. The shirt looked so well done and Jessica was very proud to share something so special with her husband.

Just as Salvador was ready to dig in to this fabulous breakfast, Jessica comes over to him. "I also have something for you." She hands a neatly folded burgundy shirt to Salvador. "I made this with my mothers buttons, off a very special shirt that once belonged to my father. I hope you like it Salvador." Salvador put his utensils down and smiles. He reaches over taking the shirt from her. He knew how much Jessica's parents meant to her. So he was extremely honored that she would share something so personal. "Jessica that was so thoughtful of you", he exclaimed. Jessica grinned as if a slight embarrassment and shyness came over her. "Those buttons were the same buttons my mother sewed on my fathers shirt for him." He unfolded the shirt and held it up in front of him. He looked closely at the buttons as to see how very special they were. He rubbed his fingers over one of the buttons the same way Jessica had once done. He could feel the ridges and smooth surfaces of each one. "Indeed Jessica, these are quite special and the shirt will fit me perfectly." Thank you so much for making this for me and sharing something so important to you." Salvador got up from his chair and went over to Jessica hugging her closely. He lingered for a moment in this hug, as to ensure her how much he treasured her. Jessica pulled away to gather herself, as she felt the need to cry. She missed her parents, as they had passed away a few years back. She gathered herself together and clapped her hands, "ok now time to have this great breakfast I prepared. The food is getting cold." Salvador knew she was missing her parents, so he let her go to the other room. He understood she needed some time to herself. She walked out of the room and Salvador sat back down and started to serve the girls their plates. "Ok Meninas, lets try this great meal." He gently smiled at both of the girls as they were oblivious to the moment and busy eyeing all the great food. After breakfast was finished, Salvador headed to his room to put on his new shirt. He was very careful to place each button securely. As he headed back out, he modeled his perfectly fitting shirt to Jessica. She was pleased at how well it fit him and how wonderfully the burgundy brought out his dark brown eyes. He headed back out to work for the day, as the girls helped Jessica clean up the kitchen.

Salvador was hiding something from Jessica. Something that for a man is so devastating his pride was served quite a beating. You see, unfortunately the farm was losing money. His crops were suffering great losses. There have not been good levels of rain in quite some time. Salvador already had to let go many of his helpers. He hasn't shared these stresses with Jessica. He doesn't want to burden her with it. However it was getting very bad for their farm. He continues to get up every morning at the crack of dawn to work the fields, hoping things will eventually turn around. In the evenings when Salvador would come home, the family would all sit out on the porch and listen to Salvador play his accordion. Something his father taught him since he was a boy. They were a close family with many friends. Many of the helpers families would join them. One particular evening while Salvador was playing, Jessica watched her husband closely. She noticed something was wrong. Later that evening after she tucked the girls in to bed, she decided to talk to Salvador. She really wanted to make sure he was ok. As she approached the bedroom, the door was slightly open and she peaked in at him. He was standing at the mirror just looking in. There was only one expression on his face and that was sadness. Jessica walks into the room. Salvador became startled by her entrance. He immediately turns to look her way and smiles. "Dinner was grande my beautiful wife." He pinches his fingers together kissing them and waves towards Jessica with a very chef expression. He was always so good at staying positive. Jessica knew him better then anyone. She knew he was carrying a burden. "Salvador talk to me. I know something is weighing heavy on you. You must tell me." He looks down to the ground, suddenly his bright smile and glowing eyes start to fade. He falls down to the ground to his knees. "Oh Jessica, I'm afraid our farm is fading away, meu amor (my love). This drought is causing our crops to die. We don't have enough supplies for the animals. I have tried to keep it going the best I can, but I am afraid we are going to have to start discussing a move." Jessica could see how distraught he was. He clenches his hands, then rubs them back and forth on his legs as he was sweating from so much distress. A cousin of mine from California offered us an opportunity with a dairy farm. They will provide us shelter and food. I can work and save. I'm so sorry Jessica Amelia. I have tried, but so many of us here with crops are facing this." Jessica could see his pain in his eyes. Losing her home and their friends, it saddened her too. "My husband, I know, don't you think I see? I have watched the other crops of our friends. I have seen the struggles you have been going through. We will get through this together." Jessica reaches over to his shoulder and rubs him so lovingly. She kneels down to where he is and holds him close to her. Salvador clasps his hands around her face, pointing her towards him and comes closer with his lips to hers. With all the stress they have been distant, with so much on Salvador's mind. They have always been very passionate with each other. This was a time they needed to be close more then ever. Salvador picks her up in his arms and carries her to their bed. "You are so beautiful Jessica Amelia, eu te amo muito (I love you so much)." That evening they spent together making love and holding each other close.

The next morning, Louisa and Maria got up at the crack of dawn, however something was different that morning. Their pappa was not outside yet. Maria goes back into the house to find him. She goes to Pappa's bedroom and knocks on the door. "Yes Maria, I'm coming, I will be out shortly." Salvador kisses Jessica on the forehead while crawling out of his bed. He quickly puts his clothes on, heading out of the bedroom door as quietly as possible. He wants Jessica Amelia to get her rest. He looks back at her once more admiring her beauty. Such a perfect complexion she has, he thought to himself. Her hair is draped over the pillow as he could see her wincing her eyes while dreaming. He smiles once more before leaving their room. Salvador walks out of the house through the screen door and can see the girls sitting on the patio waiting. "So girls, are we ready for another day of work?" Maria excitedly jumps up, "yes Pappa", they head out towards the farm together. Then Salvador has an idea as they walk towards the barn, "Maria would you and Louisa like to take a break today and play with your pet pig, Pepper?" Maria smiled with excitement, "Pappa that would be so great, you don't mind with so much work to be done?" Salvador chuckles, "no I don't mind Maria. You girls go have a restful day today." Louisa perks up with a smile on her face, "Yay! Pappa Yay!" One of the local farmers gave this baby pig to them. The Mama rolled over the baby, so the baby pig had a bad leg. The farmer had no use for it, and gave it to the girls as a pet. They called him Pepper, since he had little black and white spots. The girls thought he looked like a combination of salt and pepper.

As time went on the farm was suffering great losses. The worse things became, the more of the helpers Salvador had to send home. He finally came to the conclusion that he will have to give up his farm. It put a very big strain on Salvador. He was becoming more and more depressed as the days continued. He decided to reveal to Jessica that the time has come. They will have to leave the farm. Jessica was such a strong woman. She always made Salvador feel good about himself, no matter how bad things seemed. She always believed that as long as the family was together, they would all be ok in the end. As time went on they started to sell off many of their belongings, attempting to make ends meet. Eventually they had to sell off the farm. The Government was offering very small settlements of money to the farmers. This was to enable them to leave Portugal with at least enough money to relocate and settle elsewhere. Salvador decided that they needed to move to California. Jessica was so supportive and maintained a positive attitude. However Salvador was extremely saddened about their situation. He had so many fears as to what their future holds for them. This farm has been in his family for many generations. Leaving his home devastated him.

Chapter 2

The girls were able to maintain one box each between them of their very own personal items and a few clothes. They would be traveling by boat and some neighbor friends are taking them to the dock. Salvador made sure to pack his one most personal item, which was his accordion. Jessica kept only one tea cup and dish. She had the entire set given to her by her mother, unfortunately she couldn't keep the entire set. This porcelain set was so beautiful. They had pink roses with green leaves, hand painted in golden trim.

You could sense the sadness amongst this family. They sat on the porch waiting for the neighbor friends to come pick them up and take them to the boat dock. The girls started sobbing as if suddenly they just realized their entire life was over as they once knew it. Salvador reached over to the girls and wrapped his arms around both of them. "Meninas", he said, "I beg of you please don't be sad you make your pappa sad." Maria looking down to the ground said to her pappa, "why do we have to leave pappa? I don't want to leave." Salvador reached his hand over to Maria's chin and pulled her face upward towards him, "sometimes menina, we have to do things we don't want to do, but it's simply for the best. Do you understand Maria?" Maria hesitantly nods her head. It was early morning as they waited looking out into the sky. Salvador held his girls on each arm knelt down on one knee. He would just stare out into the morning sun as he held back his tears. Everyone knew he was devastated. Jessica sat on the porch and just watched them in front of her. Somewhere along the way through all of this she lost herself. She seemed strong, but deep inside she was also sobbing. She was always taught as a young woman to always be strong no matter what comes her way. She glanced down at the very chair she was sitting in. This chair was so special to her. Her father made the chair for her when she first got married. It was a wooden rocking chair. He even carved his initials on the bottom of it. She glided her hand across the arm of the chair, feeling every intricate design her father carved into it. Jessica was trying to hold on to the memories before they had to go.

Suddenly they all heard the horses strutting down the driveway. It was almost as if this was the scariest sound they ever heard. They all jumped, startled by the sound. That moment shook them all to the realization, that the time has come for them to leave. This is really happening. They are truly leaving their home for good. The neighbor friends rode up and jumped out of the wagon, ready to help Salvador's family place their items in. Not much was said as they put everything in and climbed onto the bench. It was a long quiet ride, as the girls took one last look back as they rode away. Louisa saw their pet pig Pepper running towards the wagon, she screams out, "Pappa, pappa what will happen to Pepper?" Louisa starts to cry while reaching out to the pig almost falling right out of the wagon. Salvador quickly grabs her waist stopping her from the fall. Salvador couldn't hold back anymore, as he starts to sob as well. He places Louisa in his lap, while holding her close. They cry together, as he tucks her head into his chest. Jessica quietly wipes her tears from her face, trying her best to remain strong.

There was nothing anyone could say to make the situation feel better for any of them. It was a very long and quiet ride. The dock was about an hour from their farm home. Once they reached the boat docks this would be yet another very long ride, but much longer then the wagon. Everyone was a little nervous about the boat ride. None of them had ever traveled in any way, their entire life was at the farm. Salvador was also reminded by his friend how important it was that they all stuck close together through this journey. They pulled up to the dock and made there way to the man who was taking the money for this trip. This would enable them a place on the boat. This man standing there tells them, "I have a cart to haul your things to the boat, just load it up." He had handed Salvador his document to enter the boat and directed them on the way to the dock. Jessica hugs her friends goodbye and grabs both the girls hands ready to follow Salvador's lead. The girls were shaking, they were so nervous. They all walked slowly following Salvador as he led them up. Maria being the older sister and very protective of Louisa she felt the need to tell her, "Louisa I will take care of the both of us. We will stick close together, ok Louisa?" Both the girls were frazzled by the amount of people around them, but Maria did her best to hide her fears. They were watching how all the travelers were in such a hurry. Everyone going in different directions with the same scared and confused look in their eyes. It seemed they all were overcome with fear of what their futures will hold. Suddenly they heard a loud horn and a man standing outside shouted in a loud voice, "boats leaving soon!" All the remaining people seemed to be rushing even more so. You could hear a sudden whirl through the water below. What the girls didn't seem to realize is all those people had once had vineyard farms and fields just they themselves had lost. The drought was so devastating for the country that many people had to leave their homes, to go the United States.

They were led down below the ship in a large area full of cots. Everyone was quietly scattering through, trying to find a cot. It was very crowded. Salvador became nervous instantly and grabbed his wife and girls closer to him. The boat they were traveling in wasn't a fancy large boat as you might have imagined. This was a small boat with a lower deck. It was a very small space for so many people, with only a few cots bunked one on top of the other. These cots were simply flat boards with wood strips nailed together and small bundles of blankets. There was one blanket for each cot. They had no windows in the lower deck. You had to store your things under the cots. An odor of fish smelled everywhere. Louisa started to come to the realization that they were leaving home and she started to cry once again. She was remembering their pet pig they had to leave behind. Jessica went over to Louisa and held her close stroking her hair back whispering, "I love you menina", in her ear. Jessica started to cry on her daughter while they hugged.

Several days had passed and by this time the girls were tired of being restrained to such a small space. They desperately needed to get some air. Louisa was getting ill from the swaying of the boat. The rations of food were not anything to look forward to. The food was gray and sloppy. Everyone would get a piece of bread with each meal. Breakfast seemed to be the only meal to look forward to, since they had scrambled eggs. Even still by this time Louisa couldn't seem to keep any food down. She had severe sea sickness and Jessica was starting to worry for her. Salvador went on a search for someone who might have some medical experience to help his daughter. Unfortunately most of the passengers were from farms and vineyards. Many of the travelers were getting severely ill. When some would throw up, it would be right on the floor amongst all of the people in the lower deck. Once in a while the captain's ship mate would get a bucket of sea water and come down to toss it across the floor. The water would help to dissipate the smell of barf throughout the deck. Salvador finally found a woman who was very intuitive to natural healings. She tended to children when she lived in Portugal. Her father was a doctor. Unfortunately he wasn't one of the travelers. The woman's name was Angelina. She was more then happy to help Salvador and his family the best she could. However she was overwhelmed since so many people were ill. As they rushed back to Salvador's bunk, Angelina brought with her a small bag. It carried only natural dried flowers and different types of home remedies. By this time Jessica was resting. She was so tired and worn from the long trip. Louisa was so weak, she hadn't kept food in her for days. She was pale, very thin and extremely dehydrated. She couldn't seem to stop throwing up. She was dry heaving and it was very painful. Angelina had a type of dried plant to help with queasy stomachs. She had her nibble on it little bits at a time and gave her water. By now they have been traveling for over a week. Louisa was finally starting to keep some food down after Angelina helped her. It was a very long trip for everyone. Even Angelina was feeling ill from traveling so long. The boat had no tubs or places to wash so the stench was getting to everyone. It was enough to make anyone ill. There were some travelers who died, it was devastating for all of them. The dehydration, lack of light, healthy food and being confined together made it tough not to get sick. The lack of water caused the captain to have to ration it by very small amounts per traveler.

Maria was sitting by the doorway when she overheard the captain talking to his ship mate. He was telling him they were very close. This trip has taken almost an entire month of travels. The ship mate said to the captain, "I sure hope so, these people are dying and we are running out of water." Maria walked over to Salvador she tugged at his shirt, as he and most of the others were sleeping. Everyone was so motionless at this point. Maria whispers to her pappa, "we are almost there pappa, I heard the ship mate talking to the captain. They said it was going to be soon pappa." Salvador looked up at her, "are you sure Maria? That would be so wonderful." He laid his head back down, as he was so dehydrated and hungry. Maria kneeled next to him and just stared off into the distance, as she started to pray. She had a tiny cross in her hand that her mother made her out of wood before the trip. Even Maria was becoming concerned about her parents, herself and her sisters well being. She continued to pray as she stared blankly at all the passengers. She would attempt to lick her dry lips trying to grasp some moisture, but there was none to spare from inside her mouth. Most of the elderly who traveled in this boat did not survive. Small children and babies were also dying. Fortunately Louisa was able to make it through, though she was extremely weak. There were buckets everywhere for them to use when needed to go to the bathroom and woman would hold up a blanket for privacy when needed. The ship mate would come down ever so often and take the buckets up and discard them into the sea. As time approached closely the ship mate came down and announced to all of them, "we should be to land by next light. Hang, in there folks." As that time approached they could hear other boats and their horns. The ship mate opened up the door and would allow only a few to step up to see the land, as to inform the others. Jessica began piecing together their things, anxious to get off the boat. It took a few hours still for them to make it to the dock, but they finally got there. People were rushing into each other, desperate to get off the boat. They were quickly maneuvering there way to the door. It was raining when they arrived and the temperature was much colder then any of them were accustomed to. It appeared to be a very busy state, people rustling around. Just as Salvador and Jessica were exiting the boat they both could sense this sudden fear in them. They were feeling lost and confused. "What will become of us Salvador?" Jessica looks down and realizes the girls are not with them. "Oh my goodness

Salvador, where are the girls?" Salvador starts to scramble throughout the crowd, "Louisa, Maria!" In a distance Salvador could see Maria waving her hands high in the air for him to see. "Pappa, Pappa, were here, were here, Pappa!" Maria quickly runs to him and begins to explain, "Louisa dropped her ribbon Pappa and when she let go of my hand I looked away. Then when I looked back you were gone." Maria started to cry uncontrollably. Salvador hugged Maria and gently grabbed both the girls hands. He realized they will have to stay close. With so much confusion he feared losing his family in this mess. He grabs hold of his daughters and leads them back towards Jessica.

Salvador was on the hunt for his cousin. They only had a short time to get to a train station by wagon and there were tickets Salvador's cousin has for them. The train will be leaving to California soon. The girls were amazed when they saw the statue of liberty. It was so large. They had never seen so many buildings and people all in one place before. Even Jessica was overwhelmed by what she was seeing. There was so much stress and concern with Salvador they couldn't really stay in one spot long enough to appreciate this strange new place for all of them. They just spent there time looking at the people and faces trying to find Salvador's cousin in the mix of so many. Fortunately Salvador's cousin in California traveled to California years earlier. He had been the one who sent word to Salvador about a dairy farm owned by a wealthy woman. Apparently she was interested in hiring more workers. She had offered to hire Salvador and Jessica since Salvador's cousin was already working there. She could always use extra hands at her dairy. Her husband had passed away several years earlier. She had to take over the business. They will be living in a small cabin outside of the woman's mansion. Jessica will be the maid and Salvador would help run the dairy farm. The woman running the farm her name is Jenine. She is a single woman. Her husband had been killed years earlier. He was involved in some dealings that were not something Jenine liked much to discuss. Though she benefited from his death greatly, since he had a lot of wealth and the dairy farm was a large part of that. Salvador's cousin his name was Phyllix. He agreed to meet them at the dock to help get them to the train station. Phyllix will travel back with them. Jenine had about two hundred men working for her. They didn't all live on her farm. She did have a few cabins on the property for some of them, Phyllix being one of them. As Salvador guided his family through the crowd trying to locate his cousin he noticed his accordion was not with his things. "Jessica my accordion where is it?" Jessica covers her mouth in shock, "Oh my Salvador someone must have taken it, oh my." Suddenly you could hear a distant man shouting out, "Salvador, over here Salvador!" It was Phyllix, he finally could see them in the crowd. He started running to them. "We have to get you guys to the station, we don't have much time." Phyllix motioned them towards him. They didn't even have time to hug and reminisce anything. They followed Phyllix through the crowd. Salvador wasn't able to even look for his accordion. He felt a sudden twinge of pain in his heart realizing the accordion is gone. The one thing he had to recall the memories of his father and it was just gone. He wanted to cry, but there was no time for even that. A horse and wagon was ahead. Phyllix started helping

Salvador grab up some things and load them onto the wagon. Phyllix started telling him about the plans ahead. He was so excited about seeing his cousin, he didn't even realize how worn out and pale they all were. He just kept chatting away at Salvador. "Believe me Salvador, you will be happy about this place. Jenine pays well and doesn't treat you like a servant, or anything. It is hard work, but we can work together and save money. I will help you, then we can get a place together, a farm." Salvador never had a boss before, definitely never a woman boss. Jessica was starting to worry, but then she tried to imagine how hard it must have been for this woman to take on her husband's dairy all on her own. She then wondered if the woman had children for her Maria and Louisa to make friends. They all quickly climbed aboard the wagon to set off to the train station. Phyllix brought along some jerky for them to eat and a canister of water. He remembered the way those boats fed people. They were all so grateful for that. It didn't take long getting to the train station, as it was near the boat docks for travelers heading elsewhere.

As soon as they arrived to the train station Phyllix informed them they must hurry. Everyone jumped off the wagon quickly. Phyllix and Salvador grabbed the bags. A man was shouting, "all aboard!" You could hear the whistle from the train they almost didn't make it. Just as the last child jumped onto the opening the train wheels were starting to roll. Salvador had to pull Louisa up by one arm. Everyone was following Phyllix. He knew exactly were their small coach room was going to be. One of the train employees was walking through the isle's yelling out, "tickets, I need your tickets!" Phyllix had all of the tickets so there were no worries for Salvador. He walked them into a small box car with bunk beds and a small booth. It had a large window looking out. There was even a tiny bathroom with a sink bowl in the car. The girls were astonished. Everyone was tired, but happy this would be a much more comfortable ride. Fortunately Phyllix has saved a good portion of money to make sure their train travels would be much better and Jenine also helped as she appreciated Phyllix bringing her new workers. Another long week they will be traveling to get to their destination. There were several box cars some larger ones fitted with tables and chairs. This was for people to come in and order a meal. Phyllix had already set it up ahead for them all to have a good solid hot meal to fill their bellies. Of course they all wanted to get cleaned up, it had been a while for all of them. Jessica and the girls stayed in the box car getting washed up and clean clothes from their bags. There was a small canister of water Phyllix grabbed and left for them with a rag and soap. Phyllix and Salvador headed over to the food car to have some coffee and get some food together for the girls. As soon as the girls and Jessica arrived to the food car the food was awaiting them. Salvador headed back to the car to get cleaned up him self.

Jessica asked Phyllix, "are things going to be ok for our family?" Phyllix could see the fear in Jessica's eyes. "Oh Jessica no worries, everything will be fine. In time you will see." Finally Jessica was feeling much better. She had been so sick for so long on the boat getting cleaned up and having a hot meal made all the difference in the world for her. Of course Louisa was anxious to play. Unfortunately there wasn't much to do. However these girls had a wonderful imagination. "Mama, may we go for a walk through the cars please, "por favor Mama?" "Don't go far and don't talk to stranger's menina, watch your sister." The girls were finished eating and couldn't wait to go adventuring around this strange moving vehicle. They bounced from car to car. Maria said, "were looking for buried treasure." They wondered around looking through all the windows. Suddenly the ticket man bumps into them. "Oh my, young ladies venturing through our train are we?" Maria was a little nervous, but she knew it was ok to talk to this man, he was the worker on the train. "Oh sorry sir, we were just looking is all." "Oh it's ok, what is your name?" I'm Maria and this is my little sister Louisa, "she said with such pride." "Hello sir, Louisa sais in a quiet voice." Louisa started tugging at Maria's dress, "we should go Maria, C'mon, let's go." "Well young ladies maybe you should head back to your car it's getting late. I'm sure the passengers would like to rest without little chillins running around now ok?" "Yes sir", Maria states, she was disapointed they didn't get to go far. Maria takes Louisa's hand and they start heading back. Maria was always such a bouncy girl and a very positive happy girl. Louisa was a little more of an emotional child, but she had a big heart. When they got back to Jessica they decided to head back to their car. Jessica was preparing the girls bed. Both of them slept on the same bunk, they were small enough to fit together in one bed. Thus making room for Jessica and Salvador on the bottom bunk. Phyllix put down the small table in the room and laid out a blanket. Of course Phyllix and Salvador had a lot of catching up to do and Salvador hadn't eaten yet. They headed back to the food car while the gals got their rest. As Phyllix and Salvador sat down, a man

came right to their table offering them hot coffee. "I....
would......... like..... some.....muito..... food...... por favor....
please." Salvador managed to mutter out mixed English
and Portugese, he was so nervous. Phyllix laughed, "you
know cousin you will get this just fine." By now Phyllix
spoke pretty decent English he had already been in the
states for some time. "I will help you through it. "Sem
problemas," (no problem) he stated with confidence. The
whole week on the train Phyllix and Salvador discussed
how things fell apart in Portugal. Phyllix was so sad for
his cousin.

It seemed to Jessica that things may be ok after all.
Finally the trip had come to an end on the train. As they
pulled into the station they could hear the whistles blowing
once again. By now the girls were ready to see their new
home and destination. Louisa was thinking deeply for a
moment then she turned and asked, "Pappa can we get
another pet pig at our new home?" Salvador chuckled at
the thought. "I don't know Menina, I guess we will have to
wait and see." There was another horse and buggy waiting
for all of them outside the station. The men started loading
up their things and helped the girl's and Jessica up to the
bench. It wasn't too far out of town. Jenines dairy was quite
popular. Many of the towns people were already gossipping
about the new arrivals at Jenine's dairy. They ended up in
a small city called Tulare, California. Fortunately there
were many Spaniard, Portuguese and even Mexican's
in that area. The spanish and portuguese language was
used by many of the townspeople. It kind of made Jessica
and Salvador feel better about their suroundings, more
at home. Salvador started thinking about his accordion

realizing that is something he will never get back. Just then he looked back at their things in the wagon and he noticed his small box with the accordion in it. He spoke out loud in so much shock, he could hardly believe it was there. "Jessica, oh my Jessica." She looks back at what Salvador was looking at and she also saw it amongst their things. "How is it possible?" Jessica shrugs her shoulders with her eyes bright saying, "Oh Salvador", she smiled with joy. She knew how much that meant to him. Just then her cousin realizes what they are looking at and said, "Oh I forgot to tell you, as we were loading up a woman...ahh... her name was ahhh... let me think, it was Angelina. She said she saw that it was left behind and she knew it was yours when she tended to your daughter. She saw it with your things, so she brought it to me to put in the wagon for you." Jessica was so pleased, "she was a good woman and honest, what a special person of her to do this." Salvador cried, "I wish I could thank her." Just then his cousin realized how important this was to him. "Well cousin no worries", he pats Salvador on the back. "I'm sure she knows how much that meant to you, she went through the same troubles as all of you. I'm sure she knew how much what little you had was to you." They all smiled at each other and the girls smiled too.

Chapter 3

When they finally arrived at the dairy they saw this big huge white house in front of them. You could see the dairy in the back and a very large field of cows all fenced in. The house was surrounded by acres and acres of land. The girls actually felt good about that. They were all use to having lots of land around them. Just as they pulled in Jenine came out the front door. She seemed so excited to see them. It was almost strange as if she was family. This made Jessica happy. When Jessica was in Portugal she had many female friends. They all use to bake together and clean together. She finally felt like maybe things will be ok after all. Jenine was seemingly very welcoming. She was a medium build woman, with long wavy blonde hair. Her nails were long and she had a very shapely curvaceous body. She had dark blue eyes with a touch of hazel green color in them. The men started grabbing all the items off the wagon. Phyllix walked up to her and asked, "Madam where are we putting the things?" Jenine turns to Phyllix, "just load it on the porch for now. I want your family to come in the house ok?" Phyllix quickly complies with her wishes, "yes madam." Salvador and his family followed Jenine in the house. Phyllix and the other men started putting his families things on the porch. You could smell fresh apple pie as they were entering the house. "Oh wow it's been a long time since smelling something so fresh", sais Jessica. Just then they entered the home and suddenly Jenine looks over to Jessica. The look on her face suddenly changes from pleasant to bitter. "Now we need to get a few things straight here and now." As Jenine spoke she waved her finger at them with a harsh and crude tone. She leads them into the kitchen, almost immediately handing an apron to Jessica and Maria. As she gives Maria her apron she scowls, "I think this girl looks plenty old enough to work in my kitchen and that other girl, well that one can tend to my chickens till she gets older." Jessica was a bit taken by her sharpness. She didn't quite know what to say, but she knew they would be her employees. *Straight to business I suppose*, Jessica thought.

Salvador startled by her discontent becomes irritated quickly. "Madam we understand our position here, but may we at least get settled in before we start?" Jenine glares towards Salvador at his rude intrution. "Understand this, my pleasantry is expected of me by people in this town so I do what I need to do, but I don't have time for wasted weight. I don't pay for wasted weight around here. You are here for one purpose, that's to tend to my needs. I will pay you fairly, but don't expect more then what you get ever. Do we understand each other?" She looks squarely into Jessica's eyes as she sais it. Jessica steps back and starts shaking uncontrollably. Salvador jumps in once again at his families aid. "Madam no problem, madam honestly we mean no disrespect." Jenine looks down at Jessica's stomach and notices a small bump. "Oh well look at that she chuckles in distaste, another bundle of joy. How disgusting you Portuguese people that's all you do is have a million kids to feed. Don't be thinking I will pay you more just because you keep spawning babies either. If they don't work they don't make any money got it!" Suddenly Salvador realizes his wife is pregnant. With all the commotion in their life neither one of them had even paid attention that Jessica hadn't had a period in some time. She was at least two or three months pregnant by this time. It was hard to celebrate such a notion considering Jenine's tone. Jenine called out her back door to Phyllix he came running to the back, "yes madam." "Get their things take em to the cabin by the lake. As for you.... Salvador is it? Don't you fret these girls I got jobs for them." Just as Salvador jumped up he looked back at Jessica with despair in her eyes. Jessica just gave him a small grin trying to impress on him her nervousness. It angered him at how she was treating his family. "Look madam I got no problem working for you, nor does my wife, but I won't have you slaving my children". Just as Salvador said it Phyllix over heard and jumps in, he was concerned Jenine may become angry. "Oh no worries Salvador", he was trying to help him out since he knew how curt Miss Jenine could be. "Miss Jenine please, give them a chance to settle in?" Suddenly Jenine notices how overly handsome Salvador was. She was even attracted to how he stood up for his own. Jenine wasn't use to anyone standing up to her ever.

She took a moment to look him over as if he was a prime piece of meat. Salvador realized what she was doing. He thought her to be attractive as well she was after all the first woman he had ever seen with blonde hair. However he had no intentions of making his attraction obvious. He loves his wife and didn't care for this womans personality at all. She was smoldering over his attractive eyes and beautiful thick hair. He had nice dark skin. She felt a shiver in her thighs impressing her eyes on his bare chest that showed through his un-buttoned bergundy shirt he wore. It's been so long since she's had any man since her husband died. When he stood up to her like that it immediately got her attention. Just then Jessica noticed how much this woman was staring at her husband. She suddenly felt sick to her stomach and threw up all over Jenines kitchen floor. The girls just stood there in fear and unsure as to what to say, or how to act. It may have been because she was pregnant, or maybe the horrible feeling she got with this woman and her husband. Nobody has ever disrespected Jessica in this manner. She just knelt there on her knees with a mess on her dress and face. Jenine turns over to see the mess Jessica has made, but at that moment realizes she wants to keep Salvador around for a while. Just then she grabs a rag off the counter and throws it down to Jessica. "Ok fine get cleaned up, clean that mess you made on my floor Jessica and you can join your family. Phyllix will show you how to get to the cabin." She turns back to Salvador, "as for you, be back here at my kitchen tomorrow morning at the crack of dawn. There is lots of work to be done around here. You make sure that wife of yours is here as well, making my breakfast. She also has to prepare breakfast for twenty men. So if you think she can do that with no help from your daughters, then I guess I will leave that up to you. It's wasted hands if you ask me. However I do expect one of those girls to collect the eggs every morning, that or you just found yourself another job. If you think you can do it all." Just then she reaches out her hand to touch his face and Salvador pulls away realizing this woman has other thoughts in her head. He wasn't pleased at all, but he knew he had to make this work. She walks into her den and Salvador runs over to his wife to help her. The girls started wetting the towel and rubbing it on their mothers face. They tried to be quick in cleaning up the mess so they could get out of that house and away from this horrible woman. "Are you ok my sweet love?" Jessica looks up at Salvador. You see the Portuguese woman have always believed that when they feel this sick sense in their soul something bad is going to come to them. She utters out to him, "my husband you know I love you?" He looks into her eyes realizing her feelings of fear. He touches her chin and forces her face to his. "Meu amor", he sais, "you are my wife, you bare my children and have my daughters. We will be ok together eu te amo, (I love you) you must trust me."

Once they got everything cleaned up they followed Phyllix to their new home. With such a bad experience meeting the boss woman the home they were brought to was even more grim. It was an empty little cabin by a lake. It wasn't far from the main house, but far enough for them to feel safer. There was only one separate room in the cabin. Jessica decided to let the girls have that room. She wanted them to feel like they had something private. She planned to set up the other part of the house by stringing a sheet across one area for her and Salvador's privacy. They had a small area with one window and one sink. There was a wood stove in the middle of the floor with a large cast iron pot for cooking. The wood stove would also be used for heat when needed. The entire floor was dirt and only one small cot was in the small private room with a very thin mattress on it. Jessica saw the children's grim faces and she spoke up saying to them, "no worries meu bebe meninas, (my baby girls) we will make this nice ok?" That was enough to make the girls feel a little better about the situation just hearing their Mama console them. Phyllix showed them an outdoor wash tub the men had put behind the cabin for them. Just then Salvador decided to pull Phyllix aside while his family is getting settled in. He was very angry at how the meeting went with this woman Jenine. "Phyllix why did you have us come here to this? This woman is horrible. My family shouldn't be treated this way." Salvador was so angry he wanted to punch Phyllix for bringing them to this situation. Phyllix waves his hands at Salvador, "look Salvador, she's really not so bad. You caught her on a bad day. She has so many responsibilities and deadlines. She is on her own. Try to understand. She hasn't been around another woman in a long time, just us men. She has had to toughen up like that. Maybe your wife can help her lighten up with her company. Even the kids might help her." At that moment Salvador realized maybe he was right. He decided to calm down and give it more time. He shook his head with so much ambivalence, "I hope your right, I really do." That night Salvador talked with Jessica sharing with her what Phyllix had said. Jessica decided she will try her hardest to be a good wife and hopefully make friends with this woman. Jessica talked with the girls as well.

The routine had started for the family. Jessica decided it would be best to have Louisa help her with gathering the chicken eggs and Maria preparing meals for the men and Jenine. She didn't feel that Louisa was quite old enough yet to do any cooking, but she did help her mom prepare the plates. They learned more as they worked in the kitchen. The men workers were constantly helping Salvador and his family with the work and understanding Jenines rules. They all understood their struggles since most of the men were from almost the same situation as them at one time. Jenine seemed tolerant of Jessica and the girls, but rarely expressed much interest in them. She was a very lonely woman and in some ways bitter of her circumstances of never having children from her husband. She was left with so much responsibility. She couldn't even consider a man at this point in her life. Even with that, her longing for affection from a man and having a child was becoming apparent more and more each day. She seemed to have developed an interest in Salvador. At first it was very small innuendos of affection she would show him. There would be a brush of her hand across his at the food table when she would reach for the potatoes. Or an extra smile in his direction if he happened to look her way. Salvador has never entertained her crazy obsession she apparently had for him. He was very devoted to his wife.

As time went on the routines, schedules and chores were expected from Jenine to be carried out diligently by the entire Cardoza family. Salvador learned everything he needed to become very experienced in his job. Jessica and the girls worked very hard, they all learned to understand Jenines harsh way. She was completely harmless or so they thought. There were always hints of something to be concerned with when Jenine would continue to show her interest in Salvador. He had managed to keep her crazy childish crush at bay. This helped Jessica to feel more and more confident in her husband and that eventually they would be able to move on from this place. Salvador continued to save his money. He would keep every bit of his pay in a bag hidden in the cabin. Phyllix also continued to save as much as he possibly could. They still had the plan to eventually buy some land and start their own family farm.

By this time Jessica is now six months pregnant and definitely showing. Ever so often Jenine would make sly remarks to Jessica stating how fat she looked, or how remarkably ugly a pregnant woman gets. Jessica had learned to ignore her comments and just continue to work on her grueling duties. The girls use to cry and want to say something back to Jenine, but Jessica has taught them to respect their elders. She let them know that nothing she said mattered. "Just ignore her and know that anything she speaks is only due to her deleterious feelings about her own life." The cabin they were living in was not far from the lake. During the hot summer months the girls would rush to the water as soon as all there choring for Jenine was complete. They loved swimming in the lake water. It was so cool and refreshing after working in the hot kitchen. One day when the girls headed out to the water they heard something in the bushes rustling around. Then suddenly they heard a small whimpering sound. Maria being such a curious child went to look deep in the bushes. There scampering around was a small blonde colored puppy.

"Oh how sweet!" Louisa shouted out to Louisa. "Look, look Maria it's a puppy." Maria came running to see. The girls loved on the puppy as he excitedly jumped onto their laps. Maria of course was the first to look and see if it was a male or female puppy. The puppy was a male. Then Louisa had an idea. "Hey Maria we can call him Pepper like our pet pig we had." Maria thought that was silly since the reason for the pigs name was because of the black and white spots it had. "It doesn't match the puppy Louisa," so they pondered on a perfect name for their new found friend. "I know let's call him Roscoe!" Louisa shouts. Maria liked that suggestion and nodded her head in agreement. The girls were excited to have a new friend.

Later that evening Jessica was in their cabin and she had noticed the girls had not yet returned. She was becoming very concerned. Jessica and Salvadore decided to go looking for them. Salvador grabbed a lantern and they went out towards the water since they knew both girls spent most of their time over there. Jessica started shouting out, "Maria, Louisa where are you!" Salvador had their lantern in hand so he could better see the trail to the water. The girls had been so busy playing with this new found puppy they hadn't realized how late it had gotten. Just then Maria heard her mom shouting for her, "Maria, Louisa!" Maria looked up as she heard her Mama, "oh no Louisa we are so late. We must go home." Louisa started to pout, "but I don't want to leave our puppy out here all by himself." "C'mon Louisa, we can always ask Pappa if we can bring him back. We have to go." Maria grabs Louisa by the hand pulling her up to stand. They ran towards the trail back to home. "Mama we are here, we are coming", Maria shouted! Jessica could hear Maria the closer they became and she felt so much better. Salvador started walking towards the girls as they approached each other on the trail. Maria was apologizing over and over to her parents. "I'm so sorry Mama and Pappa." Louisa was so excited she immediately started to tell them about the puppy. "You will never believe what we found", Louisa shouted excitedly! Jessica scolded the girls before Louisa could continue her story. "I have been so worried about you two. Don't ever do that again." Louisa began to pout feeling deflated from the reaction of her parents. Salvador was relieved the girls were fine. "What have you girls been doing so late at night?" Salvador asks. Maria was nervous about telling her Pappa about the puppy. She was worried he would not allow it at their cabin. She desperately wanted to bring Roscoe home so she decided to bravely ask anyway. "Pappa I am so sorry, but we found a puppy that was left behind out by the water. We just couldn't resist but to stay with him." Maria bats her eyes and tilts her head innocently. "Can we please, please bring him home so he will be safe?" Salvador grinned it was the first time he has seen his daughters look so happy in a very long time. Maria's cunning little face softened Salvador for a moment. "Well girls it's not entirely up to me since Jenine is the boss here, but I suppose if we build him a little house behind the cabin and we only give him scraps Jenine won't know any different." Jessica smiled she was pleased the girls could have a new pet to keep them busy. She was relieved the girls were safe, not lost in those back woods by the water. These girls have been through so much they deserved a little happiness. Jessica decided to walk back with Maria to go get the puppy while Salvador and Louisa waited behind, since they only had the one lantern. As Jessica and Maria approached the puppy it was whimpering and sounded scared. "Oh isn't he so sweet." Jessica even enjoyed the free spirit of a puppy in her presence. She lifted Roscoe up in her arms and they quickly headed back towards Salvador and Louisa. That evening Salvador built the girls a small little dog house in the back of the cabin. He also made sure to put up some fencing around the dog house so Roscoe wouldn't go running off in Jenines sights. Since Jenine allowed Jessica to take any remains of the foods prepared and not eaten by the men back to their cabin they always had leftovers available to share with Roscoe.

Jenine would ration a small amount of potatoes and rice every month for any of the workers who lived on the premises. Jessica was very good about preserving as much food as she could, so they would have decent meals. She would even sometimes sneak a few things from Jenines kitchen so the girls could actually have some treats once in while. The only thing Jenine ever did in her kitchen where baked goods. She enjoyed making pies and cookies but only for local shops. She did this to look like more of a friendly and caring type to the business owners. This would enable her to get continued business orders of her dairy products. She never much cared to share any of that with the girls. So Jessica would sneak a cookie or two once in a while. Fortunately there where times Jenine really didn't pay attention to things like that since when she baked, she drank a lot of liqueur. It was pretty obvious to Jessica how unhappy and bitter Jenine was. Jessica never much thought it was appropriate for her to be so sorrowful for so long. She felt there had to come a time when this woman moved forward. But Jessica stopped trying to figure out Jenine and just focused on her work and took every opportunity to provide for her family more if she could.

One morning when Jessica was carrying out her duties in the kitchen and Maria was helping as much as she could. Louisa went out to get the chicken eggs. Jenine had stepped out in the back patio. She called over one of her workers requesting him to go get Salvador. When the worker ran out to the barn Jenine stepped into the kitchen. She then requested Jessica to change her duties of the day. She instructed Jessica to tend to her garden all day today. This was so odd since Jenine never allowed anyone to touch her garden. jenine would only allow specific hired hands with whom she watched over closely. This was to ensure her garden was tended to in her way. She also was very strict about anyone taking anything out of her garden for themselves. "I want you to clean all the weeds out and pick all the vegetables. Leave them in the baskets on the patio in the back. Have the girls work with you and do not enter my house today." Jessica was confused, "have I done something wrong?" Which seemed like an odd question since in a way it was an honor to know Jenine would trust her with her garden. Jessica wasn't sure if she should feel pleased or offended. Jenine had a very strange look on her face, "just do as your told. I don't want to be disturbed." She looked like she was in deep thought. Jessica simply followed her orders and proceeded towards the garden. Jessica and Maria headed out with baskets for the vegetables. Maria called Louisa over to help them. Louisa ran over with a full basket of eggs ready to take into the kitchen. Just as

Louisa approached the back door Jessica looked over and saw her, "Louisa stop!" Jessica shouts to her. Louisa was so startled she dropped a few of the eggs and started to cry. She thought she was in trouble for taking too long. Maria ran over to her and hugged her. "It's ok Louisa you didn't do anything wrong." "I know it's strange, but Jenine doesn't want us to enter her house today so we were ordered to work in the garden instead." Louisa looks down at her eggs and gently asked while wiping away her tears, "what do I do with my eggs?" Just then Jenine pops her head out of the window and shouts out to Louisa, "just leave them at the door I will get them later. Now go away!" Both the girls put the basket down and Maria picked up the few eggs that broke. She wiped away the mess with the bottom of her dress, then grabbed Louisa's hand and they ran off the patio towards Jessica into the garden.

Off to the other side of the yard Salvador is approaching the house. As he takes his first step on the back patio Jessica is now even more apprehensive. She shouts out to Salvador, "Jenine said she does not want to be disturbed today!" Just as she speaks the last word of her sentence Jenine pops her head out the window once more, "don't you be concerned Miss Jessica. I have invited Salvador in and he is to enter my home today!" Suddenly both Salvador and Jessica have the same dreaded look, but Salvador knows he must comply. Jessica just nods her head at him and gives him a very gentle smile, but you could feel the fear in her from a mile away. Even the girls felt a shiver. Jessica looks over at the girls realizing they were watching their parents expressions, "girls lets just work ok", "Yes Mama", they both comply and start working at the weeds.

Salvador gets to the door and Jenine has opened it before he even has the opportunity to touch the knob. Jenine was standing at the door in a very different dress then anyone was accustom to seeing on her. The dress was a very thin white fabric and off both shoulders. She had some lace draped over her like a shawl, but it was so thin Salvador could see her breasts almost completely. He couldn't help but look, she had such perfectly round breasts. Salvador knew this was very bad. He had to go in. He couldn't risk her firing him so he enters the home. Jenine quickly closes and locks the door. All the windows were covered in the house. She rested her back up against the door and she's rolling her head back and forth looking his way then looking away from him. As if she were a damsel in distress. Salvador is just standing there. He doesn't know what to say, or what to do. He felt the temptations and desire for her for a moment. "Salvador please tell me, you must want me?" Her hair was slightly wet and hanging down over her shoulders. It was long draped down and freshly brushed. She was slightly biting her lower lip in desperation. "Your wife is as big as a boat with that baby in her belly. She is fat and has nothing to offer you? I'm quite sure not even the comfort of a beautiful woman since she is withchild. You must want me?" Jenine was breathing heavily as she unbuttons two of the buttons of her gown to show him more clearly her breasts. Salvador just looks at her in utter disgust, but as a man it was hard to fight the desire. She was truly a different beauty his eyes have ever seen, but he knows he has to reject her. Though even with his disgust she did look good to him. His nerves cause him to almost stutter as he speaks. "Miss Jenine I-I-I'm sure a m-m-man who is single out there would be h-h-happy to comply with you." Jenine then gets very angry. "I do not want a man to just comply with me. I want you." She walks towards him and pushes him into the nearest wall. She places her hand on the middle of his chest and slowly caresses him. Salvador actually begins to feel somewhat tempted by her advances. He definitely took notice to her beautiful perfect breasts, her shapley body and flower scented hair. He loved her blonde hair and in a moment almost felt himself losing control. She presses her lips onto his kissing him almost violently, pressing her body into him. He couldn't help but to begin kissing back. Salvador starts to sweat as he grabs her waist pressing her even closer to him. Suddenly he glances over through the window and could see his wife outside in the garden. Salvador grabs her hands to stop her from touching him further. "Miss Jenine please, I love my wife you must stop." As he states completely flustered. Jenine pulls back looking into his eyes, "I need you to want me." She tells him in complete desperation. She could feel his body so intimately close to hers. Salvador continues to push her away as he looks through the window at his wife. Jenine becomes very angry and steps back and yells for him to get out. She felt so rejected. She wanted him so badly and could feel him wanting her. She was so angry and flustered, "get out now, get out of my house", she yells! Salvador is now very afraid for his family and their destiny. "Please, Miss Jenine I meant no disrespect." He waves both his hands at her then clasps his hands together as if he were praying. "I'm s--s--s--o sorry." Jenine grabs her forehead with both of her hands almost ready to cry. With all her bitterness she is able to keep it under control. "Just leave Salvador, just go and don't mention this to anyone." "I will fire you and your family even Phyllix, just leave."

She throws the vase sitting on her counter at him. Salvador ducks just in time as the vase crashes into the wall and shatters into a thousand pieces. He rushes out the door quickly. He doesn't even glance back at Jessica. He simply runs back to the barn. Jessica seen him come out the back door she watched as he quickly ran. She looked back over at the house to see if Jenine came out, but she never did.

Later that evening Jenine didn't even feed the men. They all came to the table, but Jessica explained that Jenine would not allow anyone in at all today. No meals have been prepared. All the men who lived on the premises went back to their cabin's and just prepared themselves some rice for the evening meal. None of them were very happy about that. Jessica was boiling water over their large pot to prepare some potatoes. The girls were peeling them and cutting them for her behind the cabin while they played with Roscoe. Salvador walked in and just looked at Jessica for a moment. She looked up and knew whatever happened in that house it wasn't good. "Salvador tell me what happened por favor?" Salvador just looks down frustrated knowing if he tells her and some how Jenine finds out that would be the end of them in this place with no place to go. He had some guilt as well since he became so tempted by her advances. He looks up at her and smiles at her beautiful belly that's carrying his child. "Minha esposa, (my wife) I love you and this will be another one of those times you just have to trust me. I cannot say. You know how Jenine is. That's all I can say about that, but we are ok I love you." He approaches her and hugs her. Jessica stands up holding him closely back. Salvador kisses her cheek and jokingly changes the subject. "So what is our special feast of the evening, will it be potatoes or rice?" Jessica just starts to giggle and she goes on with her work. She knows something was not good about what had happened, but he wasn't in there long. She hopes whatever it was it just goes away now and they can move forward.

Meanwhile Jenine is back in her house still in her very concealing clothing. Just sitting in her den with her lantern on a very low light. She has been festering all day in anger of how that whole incident happened between her and Salvador. She wants him and she is a woman who is use to getting what she wants. There was a man in town who was very interested in Jenine. He owned a few of the local shops. He was fairly well to do with money and many people in the town respected him. His name was Richard. However Jenine was not even attracted to him. He was quite a few years older, but he was stable. He has tried to court her many times. She is friendly since he has such a grand reputation throughout the town. He orders a lot of her dairy products for his stores. He is a good prospect for marrying, but Salvador is who she desperately wants. Jenine is in love with Salvador. In her mind she owns him and she has every intention of getting him. Even if it's only in a physical manner. Many Christians in the community would not look very highly on her if they knew of her inner most sinful thoughts. She knows in her mind she will have Salvador. She has always believed she can have whatever she wants, but there will always be that part of her, of any woman who wants to be wanted. When he said no to her, it broke her heart to the core. Unfortunately Jenine is very evil and has no intention of letting him get away with rejecting her.

Chapter 4

As the weeks go by Miss Jenine starts to meet with Richard at the store more often. Even with her heart elsewhere she knows she needs to marry well. Richard is truly her only option. She finally would except his invitation out to dinner. As he is courting her she can't get Salvador out of her mind. She knows she must do this. Richard was definitely an older man. He was at least twenty five years older then Jenine. He was also widowed early in his first marriage. His wife had caught a terrible pneumonia and never recovered. Everyone at the dairy could see that Jenine was going out more often in the evenings. The crew assumed that she had finally found someone and eventually will step down as the boss and become the wife to this man. All the laborers would prefer Richard as a boss. They all hoped she would become a more pleasant woman. None of the men really liked working for a woman, but they were paid fairly well so they tolerated it with the circumstances. Salvador and Jessica were definitely feeling more relieved since her attentions seemed off Salvador, but in her heart her attentions never left. Every evening after spending time with Richard, Jenine would sit in front of her window thinking only about Salvador. Her desires would never change. She knows in her heart she has a status to fullfill. Appearances are everything in the community. It affected her dairy business greatly. Richard was mainly a good business move on her part. Even with that she couldn't help fantasizing about Salvador.

By this time Jessica is now eight months pregnant and having a much more difficult time carrying out her duties. Jessica also started becoming severely ill. This was not common this late in the pregnancy for a woman to become ill. It worried Salvador greatly. He tried to take care of her as much as he could in the evenings. The girls did there best to take on some of their mothers duties so she could sit more. Meanwhile Miss Jenine was proposed to, by Richard. The plans for them to marry where in a very short few weeks. During the engagement Jenine informed Richard for the next two weeks they will not see each other until the wedding day. She wanted time to reflect on the changes coming in her life. She was struggling with her emotions. Getting Salvador out of her mind was just not happening. Jenine truly was not interested in Richard, but she knew he had money and status.

Jenine was coming down the stairs of her home one evening as Jessica and Maria were preparing the evening meal for the men. Jenine heard Jessica in the kitchen suddenly scream and a loud thump on the floor. Maria gasped shocked by her mothers sudden whale of pain coming out of her. Jessica had a knife in one hand and a potatoe in the other. Both items fell to the floor. Maria quickly dropped the bowl full of potatoe peels from her hands and hurried to the ground close to her mothers aid. She held her hand for a moment unsure of what to do. "I will go get pappa ok mama", she announced. Jessica was in so much pain she did not even respond to Maria. Maria determined with tears in her eyes scared for her mama quickly ran out the back door to go get Salvador. Jenine rushed to the kitchen to see what was going on. Jenine was shocked at what she saw. Jessica was on the floor eight months pregnant and bleeding everywhere. She was crying while grabbing her stomach in agony. Jessica looked so pale you could hardly see her beautiful dark skin anymore. Jenine was such a hard woman that rather then rushing to her aid she just stood there with hate in her eyes. Jenine was almost wishing Jessica would just die on her kitchen floor. She smerked in Jessica's direction with so much disgust. Just then Salvador came running in with Maria just behind him. As soon as he saw how badly Jessica looked with all the blood everywhere he motioned back telling Maria to go outside. "I don't want you to see this Menina and keep Louisa out ok? Please Menina pappa will help her ok. Go now go." Maria was crying hysterically and so afraid for her Mama, but she still followed her pappa's orders. As she wiped her tears with her sleeve she knodded her head, "yes pappa." She walked out the kitchen door towards Louisa. Salvador without thinking quickly closes the door and walks into the kitchen to Jessica. He kneels to the floor by her side. "Oh my god, what do I do?" He can see the blood on the floor that was coming from jessica. Jessica quieted to a low moan, then suddenly nothing. Salvador could see her eyes rolling back, then nothing. Jessica was no longer responsive. He starts to cry as he attempts to hold her pulling her body on his lap. You could see the panic starting to take over with Salvador.

Jenine suddenly realized that her opportunity has just arrived. She has this evil grin on her face, but then she quickly covers her lips so Salvador cannot see her smile. She gently walks over to the back door and locks it. While standing behind Salvador she starts to caress her counter with her hand as if it was Salvador's chest right in front of her. Salvador heard and saw her lock the door from the corner of his eye and in that moment he realizes that she is up to no good once again. And she is up to no good while his wife and baby is apparently dying on Miss Jenines kitchen floor. Salvador is desperate so he turns to Jenine while he is still kneeling with his hands clasped together, "please, please Miss Jenine she needs medical help she needs help. I don't want her to die please." Jenine drops down on the floor with him and grabs a hold of his shirt and pulls him up to her. "This is it my love, my sweet, sweet dark beautiful man that you are." Salvador falls back, "what are you talking about Jenine, my wife and baby they are dying?" He is so disgusted by her at this point, but desperately wants his wife to be ok. "Do you want my help Salvador?" Jenine said it so carelessly to him, but very intently. "Yes of course please," "Then Salvador you must come in the den with me now." As he slowly places his wife down on the ground positioning her head for her, he walks over to the den as Miss Jenine instructed. She is very stern with him so he believes that she is intending on helping. When they enter the den she informs him of what she desires. "I have a friend who can help her right now to save her life and your miserable baby.

I will only help you if while my friend is saving her, you do something for me?" Salvador knows exactly what she is referring to. "You can't be serious.. this is wrong.. this is blackmail. You can't be this evil?" Salvador cannot believe what he is hearing. He begins to pace shaking his head flustered looking over at his wife, then back to Jenine. He begins biting his tongue in frustration and grinding his jaw. He is so desperate he doesn't know what else to do. "Fine damn woman fine, just help, please hurry." Salvador is so angry, but he knows she will die so he complies. Jenine informs Salvador he is to stay in her den and she will be back. Jenine rushes out the door has one of the men fetch a horse. She instructs one of the workers to go get the doctor. Miss Jenine has known him for many years. This particular doctor dealt with many situations concerning bad births. The worker does as he is told. She has already informed the worker to let the doctor know to come in the back door and do not enter any other part of her home. She points at him agressively, "do not allow anyone else in my home. When he has done his job, he is to put Jessica back in her cabin with the girls." Honestly Jenine doesn't even know if she will survive at this point since so much time has passed, but she does not even care. She figures as long as Salvador has hope, she will get exactly what she wants. She then looks over to her house realizing the time has finally come for her and she intends on ceasing the moment at its best. She quickly heads back in to her home and straight to the den. As soon as she walks in Salvador is pacing back and forth, so concerned for his sweet Jessica. "You will go to my spare room upstairs and stay in there. I will be in shortly. I won't be having you all crazed about your stupid wife either. I will wait until word that your wife is fine, then we will pursue our little venture. Are we clear my fine Salvador?" Salvador looks at her with complete hate in his eyes. He knows he has no more options at this point, so he complies with no words to even speak to her. Salvador heads up the stairs and Jenine points to the room he is to enter.

While Jenine is busy admiring herself in the mirror, she can hear the commotion down stairs in her kitchen. She throws a robe on over her sheer white nightgown that drapes over her shoulders. She gently and quietly goes down the stairs just to peek in and see if things have gone successfully with Jessica. She is anxious for them to leave her home and venture up the stairs to touch Salvador and caress every part of his body. As she peeks around the corner to look, it appears the doctor has been able to successfully deliver Salvador's baby. Jessica appears to be coherent once again. She could hear the doctor as he spoke to Jessica telling her he was able to save the child. Her and the baby will need lots of rest, particularly Jessica since she had lost so much blood. The doctor was concerned for her well being in the following days. Just then Jenine shouts out to the doctor, "now get her out of my house and that stupid baby." The doctor looks up realizing Jenine had been standing over the stairwell. He's always known Jenine and how terribly hard she had become since her husbands death, but he never imagined she would be so cold to another human being. He had no idea she had Jessica's husband upstairs in her bedroom ready to completely take advantage of him. "You will receive my bill in the morning, I promise you that" The doctor states, irritated by her complete steel, cold heart. Jenine grunts at him with disgust and total disregard she doesn't even care about the bill. "Just go", she states, so the doctor lifts up Jessica with the baby in her arms and carries her out the door. Maria and Louisa were both waiting outside crying uncontrollably. Phyllix had been comforting both the girls through it. Even the men workers completely forgot about the evening meal. They were so concerned about Jessica's well being. She was always the one bright thing in their day. She was so pleasant to everyone, it was a joy for them to know a new baby was coming into the ranch for all of them to appreciate. As the doctor walks out to the porch and down the stairs with Jessica, all the men come together to help him get her to her cabin safely. The doctor announces to all of them happily, "she's had herself a beautiful baby and they are both going to be ok." Everyone was cheering and relieved. Maria and Louisa both smiled and ran to their mothers aid. As they all followed to the cabin Maria and Louisa both insisted they put her in the cot in the room, since it was the most comfortable spot in the cabin for her to rest. As all the men headed back to their cabins and homes Phyllix looked over to the girls, "you girls make sure you get your Madre plenty of water in the cabin next to her bed, for when she needs to drink. Don't let her get out of bed ok?" "Yes uncle Phyllix we will take care of her we promise", Maria announces proudly. Just as Phyllix was heading out he noticed Salvador was nowhere to be found so he looks back at Maria, "where is your padre?" Maria knew he was still in the house, but she completely forgot. "He's still in the house with Miss Jenine Uncle Phyllix." Phyllix at first had a puzzled look on his face, however he knew Salvador would always stay by his Jessica knowing how ill she is. Then he remembered

Jenines crazy ways, so he didn't want to push Miss Jenines buttons and get too involved. "No worries Maria, I'm sure he is fine. Maybe Miss Jenine needed him to help her with something tonight. Just take care of your Madre. I'm sure pappa will be home soon." Honestly Phyllix had no idea what horrible circumstances Jenine had put this family into.

Meanwhile back at the house Jenine meticulously locks every door in her home and makes sure every drape is drawn on every window. She heads back up the stairs with her lantern into the spare room where Salvador is hesitantly awaiting. She walks into the room and throws her robe off in front of Salvador. He frantically shakes his hands at her, "please Jenine my wife, is she ok, my baby?" "Of course Salvador she is fine and the baby is born. She is back at the cabin as I said she would be. She will be busy resting out the evening." Salvador lets out a huge sigh of relief. Just then he is distraught. He cannot be there with her to watch over her. "Please Miss Jenine you can't be serious about what you want from me?" "Oh but I am. If you try to walk out of here, I will make sure your good fortune turns around in a very bad way. So don't play with me." She walks up to him and holds the lantern up closer by her so he can see her breasts through her nightgown. She had been ready for this moment for a very long time and she has no intentions of allowing him to just walk out. She approaches his lips to kiss him and Salvador pulls away by habit of course. Jenine begins to get angry with him. "Don't play with me you fool comply, or you will find that I will scream rape to this whole town. Believe me they will believe a wealthy woman over an immigrant from another country. One who simply works a dairy farm. You will be hung in a matter of days." Suddenly Salvador realizes she means it and is fearful of what she is capable of. He manages to set his thoughts aside and attempt to appease her. "I'm sorry, I...just...can't...." Salvador looks down to the ground in complete disbelief what he is about to do. He feels completely helpless in this, so he complies as best he can. He is so afraid she is going to hurt his family. He reaches up to her face and attempts to kiss her on her lips. Just then Jenine pulls away from him. "You will have to try harder then that if you expect me to ever leave you alone again. I want a baby and you will give me one and you will enjoy every moment of it. Do you understand?" Salvador gulps as he is sweating from his forehead. "I... will...do... ugh what you ask of me...he is so hesitant, but he knows he can't get out of this anymore. He decides to close his eyes and try to envision his wife in his mind so he can cope with the moment that is about to happen. "Fine damn it Jenine," he is so frustrated. After having so little closeness with his wife in months due to her illness from the pregnancy, seeing Jenine's naked breast behind the white gown has even made it difficult for him to keep fighting her. He grabs her face and pulls it close to his and violently kisses her and throws her onto the bed.

At first Jenine wasn't appreciating how rough he was being, but then she realized he couldn't help himself at this point either. She finally got him right where she wanted him. She was so pleased with herself she got completely caught up in his strong arms holding her down the way he was. She ran her fingers down his shirt touching the intricate buttons that Jessica had sewn on Salvadors shirt for him. She could see how very special these buttons were as she rubbed them between her finger tips. She pulled his shirt open so she could touch his chest with her bare hands. Just as she pulled it open, one of the buttons flew off the shirt onto her floor. Salvador saw the button on the floor and felt a sudden rush of sadness knowing how special that button was. In Salvadors weakness he tells Jenine, "I have to get that button." Just then Jenine looks crossly at Salvador for interrupting the moment with something to her as so trivial. "Why Salvador, what difference does it make?" "My wife made that for me she sewed each button...you don't understand." ....Just then he realizes he is telling the wrong person anything regarding how special that button was to him. Jenine becomes very annoyed that he is even discussing this and grabs his face. "Enough Salvador..... please just enough... give me what I want." There was nothing he could do at this point he was trapped in this womans passions. He ripped her gown off and took her the way she wanted to be taken. She sucked on his strong arms as he took her, she kissed every part of his body she could grab hold of. As the night went on she forced him to give her more and his sexually rough pattern continued with her as he had never been this way before. He couldn't even understand his own body at this point. He was letting out every frustration, every bit of his life's anger of loss and tragedy he suffered. Somehow all just would waterfall through him onto her. She insisted this night will be hers. For she wanted to make absolutely sure he got her pregnant. That was the deal in her eyes and that was going to happen, or he would have to come back. He didn't want that at all. He loved his wife with everything in him. He knew things will never be the same again now, for him or his wife. He knew he could never fix this. In his heart he just kept trying to convince himself he was saving his families life, but he knew it would never matter for his Jessica. Things will never be the same again. There were points in the night were Salvador just wept in silence. He knew his life was over as he knew it. And he somehow wasn't able to stop this. He kept reflecting on all the promises he had made to Jessica and now he knows he has completely broken that trust forever.

The next morning Jessica is completely worn out. The entire evening was so eventful she was exhausted. However she was extremely satisfied. Salvador was accustomed to waking in the early morning light so he gently tapped on her shoulder, "Miss Jenine, Miss Jenine." She finally opened her eyes realizing Salvador was attempting to wake her. "Yes my sweet Salvador", as she moaned and purred to him. "Miss Jenine I would like to go to my wife now?" Jenine lifted herself up out of the bed as she sat up with her back facing him. The only thing Salvador could see was her bare back. She had rested the blanket on her front side as she was chilly. She peered sideways at him with her eyes, "you have given me everything I could ever ask for. You may go, but this business is ours and not the other workers are we clear Salvador?" Salvador didn't even care any more. He just wanted out of her home at that point to tend to his wife. "Whatever you want Miss Jenine now can I please go?" Jenine took her blanket with her as she walked to her dressing room, "just go Salvador." He quickly got up and clothed himself. He rushed down the stairs and out the back door back towards their cabin. He completely had forgotten about the button at this point.

He was so worried about Jessica and he wanted out of Jenines house. As he left Jenine watched him. She silently fantasized him saying I love you to her. In her own sick way in her mind she wanted to believe he loved her and she loved him. She kept replaying the night in her mind. The passion was so intense and so real for her. As the sun was rising through the window she saw something shiny on her floor. She looked down and saw the button on her floor that she had ripped off his shirt. She reached down and picked it up and just then she realized it's a piece of him that she now holds in her hands. Something that Jessica did for him and she took away. She grinned rubbing the button close between her fingers she was pleased. After a long morning of Jenine relaxing and reflecting she took the button and placed it in her special trinket box. With every intention of utilizing that button at some point to her advantage.

Salvador quietly entered the cabin. He knew his Jessica would be resting from such a very rough evening of birth to their child. He quietly entered the room with the cot. He saw his sweet Jessica Amelia lying on her back with their new born baby in her arms. He just stood over her for a moment to attempt to recapture her beauty in his heart. He felt so much shame and he had to tell her, but he struggled with that reality. He questioned himself over and over as to how to even speak the words. Jessica's hair was so beautiful and draped over the opposite shoulder of where the baby was lying on her. They looked so peaceful. He could tell by her skin color that she was still very frail and weak. He sat down next to her bed and just patiently waited for her to awake to him.

It didn't take long and her eyes started to flutter. She could sense him next to her. As she opened her eyes and looked over at him she was pleased he was by her side. As soon as he looked at her she could sense a pain in his eyes. Somehow she knew something was terribly wrong. "Salvador were have you been?" Salvador turned over to her, his hands where shaking uncontrollably. Maria heard her papa in the room and ran in, "pappa, pappa your finally here. Why did you stay at Miss Jenines last night?" Jessica jumped up from her bed with the baby close in her arms. She sat up and pierced directly at Salvador. She knew in that moment what had happened to Salvador. Why he was gone. As she looked down at his shirt she saw that a button was missing. Salvador snapped over at Maria, "Maria please go in the other room now." Maria ran back over to Louisa and didn't say a word. Jessica immediately looked away from Salvador. "My sweet Jessica Amelia please," he knew she was not interested in hearing him at this point. Jessica held there child up for him to see as she held him up she showed him, "this is your first born son. I will not honor you with giving him your name. His name will be Manuel." You could hear the disgust in her voice. Jessica has lost him in her heart and she will never forgive him. Salvador reached out his hand to hold his son and Jessica pulled their child away. She put her head back down in the cot. She had so little strength and it will take more time for her to get up from the bed. She nestled Manuel in her arms and turned away from Salvador with no interest of speaking another word to him. Salvador felt so ashamed and he knew he lost the right to his son taking his name. He was totally defeated. He stood back up and walked out of the cabin with no interest of working that day. He just walked down the trail to the water. While he walked he sobbed uncontrollably. He didn't want anyone to see his shame in his heart. Jessica was back at the cabin sobbing as well. Her heart was torn apart. She just cried and cried as silently as she could. She didn't want the children to hear and she didn't want Salvador to come back in. She didn't even want to look at him. Maria knew that something was terribly wrong she was old enough to know that her pappa staying at Miss Jenines was not a good thing, but she had hoped there was an explanation. Judging from what she saw unfold with her pappa and Mama she knew things would be different for them in a way that it had never been.

Chapter 5

As Salvador walks down the trail alone his heart is tearing into him. He feels completely lost with the weight of the world on his back. He collapses to his knees in absolute despair. He continues to sob throughout the entire day. Eventually he lies back against a large oak tree and falls to sleep. He is so exhausted with the heaviness of his life's disappointments.

Phylix had noticed Salvador had not shown up for work that day. He became increasingly concerned for his family. Eventually he left the barn to investigate the troubles of his family. Phyllix peaked in at their cabin, "Jessica," he said in a soft voice. Phyllix knew Jessica was still resting. He really did not want to disturb them, but he was concerned. He crept into the cabin silently and whispered yet again, "Jessica are you doing ok?" Jessica was still resting, but his entrance into the cabin alarmed her. She sat up slowly as she was still feeling very weak and sore. "Oh Phyllix you frightened me." "I'm so sorry Jessica, it's just we haven't seen Salvador all day and I was getting worried." The moment Phyllix spoke Salvador's name Jessica became angry once again. She pierced over at Phyllix in a way that he had not seen her ever before. It surprised him he stepped back just as he saw her expression. "Is everything ok Jessica?" He asked hesitantly, one thing you did not do in those days was pry into other people's personal affairs and that included marriage issues. Jessica realized she had made her feelings very obvious and took a deep breath for a moment to compose herself better. "Umm well Phyllix it's nothing we can't handle ok." He knew he overstepped his bounds however he was still concerned as to where his cousin might be. He pressed a little further only to have a better understanding as to where Salvador is and that he is ok. "I'm sorry Jessica I understand this is none of my business. However he has not shown up for work and I need to talk to him about this. He certainly can't chance Miss Jenine firing him." As soon as Phyllix mentioned Jenines name Jessica became even angrier. She didn't want Phyllix to know what Salvador had done so she had to keep her composure as well as she could. She had Manuel in one arm sleeping and she knelt forward putting her elbow to her knee and leaned down into her hand. She was covering her eyes as well as she could. She truly just wanted to bawl her eyes out and scream. In that moment she could see Phyllix had became even more concerned for his cousin. He truly didn't understand the extent of troubles they were in. "It is ok Phyllix, it's fine, were fine umm look he probably decided to walk down the trail by the water. You will probably find him there." Jessica really didn't care if he found him, her anger consumed her. Bitterness started to take over any love she had for Salvador. Just then Phyllix nodded at Jessica, "get some rest Jessica ok I will look into this ok and make sure everything is good I promise."

Phyllix headed out of the cabin door and proceeded down the long trail towards the water. As he was approaching closer to the end of the trail he noticed Salvador lying against a large oak tree. Salvador was leaning there with no motion to speak of. He had fallen into a deep sleep. Phyllix walked over to him and noticed he was a mess. His face was pale and you could easily see streaks going down his face where tears had dried up. He honestly didn't know quite how to approach this situation since in those days men were men. They didn't talk about feelings to each other. He knew he had to do something. He loved his cousin and the family so much. Phyllix knelt down on one knee and started lightly shaking Salvadors leg. "Salvador wake up, Salvador we need to talk." He started to open his eyes. He was so tired emotionally and physically it took him a minute to piece together who was kneeling in front of him. Salvador leaned forward and started rubbing his hands across his face and through his hair. He tried his best to compose himself and stood up rather abruptly. "I'm good, everything is good Uh yeah.. Uh what's up.. Phyllix what are you doing out here?" Phyllix stood up meeting Phyllix more equally in front of him. "Look Salvador I don't know what's going on and I'm not going to pry I assure you that, but you have a wife who is still recuperating from a very rough delivery and a job to do for a very strict boss. You didn't show up for work today and fortunate for you Jenine hasn't said a word yet. You really need to compose yourself and get back on the horse as they say. Do you understand cousin?" Salvador looked down to the ground. Everything started racing through his mind that has occurred in the last few days. He wanted so badly to tell Phyllix what had happened, but his shame took over just as quickly as the thought to speak of the whole night before. Salvador knew that he couldn't possibly tell him. He couldn't tell anyone. He looked back up at Phyllix with such an empty expression. Phyllix knew whatever it was it was bad, but he wasn't going to push the issue. "Alright Phyllix lets just get back on that horse then I suppose." They both started heading back down the trail back towards the barn to the milking cows.

In the following weeks Jenine spent most of her time planning the upcoming wedding. She wasted no time getting the plans under way. She knew if she came up pregnant she had to make sure she was married. Quick enough as to not raise anyone's suspicions. Due to the very prominent reputation of Richard and her. The wedding was to be very high society. They had a reputation to up hold and both of them intended on impressing that reputation upon the towns people. Jenine ordered the finest of china, crystal and foods. She had no intentions of inviting any of her workers. The only guests were people of stature, wealthy, and well known. When combining Jenine and Richards wealth together that then would make them the wealthiest couple across several towns and cities. Even the local mayor and some out of city politicians where to be present at this event. Between the two of them, her owning the largest dairy across several towns. Richard owning several stores and other property. They were almost like royalty. With all the chaos that had been going on it left Salvador and Jessica free to keep some distance with

Jenine. Jenine actually had informed Phyllix she wanted him to handle the dairy while she was planning this wedding. She did not want to even see Jessica, or her kids during this entire event. Salvador and Jessica didn't talk much anymore. It was very obvious to Louisa and Maria. The girls kept busy helping their madre with the baby and doing chores. They also spent a lot of time with Roscoe. Louisa hated how silent her parents had become with each other, but she knew not to say a word. It made her very sad. Maria had to grow up so fast taking care of her sister and the baby. She carried a weight within herself. She knew whatever had happened that night it would be a night that will carry in their lives forever. Anytime Salvador attempted to hold Manuel, Jessica would grab him away. It was as if she didn't want him to touch his son. Salvador was completely detached from his children after this. He just got up and went to work every morning. Without so much as a kiss on his wife's forehead. Anytime he had tried she would pull away from him. He eventually gave up and just carried out his duties to take care of the family. Phylllix knew he had to help them get enough money to leave this place soon. He saw that everything they once were, was just slipping away day by day.

Jenine had almost had everything ready for the wedding. The yard was decorated with wild flowers. Everywhere you could see multiple colors of yellows, purples and blues. She had several small white flowers throughout the entire back yard. She had crystal everywhere. Beautiful vases filled with flowers on all the tables. The area where the preacher would be standing awaiting the bride had an awning arched over him. It was decorated full of flowers. The tables were covered with linens and sterling silver tableware. The chairs that where set up for the guests to watch them wed, where covered with white fabric and draped with a bow. A few flowers were on the back side of every chair. Jenine had hired several women to come in to her kitchen and prepare foods and drinks for her guests. The local preacher had met with Richard and Jenine several times for councel prior to the wedding day. Everything seemed to be coming together quite well. Jenine was proud of herself. She felt very accomplished in her plans. She had a thin long white dress. It was a very simple and elegant white dress. The dress was taylored made in shiny silk material. She had a long vale that cascaded down the length of her dress. The dress will completely cover her. The long sleeves will adorn down her arms in silk. She will leave her hair down and draped with small wild flowers through it. The dress will fit her petite frame perfectly. She had the dress hanging and was silently admiring how beautifully it had turned out. She held the dress close to her while looking in her long mirror. The wedding was only hours away. The only thing in her mind, "am I pregnant?" She has wanted a baby for a very long time. While stroking her belly and looking in the mirror sideways she was excited to think there could be a beautiful baby in there. She still continued to fantasize about Salvadore being her husband to be. In some ways she was sad that he couldn't love her the way she truly loved him. Some place deep in her sole is a once good woman a long time ago. She became so hard emotionally. She protected and shielded herself from allowing any feelings. So many years had passed with so much sadness. Eventually her anger over powered any happiness. Any part of good in her, got lost a long time ago. Yet somehow she managed to fall in love with a portugese worker. She sighs and shakes her head in disbelief of even herself thinking about that. The inner conflict she is having with herself. She angrily throws the dress down on the ground and thrusts herself on to her bed. She's still looking in her mirror, but you can see her complete mixed emotions. She's angry, sad, disgusted, emptiness. She started reflecting on her night of passion with Salvador and how amazing it was to her. She remembered the button she had saved in her trinket box. She got up from her bed and pulled it out of the box feeling the layers within the button. Then realizing she could have Salvador with her in this wedding. She pulled out her sewing kit and picked up her dress. She decided to sew the botton into the inside fold of her breastline of her dress. For her that was a moment she would treasure. Just then one of Jenines helpers peeks into the room. Jenine quickly bites off the string of the thread as the button is completely sewn in now. Her helper heads over to Jenine. "Miss Jenine can I help you with your dress, shall I hang it for you so it stays pressed?" "Yes of course, please yes." Jenine hands her the dress and leaves the room.

The workers had picked up the piano from the church and placed it on a wooden platform they made on the property. It was a perfect location for the pianist to play the wedding song. Everyone was frantically getting all the last minute touches done as the guests will be arriving soon. Jenine and Richard had special ordered wines for the occasion. They had a large selection of the finest wines available. Jenine observed all the kitchen activities looking over the different assemblies of foods laid out. She was waiting for Richards sister since she had insisted on helping her get ready for the wedding. Jenine was not happy about it, but she had to be compliant as it is Richards adoring sister. That's what Jenine would keep echoing to herself about this woman. Jenine certainly didn't fancy her. She was quite annoyed by her involvement in her life. However she never showed it out of respect to her future husband. She knows she has to remain proper for this marriage to go smoothly. Jenine has no intentions of continuing the game after the marriage. She will privately get rid of the annoyance some how. Jenine was always very meticulous in her planning. As soon as she discovered Richard had this latched on sister she had already started planning a way after the marriage to get her out of her hair. For now she will tolerate it, but only for now. Richard had introduced them a few weeks ago at a dinner party. Her name is Suzanna Elizabeth. Richard always called her Suzy. She is Richards much younger sister still in her young twenties. This annoyed Jenine even more. The last thing Jenine wants is a younger woman floating around her. Making her feel older yet. Jenine considered her very uneducated, since Richard has never allowed Suzy any independence. He has always been very over protective of her, so he always has kept her close. Thus meaning Richard intends on moving little miss Suzy into Jenines Dairy home. That was the arrangement that was made. Richards other businesses are managing well without his presence. He set up such good management that he only needs to check on things periodically. Richards plan is to handle Jenines dairy business. He feels he can make better profits. It naturally made sence to him for them to all live there. Thus enabling him to manage the dairy more efficiently. One thing Richard is unaware of, is how very intelligent and conniving Jenine is. She always has a plan that will benefit her. To the world Richard has the upper hand on this situation *for now*, as Jenine would utter to herself. One thing is for sure, Phyllix has been around Jenine long enough to know she can handle men and business. This is why Phyllix has been very careful about saving as much money as he can. To get free of her as soon as he can. He knows things will be changing very soon and not in a good way. His trouble is trying to figure out how to get Salvador and his family enough money so they can all leave together as a family.

Just as Jenine was getting ready to exit the kitchen door to look at the progress of the yard. She could hear a screeching voice behind her. "Oh no, oh my goodness sister you come inside before the groom see's you, bad luck, bad, bad luck get in here." As Suzy reaches out and grabs Jenines arm. Just as Jenine could feel her scrawny little hands on her arm. She wanted to smack her. Jenine has had to seriously hold back emotion lately and she's about to explode on this little Suzy. As Jenine grits her teeth and looks over at her. "Alright, alright I will go get ready." Jenine pulls away from Suzy and stomps up the stairs. Suzy follows directly after her. While Jenine is pulling up her dress, Suzy is helping her tie the strings up in the back. Suzy was feeling uncomfortable with Jenines tone earlier so she contemplates talking about it to her. Jenine could see the discomfort in her face. "What is it Suzy?" "Well Jenine you seemed a bit sharp with me." "Well yes Suzy I...." Jenine stops for a moment to think how to appropriately handle this. I am nervous. I am after all getting married today...no worries now ok?" This sounding easily dismissable. At least Jenine was hoping it was. Suzy seemed accepting of her explanation and moved on to helping her string up her dress. As Suzy is stringing each piece Jenine rubs her breastline of her dress feeling the button. She closes her eyes envisioning herself walking down the isle to Salvador. *If only it were him.* She ponders in her mind.

The guests have started arriving and Jenines helpers have been escorting them to their seats while offering wine as they wait. Every once in a while Louisa and Maria would get caught peeking out the door to see the progress of this event. They were both giggling and teasing at each other about how different the guests look to them. Little Louisa tells Maria, "look, look that man over there. He has a shiny gold watch in his pocket. Look he pulls it out, like a lot of times to look at it." Maria laughs, "he's just showing it off sister and look at those clothes. They are so pretty on the ladies." Jessica became very annoyed. She smacks her hands together, "children get away from the door. Miss Jenine would have your hides if she saw you." In many ways Jessica didn't care what Miss Jenine thought, but she knew they had to remain living there. She didn't need any trouble with that woman. Even she secretly hoped that Mr. Richard would be a kinder man and treat them better. She even hoped Jenine would then leave them alone for good. She knew that was probably too much to ever expect. Jessica hated that Jenine was having this beautiful wedding. She hated any thought of happiness for Jenine. Bitterness had built up in Jessica that was very noticeable to her children.

Chapter 6

Back at the house Jenine and Suzy are working on her hair brushing it out so meticulously. The flowers for her hair are sitting on the bed. Each flower was picked out perfectly for their colors and perfect conditions. Suzy pulled up a small strand of her long thick blondish brown hair on each side. She braids the strands and pulls them to the back of her head. Then continues the braiding all the way down her long hair and lays it down. She then grabs the beautiful white small flowers and tucks them inside the braids. She gets the beautiful long vail and attaches it to her braid with a small comb so it lays perfectly down her hair. Jenine stands in front of the mirror to get a full view of her final look. The helper puts some powder on her face and neck. The dress hugs her body perfectly in white silk. Her arms look elongated with the beautiful silk hugging down to her wrists. She turns sideways to see the vail. As it drapes down the back of her dress, all the way to the floor. She looks absolutely enchanting. Even Suzy was taken back by how beautiful she looked. Meanwhile

Jenine is caressing her breastline of the dress feeling the button sewn inside. Her mind can't help, but to continue her fantasy of Salvador being her groom waiting for her.

Suzy claps her hands together with excitement, "well I think the time has come. I think we are ready. What do you think Jenine?" Jenine snaps out of her deep thoughts and looks over at Suzy, "well lets take a look out the window and see how things are going out there." They both walk over to the window with anticipation. It appeared that everyone was seated and Richard was standing by the pastor waiting patiently for things to get started. Jenine looks over at Suzy and announces, "I guess you should go down to the pianist and let them know that we are ready. I will head down the stairs to the back door." So Suzy goes down to inform them to start the event while Jenine follows behind her. Unfortunately Jenine did not have anyone to walk her down the isle as both her parents were long past away many years earlier. She was far too stubborn to be close enough to anyone to walk in her dead fathers place. As Jenine is patiently waiting she could suddenly hear the piano playing the wedding tune. She decided to wait just a moment as to allow the guests to turn in the direction she would be coming. As she steps out of the back door and is completely revealed to everyone the entire group of people including Richard are taken back by how beautiful she looks. They express the sounds of delight outward to her. Richard starts to tear up and is extremely pleased with the pleasantry of her look. Salvador had been working. He was on his way back to their cabin when he saw Jenine stepping out onto the back porch. He heard everyone outside sounding in aw of her beauty. Salvador glanced over and happened to see her. In that moment Jenine had glanced over and saw Salvador standing there in the field. It was perfect to Jenine to see his face in that moment. She almost escaped enough in her mind to think it was him she was walking towards. Salvador was honestly taken back when he locked eyes with her. He didn't love her by any means. He was still madly in love with his Jessica. Something triggered inside him that he didn't quite understand, or recognize. He thought she looked beautiful as well. Since they had shared such a level of intimacy he almost couldn't help, but reflect on all the emotions that night brought into him. He realized he had to look away. He had to get some sence of control over whatever it was that was affecting him with her. As Jenine realized the same in that moment that all these people are watching her, as is Richard. She looked away and closed her eyes for one moment. She was able to re-focus and started her walk down the stairs of the porch towards her future groom. Salvador decided to leave the area and go down the famous trail that he became very familiar with. This is where he spent most of his time when he did have free time from work. His relations with Jessica had become so isolated away from him that he spends a lot of time at the lake by himself. He knew he needed to get as far away from Jenine as possible. As he walked down the trail he couldn't help, but take one last look back at Jenine. He could see her dress cascading behind her. Her beautiful long blonde braid full of flowers. Part of him knew a connection was deep inside him. He had to fight himself from allowing the feelings. He was so frustrated he turned away and kicked a tree.

The wedding was a huge success. All the guests were impressed by all the fancy crystal. No expence was spared. Suzy spent most of her time monitoring that everyone was receiving the best attention. She made sure the food was perfect and served quickly. Everyone had their wine and whatever they needed to keep them all widely impressed. They had a reputation to uphold after all. Richards sister had been use to the role to keep up that reputation of her brother. As the party was finally winding down and the guests were leaving Jenine was becoming very agitated. She knew that evening her and Richard would be alone. He would have expectations to sleep with her. She also knew she had the responsibility of sleeping with him. She had to be sure to do it since she suspected she would be pregnant from Salvador. Though the thought of it almost disgusted her. She wasn't entirely attracted to him. She had other motives, but she sighed in her mind and knows what she has to do.

Suzy had already been set up in the downstairs guest room since she now has become a permanent resident of this household. The last guest had left and Suzy proceeded to her room. She wanted to set up her personal things as to feel more at home. Richard had already headed to his and Jenines room to get into more comfortable clothing. Jenine stood at the bottom of the stairs peering up at the door to her room. She knew there was no escaping this. She sighed and headed up the stairs. By now most of her flowers were wilting in her hair. The braids were loosely swaying as she pulled the comb out. She had already took out the vail and had it in her hand partially folded up. It been a long day and she was definitely tired. She entered her room and closed the door behind her. "Richard would you please help me with my dress?" His friendly demure seemed to have changed. He suddenly turned from the mirror where he was untying his tie and looked sternly at Jenine. It seems that Jenine was equally fooled by this man. It appears he had the same cold soul that she had. "Jenine there is an understanding that you and I will have from this day forward. You served a great purpose for me. I am already a wealthy man, but by marrying you I am the wealthiest man in this entire county. You do well to be my partner, but you and I..... I have no interest in you except for what the world see's. Do you understand what I am telling you?" Jenine was shocked that she had been fooled so well since she was always that evil person. She never expected that another person could take advantage of her in the way he apparently has done. Richard continues on telling her there was only one love in his life and that was his wife and she died. Apparently Suzy was not really his sister, but nobody knows this. Suzy is Richard's companion and has been for many years. He refused to marry her since she had absolutely no financial value to her. So Richard goes on to explain. I will only sleep with Suzy. You are simply for status and I will take over your Dairy. I will definitely make you money, but in moderation. You will receive an allowance. Just remember I am the man in this house. I rule this house. You will simply just be my trophy wife. I will do what I do best. Jenine was so shocked and almost afraid at this point. She had so many things rushing through her mind, "but Richard you looked at me in almost tears when I came out in my dress. You seemed so sincere with me in your feelings for me?" Richard grins evily, "well of course Jenine. I know what I'm doing.

How do you suppose I am such a rich man." Since all the household helpers always left the house by 7pm and never entered the house until 7am they would never know that Richard would not be sleeping in Jenines bed with her. Richard proceeds to walk out of the room. "I will be leaving my clothes in here. We need to give everyone the impression that I do share this room, but I have no intentions of sleeping with you." He throws his tie down and exits the room. He heads straight for Suzy's room down the stairs. Jenine was completely lost. She knew she was going to be showing as a pregnant woman. Richard would then discover she slept with someone prior to their nuptuals. He will know it would not be his child. Even with that thought in her mind she also felt completely alone. She didn't love Richard by any means, but she did like him. She thought he cared for her enough that she would have someone in her life that cared for her. This totally broke her heart. She fell to the ground on her knees in her dress and just cried quietly. Until eventually she went into a deep sleep.

As time went on Richard and Jenine were able to function in front of people like a couple. Behind closed doors it was always the same. Richard would undress in Jenines room and change into his night clothes leaving his clothes behind. Suzy very rarely spoke to Jenine. They just simply co-existed in the same house. A few months had passed and Jenine was most definitely pregnant. She honestly did not know how to deal with the situation. The whole world outside had no idea that Richard was not acting as her husband in the house. It wouldn't matter with everyone else they would all assume it was his. She had to go to Richard and tell him of her adulteress actions. She was sitting up stairs on her bed one evening waiting for Richard to come up to change. When he came in he went on with his business of changing. Acting as if Jenine wasn't even in the room. "Richard I must talk to you. There is something I must tell you." Richard rolled his eyes as if anything she ever said mattered to him. He made it very obvious that he had no real interest in her. "Richard I'm pregnant." Just as she said it Richard stopped working on his tie while looking in the mirror. He chuckled and glared over at her looking at her reflection in the mirror. "Well I guess you and I have something in common in characteristics don't we?" Richard smerks, "well this will work out to our advantage. At least in everyone elses eyes we are congregating as we should as a married couple. However I'm not supporting or caring for an illagitament child. We will carry on till your at about six to eight months along. Then I'm sending you away to a mid-wife in another county to birth your child." Jenine was disgusted at how uncaring Richard truly turned out to be. She put her face in her hands and couldn't help but to cry. It was difficult for her to hide her emotions being in her present state. She felt completely like a fool and totally alone. Richard had no interest in her, or her issues. He simply turned and left the room. A part of him was annoyed at the fact that she had slept with someone else. It was more an insult to him, then anything else. At the next public dinner party they had, Richard announced to all their guests that Jenine was now with child. Nobody suspected anything out of place since the timing seemed appropriate. As time went on Richard had a good handle on the operations of the dairy. Jenine kept to herself in the house most days. She was more lonely then ever and now she truly felt useless in this world. Now that she's lost control of everything. She would sit in her bay window at the side of the house while caressing her belly. She could catch a glimpse of Salvador every day. She noticed that Jessica and Salvador rarely were even near each other and that pleased her immensely.

As the months went by she had begun to notice how often Salvador would spend his evenings walking down the trail to the lake. Jenine often wondered if he even cared that the baby she was carrying was his. It never truly entered Jessicas mind as to the connection of Jenines pregnancy and the possibility of it being her husbands child. One evening Jenine had dinner, she generally ate alone. Jenine decided she wanted to follow Salvador down the trail. She couldn't stand to wait any longer. She felt such a desperate need for companionship. By this time Jenine is four months along. She still had a beautiful figure with a small bump in her stomach. She hadn't gained much weight at this point it's been difficult for her to eat. She hasn't felt well with such a disappointing turn out of her life. It was early evening. Just enough light for her to see her way through the trail. Just as she seen the opening of the waters she could see Salvador's legs stretched out on the sand. His feet were emersed in the water. Salvador could hear the footsteps coming closer. He looked over and there Jenine stood. She had a beautiful full length dark blue dress on. It was warm weather this time of year so she had off the shoulder sleeves with white lace wrapped across her breastline. The sleeves hung loosely on each shoulder. You could see a modest amount of her cleavage. The waist line hugged her hips closely with just enough room for her baby bump in her stomach. The lace traveled down her dress like a fancy cake. It was such a beautiful shiny blue that worked perfectly with her eyes. Even Salvador couldn't help but notice. Her thick hair so long it touched her hips and flowed down her back. She had strung four sections of her hair from the front to the back in beautiful braids. Something about her being pregnant made her glow. Jenine wanted so badly for Salvador to give her some ounce of compassion. She was completely alone in the world. Salvador didn't quite know what to say. He saw her stomach and it moved him deeply. He always knew it was his baby, but was afraid to even acknowledge this. He didn't ever see himself able to father this child. It was such a sick twisted situation. Jenine fell to her knees facing Salvador. "I'm so sorry for hurting you. I'm so lonely. I've fallen in love with you." She put her hands in her face and started to cry uncontrollably. She's not much on showing her vulnerable side. Salvador actually started feeling sorry for her. He was desperate for some level of compassion also. It made this situation very bad for both of them. Somehow they both found themselves in each others arms. Suddenly they both met each others eyes. They couldn't help but touch lips. Salvador was different this time with Jenine. He was gentle. They kissed passionately and held each other so tightly. It was as if both of them were the only two people in the entire world. Jenine laid down in the sand on her back and Salvador lied down on top of her as they kissed. His hand caressing her breasts. His other hand gliding up her leg to her inner thigh. Jenine starts to moan with extreme joy and pleasure. It seems they have both lost total control of reality and became completely lost in each other. What Jessica doesn't realize is that she has completely pushed her husband right into the arms of this woman. Their kisses so passionate, so intense. Salvador starts to sweat in anticipation of completely letting lose in Jenines body. He thrusts himself into her as he holds her hips close to his. He can feel her pregnant belly next to his body. That somehow makes him feel close to her intimately with their child. As he completely loses control in her, she moans with words of complete satisfaction.

Salvador lies down beside her and they both lay silent while clenching each others hands. Suddenly Salvador takes this opportunity to feel his baby in her stomach. He caresses her belly and suddenly feels a guilt inside him. Jenine starts to cry once again. "Salvador please go away with me? We can be a family together." Salvador holds her hand for a moment then realizes he is making a huge mistake. He pulls himself up and stands putting his clothes back on. " You know Jenine I don't understand what it is you do to me, but I have to face reality. This is just so wrong. I love Jessica, I do..... this is such a mess." He leans forward and hits a tree with his fist. He's so angry and frustrated. "This should not have happened, I have to go." He leaves down the trail. Jenine just sits there and cries. Salvador can hear her as he is walking away. Both of them in their own personal despair.

Several days pass and after work one late evening Salvadore gets back to the cabin. He is so angry thinking about his relationship with his wife. He walks in and can see the girls are sleeping. He looks over at Jessica. She can see him looking flustered and angry. She tries to turn away quickly as to ignore him. He isn't having it. He rushes over to her and grabs her arm. Jessica becomes startled attempting to step back from him. He no longer cares if she wants him, he's decided he's taking her. He throws her down on the cot and tosses her dress up. Jessica knows what he is going to do wether she wants him or not. Salvadore announces to her, "your my wife and I'm taking you." Jessica doesn't fight him. She just turns her head as to not look at him. She nods and sais, "your right I am your wife and you can do this, but it doesn't fix our problems." He proceeds to take her and do as he pleases. Jessica could feel his anger, but only just lies there disinterested in his actions. When he was done he simply got off of her and left the cabin. He felt completely thrown away and was disgusted in his life. He impregnated Jessica once again on that night. When he left, Jessica sat up in the bed. She wanted so badly to want him and be close to him again. In her heart she felt dead inside. She realized she had to continue to be the proper wife to him, but cursed him in her heart.

Chapter 7

As the months go by Jenine spends most of her time in her room away from everyone. By this time she is close to eight months pregnant. Richard informs her that the time has come for her to go to the other county with the mid-wife at a convent. "I already sent word for her to come for you." Jenine is disgusted by his commanding ways and that he is able to discard of her so easily. For him to take her money and her dairy the way he has. Leaving this dairy seems to be the best thing for her at this point. She is ready to leave. She proceeds to packing her things. She runs across her trinket box and finds the button that she had ripped off Salvadors shirt. She had removed it off the wedding dress and placed it back into her box. She had a few days before the mid-wife was to arrive. She decided to crotchet her babies first nighty and sews the button on the chest of the top. In her mind she knows someday Jessica will see this. That would be the moment Jenine would feel justified. To show her Salvador has become hers, in some twisted fashion. After a few days the mid-wife came to the door. Richard brought her in and took her into the library to discuss the plans for Jenine. She grabbed her bags and called down for help to carry the remainder of her things. Before she left she wanted one last opportunity to see Salvador. She headed out the back door towards the trail. Salvador still spent his free time there. He was leaning up against a tree looking out at the water. "Salvador I'm leaving." Salvador looks over at her realizing she's close to having their child. He's worked hard on convincing himself he doesn't care, but deep inside he does. He looks over at her and stands to her level. "I don't know what to say Jenine. I wish I could figure this out, but I .....just can't." Jenine looks down to the ground in some form of shame. Something has changed about her. She doesn't seem to have anything left to give. She turns to walk away and Salvador grabs her arm. "Wait...wait Jenine, I'm so lost." You can hear sudden desperation in his voice. Jenine looks up at him meeting her eyes to his. She leans forward and touches his face to etch the memory in her mind. She kisses him delicately on his lips and turns as she walks down the trail. She whispers to him, "your free Salvador." Jenine left her home and everything it ever was behind her as the coach of horses pitter patter down the long road.

Over a year and a half has passed since Salvador and Jessica arrived at the dairy. Phyllix has saved enough money to start discussing a purchase for his cousin and their family at a farm of their own. Salvadore had been saving as well. Salvador and Phyllix had made a few trips to town looking at different farm options. They heard about a large amount of property in Fresno. About five hundred acres with a small dairy already in operation.

Their was a man by the name of Lucas Danielson who had inherited this farm land and wanted to have some form of partnership for the farm. The price seemed right so they set up a meeting. They had been told to contact Lucas at the local pub around five in the evening. Lucas was only thirty years old and unmarried, but he was never a very kind sort so not many women took to him. He spent his free time at the ladies lounge. He wasn't much on love. He was 5'9" and very well built, but did have a bit of a gut. He frequented the bars. He had thick, short light brown hair and small hazel eyes. When they arrived and came into the pub it was apparent Lucas was the most popular guy in the place. He had been told Phyllix and Salvador wanted to meet with him, so he was looking out for them. Lucas waved his hand at Phyllix and called out for him from the center table. He had a few lady friends sitting at the table with him. It was apparent they were working ladies. They both had thick make up on and the smell of cheap perfume that hit you in the face if you get too close. Both the ladies had their bossoms pushed up so tight you could see more then a lady should be showing. Phyllix saw Lucas waving them over so he headed in that direction. Salvador just quietly followed. This definitely wasn't a place Salvador had ever really been to. He was very out of his element. They reached the table and the two ladies started to giggle. Lucas was irritated that the girls stayed in the seats. "What's the matter with you two, are you dence? These gentleman aren't here for you, now scatter." Both the woman jumped up from their seats quickly and they still had grins on their faces. Those type of woman will take any prospects. One of them winked in Salvador's direction. He just quickly looked away as if not to see her slutty advances. Both the woman slithered away and quickly found another gentleman visitor in the corner of the bar.

Lucas stood up to greet Salvador and Phyllix properly as they shook hands and sat back down. Phyllix introduced himself and Salvador as he was sitting. Lucas got right to business, as he is not someone who cares to have idle chit chat. "I hear you work at Jenines Dairy?" Phyllix looks over at Salvador and assumes himself to be the talker in this business transaction. "We do, but we have been saving and would like to talk about what you got available." Negotiations started almost immediately. Neither Phyllix nor Salvador were interested in drinking. They just wanted to get down to business. It turned out Lucas wasn't interested in doing an out right sell. He did want someone to take over the dairy so he could move on to other investments. He had been left a hefty settlement when his father passed away. He had plans and he didn't want the dairy holding him down. Phyllix and Salvador became concerned they didn't want just a job. They both wanted freedom from that. Phyllix leaned forward facing Lucas. He tried his best to look professional and seem to have a clear head about him. "Well Mr. Danielson we are only interested in ownership. What would interest you in this transaction?" Lucas scratched his head thinking intently about what Phyllix was proposing to him. "Well Phyllix I'll tell you what, theirs a good size house and barn as well as a decent size dairy. You can both run a small business that could potentially grow. I will let you and your family live there and make some profits. I can give you a better pay. We will call it a cut of the profits.

Better then what Jenine could offer you. We can work out a partnership. I need some money up front and you both can have a shared 20% ownership for now. We can always come back to the table and renegotiate later. See how things go." Salvador was irritated, but the reality was neither Phyllix nor Salvador had saved near enough for any decent amount of property. It turned out the cost was a lot more then they had anticipated. Lucas proceeded to give them the price for the 20% ownership and the men barely had enough to cover it. "What do we own with 20%?" Phyllix was getting angry and extremely irritated. He tried his best not to show it. Lucas smirked, "well now I can't sell it and I cannot control who you hire. If you choose to hire any help. Plus if you get some customers your keeping 20% of the profit. I will cover a salary that is more then Jenine gives you also. Plus you aren't paying to live there. My benefit is, I don't have to run it and I'm still making money." Salvador quickly nudged Phyllix and whispers to him, "we need to talk." Lucas immediately noticed they needed a minute to talk over everything. He stood up and called out to the bartender, "hey I need a fill up." Lucas looks back at Phyllix, "I guess I will go pick me up another drink, be right back." As soon as he walked away Salvador got right to the point. "Look Phyllix this might be are best option. It gets us off that terrible Dairy. My wife can finally have some freedom. Maybe we could actually be happy again in our own home. At least here we would have more control." Phyllix scratched his chin thinking intently as he lifts one of his eye brows. "Well Salvador, I still think 20% is too low. Maybe he would consider a higher percentage if we give him some control of the business." Salvador was not pleased with that idea.

"I do not want anyone controlling us ever again!" As he recapped in his mind the entire years events and how much it has hurt his family. Phyllix saw the disgruntled look in Salvador's eyes. "Well Salvador I guess we need to really go over this and make sure that our opportunities to have more ownership down the road will be open to us." Both the men agreed and Phyllix stood up and waved Lucas back to the table. Lucas grabbed his full mug and heads over. As he sits down the men start discussing the plans to go take a look at the property and how to go forward from here. They will be spending at least a few more days in town going over the details.

Meanwhile the bartender Joe had been observing the men. He starts to chuckle loud enough for one of the patrons William, Joe called him Willy sitting at the bar to hear him. Willy was a regular at Joes place they were pretty good friends. "What's you looking at over there Joe?" Joe was a big man. He stood about six foot tall and very robust. He was kind enough for a bartender, but one thing about him he always knew everybody's business. Joe had been drying out all of his clean glasses and mugs with a dry towel. Then putting them up on his open shelves and some under the bar. Joe proceeds to tell his pal Willy what's been going on at Lucas's table. Joe knew Lucas pretty well since he spent a lot of time there. Joe never cared much for Lucas, but his money was as green as anybodies. He wouldn't complain. He didn't care for Lucas and his crooked ways. He knew Lucas always had an alternate motive. He was never generous with anybody. "Too bad these two men are gonna find out Lucas don't make fair deals." Willy peeks over and takes a look to see who Joe was looking at. Willy shakes his head, "well Joe at least Lucas won't be spending as much time around here. Maybe he will move along some. Find some other project and give these guys a chance." Joe chuckles again lifts himself a glass with some beer he had poored himself earlier and sais, "I'll drink to that."

After a few hours of negotiations Lucas and the other two stood up from the table. As Phyllix was shaking Lucas's hand Salvador sais, "we would like to ride out and look at the property." Lucas smiles he knows in his mind he's got a deal, but he's happy to get them out there to see the place. "I'll tell you what, at first light meet me out front. I'll have some horses and take you out there." Both Salvador and Phyllix felt like all was accomplished and were looking forward to the tour. "Were gonna need room and board for the night. What's available here?" Salvador wasn't anticipating staying and neither him, or his cousin were familiar with town. Lucas shouts over to Joe, "hey Joe any rooms for these gentleman around town?" Joe puts his glass down as he shouts back his way. "Yeah Miss Jonsey, she usually has a couple spare rooms available. I'm sure she would be happy to ablige. It's down by the shoe repair shop." Lucas looks over at Phyllix and Salvador and smiles, "well boys, I guess I can walk you over that way and you can get settled in." As they walk through town Salvador notices a few cars ride through. He was amazed. He had never seen one yet. Phyllix had seen a few since Miss Jenine had wealthier people in her surroundings. Generally only people with money were able to invest in these new machines. Things were changing and Phyllix was hopeful they would finally be a part of the changes. Lucas points them in the right direction. As they get closer to Miss Jonsey's place he heads back to the saloon. Miss Jonsey's place was basically an older beautiful two story home with a big rap around porch. They entered through the patio and knocked at the door. There was a big wooden sign carved into it with the name Jonsey's. It was hanging on the porch all crooked like with one nail barely hanging on. A short woman answered. She had an apron on and looked like flour in her hair. I guess she was busy in the kitchen getting some bread made up. She was an older woman probably in her 60's or so. No children, but a grumpy husband. You could hear him in the back yelling. "Jonsey where's my pipe?" Jonsey had only a minute to say, "welcome, welcome." Then she yells back, "I got customers give me a minute," in her sour irritated tone." You could hear her husband grumbling from the back room. Jonsey quickly rubs her hands into her apron getting as much flour off her as she could. As she extends her hand out to introduce herself. "Hello gentleman, please come on in." She shakes Phyllix's hand and Salvadors as she directs them in. Salvador was relieved they would be getting a good meal that night. Both of them were very tired and looking forward to a good rest. The next morning would bring a lot of hope for both of them. Jonsey was a great hostess and a great cook. When morning came, both Salvador and Phyllix were up and ready to go at first sun up. They barely even gave Jonsey time to get them some coffee. She had prepared a big breakfast, but they were so excited they could barely eat much and were ready to head out the door. Jonsey wasn't having it, "now boys, you gotta fill them tummies or you ain't worth much to nobody before you go making big deals out there." She wasn't shy about getting in other peoples business, but she meant well. She actually managed to get them to take a few more bites. After all her food smelled fantastic. It made it hard to say no.

They got back to the front of the Saloon and waited it seemed like forever for Lucas to show up. He finally road up with the horses. Phyllix laughed and said, "I figured you would be one of them with those cars they got around here." Lucas laughed back at him and said, "yeah well maybe some day, but for now I stick to my horses." Most of the farmers utilized the horses for most of their travel needs. It was usually the city people with money picking up on all this new stuff coming out. The 1920's were a new time with a lot of new technology coming out. Change was becoming very evident. They called them days the roaring 20's. "This farm is a little out of town so relax and enjoy the ride." They all climbed on and headed out. It did take a while to get there. As they rode closer to the long dirt driveway you could see the house from the road. It was looking a little rough. There were some men going in and out of the dairy house were the cows where. Phyllix was surprised, "you have workers here now? It's a running dairy?" Lucas smiled, "well yes, but your option to keep em around if you want. Or not your choice. I got about fifty cows so somebody had to milk em. Till I figured out what I was gonna do with the dairy." The house was definitely gonna need some work. The out house was just behind the barn a few feet back. The part that was in the best condition was the dairy, were the cows where. It was obvious nobody lived in the house for a while. They spent a few hours looking everything over and talking to the men that were working there already. They came to the conclusion that this was a good start for them. Lucas agreed to get the papers written up. Salvador was anxious to get home and pack up his family. He was a little sad for Jenine. He knew he probably wouldn't be seeing her ever again. He needed closure and desperately needed to work out his relationship with his wife Jessica. He sighed for a moment before they climbed back onto the horses to head out. He looked over at the farm they purchased and said to Phyllix, "this is it Phyllix. It's a new start for all of us." Phyllix grinned and patted Salvador on the back. "I told you we would do it. I told you we would be ok." Salvador sat up, "the Cardoza ranch," he announced proudly.

Chapter 8

While Salvador and Phyllix headed back home to get ready for there big move, Jenine had been spending time at a convent with the mid-wife. She still had a few weeks before her child was to be born, but she was growing impatient with the process. She was very uncomfortable. They had set her up in a room with a cot and dresser. She had a small mirror over her dresser and no pictures except what the nuns put on her wall. A few simple scenery paintings and of course a cross on her door. Jenine was never really a religious woman, but she was respectful either way. They have a beautiful garden that Jenine was spending her time in during the day just to get some fresh air. On this particular day she wasn't feeling well. She sat back on one of their benches and just sighed. Depression definitely became a regular thing for her. She was looking extremely pale and could never quite get enough sleep. Her hair was a mess. The braids were so loose she had attempted to tuck some of it back in. It would just fall back out. She didn't have the energy, or the care to fix it anymore. One of the nuns noticed Jenine wasn't looking so well. She headed over to check on her. Before she walked over the nun whispered to one of the other nuns to go get the mid-wife. She could sense something was just not right. It was way too early for Jenine to have her baby, but it was obvious she was starting to have contractions. At least to the nun it was. Jenine had no idea what was happening to her. She was never one to complain about pain, or discomfort. She always felt that people are way to sensitive and weak. Pain is not an option and complaining is definitely not an option. When the nun came over to her she could see that Jenine was sweating and grasping on to her stomach. She kept swaying back and forth trying to coddle herself like a child to make her pain go away. "Jenine are you feeling pain sister?" Jenine was so weak and the pain was getting so intense. She had no choice, but to be honest. "Yes oh yes, it hurts and I'm sooooo dizzzzy." Just as she uttered her last words, suddenly Jenine started to faint and fell over right off the bench.

The nun grabbed her just before she hit the ground. She started to yell out for the other nuns assistance. The mid-wife was heading out just as the nuns were trying to steady Jenine on the ground. The mid-wife stepped out. She could see some blood on Jenines dress and water everywhere. The mid-wife was also a nun, but she spent all of her time taking care of pregnant woman and the homeless babies that were left at the convent. She loved children and this was her calling in her heart. She called it gods job for her. She had a type of apron on to keep her clothing clean. it would allow her an easier change after helping to deliver a baby. She could simply change out of her apron and still remain in clean clothing. She also wore a red cross around her neck. The other nuns would call it her doctor clothes. They loved what she did and admired her for it. They would always assist her when ever they could. The nuns always helped her with the orphan babies.

The mid-wife's name was sister Abbey short for Abagale. She started her life very young in the convent. She was about seventeen when she decided this was her calling. She had long blonde hair with strips of gray throughout. She was in her early fifties now, but you could barely see her aged life. She was a natural beauty. The gray simply streaked through her hair so naturally with the blonde you could barely see it. Unless the sun hit her hair just so. She had smooth skin and light blue eyes, with long eye lashes. You could see faint wrinkles in her face. She still held her youth so well. Her hands served the worst punishment in her life's work. She was a short woman and petite, very sweet personality. She was suppose to wear a cover over her head like the other nuns, but so often she had to rush in for such emergencies like this one that many times she wouldn't have her full cover on her head. The nuns always laughed that she would be late and out of uniform for her own funeral. They never gave her trouble. They knew she did great works for the church.

Sister Abbey rushed to the ground where Jenine was lying. She immediately went to work and started ordering the other sisters what they needed to do. "You must go get sheets and towels. I need a bucket of warm water." The nuns hurried to their duties. Sister Abbey yelled out, "get the kit sister's hurry." When she wanted to get the exact tools she needed for delivery she made the job much simpler for the nuns by making a kit for them to simply grab. It would have everything she would need for any delivery emergency. Within minutes the sisters were back with everything Sister Abbey needed. One of the sisters asked, "sister Abbey it is too early is she going to be ok?" Sister Abbey didn't even spend a moment to answer. Even she was unsure what could happen. She did inspire the sisters to pray for her and her baby. As sister Abbey started to uncover Jenines dress so that she could get a closer look. She saw a head coming through. She grabbed the towels and sheets and started stuffing them under Jenine as to protect the baby from germs and dirt on the ground. She had a towel in her hand and started instructing one of the sisters. "Put Jenine's head on your lap. Sit her up some. Wet her head and try to wake her if you can. Put a wet cloth on her head hurry." Sister Abbey reached in and started to put pressure under the babies head. Attempting to pull the baby through. She couldn't get the baby through and with Jenine not pushing it poses a real problem. Getting this baby that's partially out, to get all the way out. "We must get her to push somehow, try to wake her." The nun who was assisting started to cry. "I'm trying sister, I'm trying." Just then as the nun was about to panic Jenine started to moan. "What.. what is happening, oh the pain?" As Jenine started to cry out sister Abbey yells out to her, "Jenine listen to me. You must push. You must open your eyes listen to me." Jenine suddenly opens her eyes in complete disbelief of what was happening around her. She saw all the nuns around her and sister Abbey pulling at her baby between her legs. Just then Jenine starts to push as hard as she possibly can. Sister Abbey immediately pulls

Jenines baby out and starts to wrap her in the towel. The baby let out a loud roar and cry as sister Abbey goes to work cleaning the babies mouth out after she slaps the babies back. Jenine looks up and starts to cry. Sister Abbey announced, "you have a beautiful baby girl Jenine. May the lord bless her." The baby was so beautiful. She had fair skin like Jenines with a good amount of medium brown hair. She was approximately six pounds. A decent size baby for the norm in sister Abbeys experience.

Just as sister Abbey was about to hand the baby to her. Jenine starts to moan and cry once again. She grabs at her stomach in pain. Sister Abbey grabs the baby back into her arms and looks down. There was another head coming out. Abbey hands the baby to one of the nuns, "here, here, oh lord in heaven. We have another baby. She has twins. Push Jenine, push." Jenine starts to cry and panic, "I can't, I can't. Oh my god it hurts." Sister Abbey realizes something is terribly wrong. As she looks closer she can see blood coming through. The birth cord was wrapped around the babies neck. Sister Abbey yells over at one of the nuns. "In my kit, get the medicine quickly!" The nun knew exactly what she was talking about. It prepared the nun to be ready and give her a shot that would help Jenine through it as much as they could. The nun rushes over and waits for instruction to give Jenine a shot into her thigh. Abbey instructs Jenine to stop pushing. She puts her hand in and starts to move things around. She was trying to help the baby through. She gradually untangles the cord from around the babies neck. Suddenly Jenine yells out a screech of pain. The nuns are holding Jenine down and praying so loud everyone in the convent could hear it.

It seemed as though it was taking forever. Sister Abbey was growing very concerned. She tried her best to remain calm. "Don't push Jenine. Just hold on ok. Please don't push." Jenine starts to cry. She was so tired and in so much pain. Sister Abbey managed to get the baby unwrapped and pulls ever so slightly. Just then the baby just falls through into Abbeys hands. Even she then started to cry in amazement. She pulls the baby out and shows her to Jenine. "Lord in heaven, bless you and bless this baby." Jenine just cries in amazement as do the other nuns.

This little girl was actually darker skinned tone and had big beautiful brown eyes. She was much darker with black hair. It was thick and beautiful. She looked just like the other baby, but everything was darker skin and hair. Her body was so tiny, maybe four pounds and a very tiny frame. Sister Abbey hands her the baby after wrapping her up. Then she reaches over for the other baby and hands her over to Jenine. As she was holding them she's flooded with emotions. The shock of having twins just took over. One thing Jenine noticed in this moment was the second baby looked so much like Salvador. You could see his face in hers. The other baby had such fair skin. Both the babies were an absolute dream. Sister Abbey starts putting all her things away and cleaning up. She instructs the other nuns to get a wheelchair to assist with getting the babies and her to the room. All of the nuns start to get to work. They knew there was so much to do getting the babies cleaned up and helping Jenine.

A few weeks passed and one specific evening Jenine pulls out the special nighty she made just for her baby with the special button. She has both the babies lying on the bed. She starts to dress the smallest baby and secures the button together. She began to realize this baby looks so much more like Salvador. It seemed more appropriate to dress this one in the nighty with the button, Salvador's button. As she is working with her babies, one of the nuns enter her room. The nun places some clean towels on her dresser. "Well Jenine, I guess it's time you name your babies and enter their dates of birth on our paperwork." The nun places a form on her dresser with a pen, "whenever your ready." Jenine chuckles and looks down at her two beautiful daughters. "What shall we call you little angels?" She said with a smile. While she plays with them caressing their little faces. She looks closely at the tiniest baby. "I think I will call you Annabelle, as she rubs the button on Annabelle's nighty. As for you my little angel. I will call you Serena. Yes that sounds just wonderful." She picks each of them up and places them in their crib together. They look so similar, but so different. She admires their differences. It's almost as if Serena was so much more the look of Jenine and Annabelle was so much more Salvador. Jenine suddenly realized it was like putting her back with the man she loved so much. Then she heads over to the dresser to start filling out her paperwork for the nun. "Let's see... date of birth January 21, 1921, at three p.m. my little angels arrived."

Just as Jenine was filling out the papers Richard walks into the room. Apparently sister Abbey was instructed to inform Richard as soon as the baby was born. He was very surprised to hear she had twins. When he entered Jenines pleasant feelings started to simply slip away from her. She felt a huge pit in her stomach as he entered her room. He had no pleasantries about him when he came in. Sister Abbey was standing directly behind him. "Sister Abbey, will you please leave us alone for a moment?" Abbey quietly closes the door in front of her. Richard looks over at the crib and can see two tiny babies kicking their little feet up in the air. He walks over and looks into the crib. He could see the darker skinned baby and immediately recognized the faces. He looks over at Jenine in complete disgust. "You slept with a latin man, are you kidding me? This is completely unacceptable Jenine. I will not be raising your illegitimate children. Let's get that straight right now. This convent has the facilities to find parents for them. They have an entire orphanage here." Jenine looks at Richard in complete disbelief of what he was even suggesting to her. Jenine stood up from her bedside, "absolutely not... I am not giving my children away no...!!" Richard regains his stern look, stood up tall and came closer to Jenines face. He slaps her across the face so hard she falls onto her bed. Just as he slapped her the sound of the slap was so loud sister Abbey could hear it and quickly enters the room. "Mr Richards excuse my interruption sir please." Abbey was feeling a bit of desperation as she never cared for abusive men. Though she knew her place and could only speak up so much in others personal affairs. Richard looks down at the papers Jenine was filling out. He picks it up and takes a closer look. He realized the papers had to do with her babies. All the information was regarding their birth. He hands the papers over to sister Abbey and promptly instructs her. "These papers will read the date of birth and will state... THE CHILD was STILL born. THE CHILD did not survive the birth! Do you understand sister Abbey?" Abbey was surprised at the suggestion of which Richard was making. "You can't mean this Mr. Richard sir?" Abbey was aware that she had to step very cautiously. Richard Danielson was providing large funds to their church. They desperately needed those funds.

Richard became very stern in his voice, "yes sister Abbey I do. These babies will be left here and you will find them a home. They will not be leaving with us. I do not want any papers stating these babies lived. They will not have a recourse to find us ever. Do we understand each other?" Jenine started to cry. She was feeling completely lost and hopeless. When Richard hit her in the face, it was so hard a bruise was already starting to form. It cut into her cheekbone just enough to cause a small amount of blood to stream down her face. Sister Abbey was feeling so much remorse for Jenine in that moment. She knew she had to think quickly. She realized these babies must not be his, but she knew Jenine would be suffering emotionally leaving her babies behind. "Yes.. yes of course. I will Mr. Danielson of course I will take care of everything sir." She quickly grabs the paper out of his hands. "I do have a suggestion, if I may sir? Miss Jenine had a very difficult delivery. She will need a few more days before the long travel back home if she may stay sir?" Abbey was hoping to give Jenine a little more time with her babies, before she had to go. She came up with any possible excuse hoping to giver her that time. Richard chuckled ever so quietly in his brass cruel manner and looked over at Jenine. He didn't much care either way, but he knew he had to get her back home. He wanted things back to normal. He could then go on with life as he chose. Richard had some business while he was in town. It didn't much matter to him if she stayed a few more days. At least in his mind she would be out of his way during that time. A part of him was angry at her for sleeping with someone prior to their marriage. Even though he had bad intentions through the process. He still was insulted by her actions. He had no respect for her in any way. "I will be returning then in a few days. Have her packed and ready." He looked over at Jenine and barked at her once more before he left the room. "Clean up that face you look despicable."

As soon as Richard left, sister Abbey ran to Jenine's bedside. "My poor child," as she grabbed a cloth from her apron to wipe the blood from her cheek. Jenine cried uncontrollably for a very long time. After a while Jenine started to open up to Abbey about her life and how things had unfolded with the pregnancy. This was the first time Jenine had ever shared anything in her life with anyone. Sister Abbey listened quietly to Jenines life story. Sister Abbey was made aware of Salvadore Cardoza. Who he was and where he was from. Of course she didn't agree with the adultress actions of Jenine, or Salvador. She still had sympathy for her situation. "I will do everything I can to make sure your beautiful daughters have a good home. I promise you that my child." Abbey stayed with Jenine the entire night listening and consoling Jenine through her pain. After a few days Richard returned as promised to pick Jenine up. She was packed and ready to go, but her heart was so torn. She didn't want to leave her daughters. She knew she had no place to go and not near enough money to run away. It was absolutely unheard of for a woman to leave her husband. Sister Abbey promised her she would make sure her daughters were safe and loved.

Some day she would help her find them again. If Jenine ever became strong enough to leave Richard. Jenine was holding Annabelle when Richard entered the room. He was immediately disgusted by the dark skin of the child. "Of course you would hold that one." He grabbed the baby out of her arms. He already had brought two of the nuns with him and instructed them to take the babies away. He didn't want Abbey in the room since she tended to butt in to his affairs. Jenine reached for her baby and started to cry. "No please, Richard please, don't make me do this." She fell to the ground on her knees begging him to reconsider. "Nobody will know. Please we can tell them they are yours. Nobody will know." Richard grabs her arm and her bag. He yanks her to her feet, practically dragging her out of the convent doors. She continues begging, as he pulls her outside. The nuns were crying for her pain as well. They coddled the little babies in their arms. Sister Abbey was in a back room peeking through a door and crying.

The ride home was silent. Richard had nothing to say to Jenine. Jenine was so sad, she couldn't speak a word. They were in a car this time. Richard had purchased a 1921 Ford Model T. More and more people with money were starting to utilize this new form of transportation. It didn't take quite as long to get home in a vehicle as it did with horses and wagons. Richard was quite proud of himself. He loved his car. As they were coming down the driveway towards the Dairy Jenine felt her stomach sinking. It felt so hollow to her. She didn't quite know how she would even face Salvador anymore. Richard finally had something to say to Jenine, but she didn't much care to hear his voice anymore. "Remember what I told you. THE BABY died at birth. End of story. Do we understand each other?" Jenine had nothing to say. She just kept looking out the window. Richard stopped the car and turned to her. He grabbed her face by the chin and faced her to him. "I'm not kidding Jenine, you better answer me!" Jenine became angry and snapped back in her disgruntled voice. "Let go of my face!" Richard pulled back his other hand and made a fist. He socked her so hard, her head hit the door. It knocked her out cold. Richard obviously turned out to be a terrible person. He wanted no problems with Jenine. I think part of it was that he preferred to marry Suzy. They had carried on this charade for so long that Suzy was his sister. It would be difficult to bring that reality out to the public. Richard liked his wealthy status at this point. He enjoyed the level of respect he received from this town. He was a con artist at his best. He accomplished everything he set out to accomplish. After knocking Jenine out cold in the car, he proceeded down the driveway. When he got out he went in and told Suzy to get Jenine in the house. He didn't want to deal with Jenine anymore. Suzy was even shocked when she saw how badly bruised Jenines face was. She knew how brutal Richard could be. She had even dealt with his rath a few times in her life with him. It was never this bad though. She got the workers to help her and they carried Jenine up to her room. Just as Suzy was covering Jenine up in the bed, she could hear someone at the door. Richard had already headed out to the Dairy to check on things.

Suzy rushed down the stairs and saw that it was the town mayor at the door. As the maid was getting ready to answer, Suzy rushed over. "I will answer the door." She pushed the maid aside. He was actually there with flowers and a pie his wife made for Jenine. To celebrate the new baby. Suzy wasn't quite sure what had happened regarding the baby. Richard hadn't even taken the time to tell her anything. Just as she was about to speak, Richard showed up on the front porch. "Hello there Richard. I was just about to say congratulations. The wife sent me over with a pie." Richard had to compose himself. He had to appear that he was mourning the loss of a child. He lowered his head down as he spoke. "I'm terribly sorry Mr. Mayor to inform you, but unfortunately the baby didn't make it... The UH wife, she is resting now." Just as he said it Suzy had a look of shock on her face. She knew Richard was lying, but she wasn't about to speak at that point. The mayor took a few steps back and almost started to stutter. He was very sad for Jenine and Richard. He never had any reason to believe Richard would deceive him. He completely believed what he had said. "I'm so sorry for your loss Richard. Please take these flowers and pie anyway. Call it comfort food I suppose." He handed the items over to Richard and patted him on the shoulder, as if to console him. "Thank you kindly," Richard exclaimed. The mayor quickly exits the porch. He was very uncomfortable with the situation and felt terrible for both of them.

It didn't take long for the rumors to travel. People everywhere in town knew it was said that Jenines baby died at birth. Even Salvador had heard the rumor. He was very sad for the loss. It even took him a few trips to the river to cry as he realized he had lost his child. Nobody saw Jenine after her arrival home. She never left her room. Salvador had been busy packing up their things. He was getting ready to leave to their new found home they had purchased. Phyllix had already informed Richard that they were all leaving. Jenine had heard in passing conversation about Salvador leaving. She never had the will to face him. She felt ashamed that she allowed Richard to do what he had done. Jenine knew if he knew the truth there was nothing he could do about it anyway. Her depression took over to a point that Jenine stopped caring about anything, even herself. She did hear about where Salvador and his family were headed. What farm they had purchased. She took the time to write a letter to sister Abbey. She wanted to inform her where the babies father would be. Her reasoning for this letter was that Jenine had lost her will to live. She wanted to be sure that Sister Abbey would be able to someday bring the girls to Salvadore. Unfortunately Jenine has now reached her point she has given up. She has very grim plans for herself.

Chapter 9

At the convent sister Abbey has been working very hard to find a good home for Annabelle and Serena. Unfortunately there are so many unwanted children at the orphanage. When they had an opportunity to be adopted the nuns took what they could get. A far distant couple from Germany was coming to the states on business. They had tried for many years to conceive a child unsuccessfully. They had been told there where two homeless babies at the convent. Both of them were excited to enter the convent. They had high hopes to adopt a baby. Sister Abbey set up a meeting with the couple. She bathed and dressed Annabelle and Serena. She wanted to prepare them for the visit. They had two beautiful cribs for both the girls, but every time Abbey attempted to separate them in the crib they would cry. Sister Abbey knew that these twin girls loved each other instinctively. They were both so beautiful. Many months have gone by since Jenine had been taken from the convent. The girls were growing so quickly. They both started to develop a bit of a personality. She had noticed little Annabelle was always so curious. She wanted to touch and feel everything. Her eyes were so big and brown. She smiled and cooed so sweetly. She was still very tiny compared to Serena. It took more time for Serena to move around. She was the sleeper. Annabelle always wanted to stay awake. She was the stubborn baby. Sister Abbey loved caring for the twins. She had not yet received the letter from Jenine regarding their father. When the new couple arrived Sister Abbey was just getting finished with dressing the babies. One of the nuns came in to inform her the couple was there. She placed little Annabelle down in the crib next to her sister. She covered both of them and placed the bottles in their mouths. It was delightful watching them together. They would stretch their little arms out to each other. You could feel their attachment when you watched them.

The couple was sitting in Abbeys office where the nun had brought them to wait for Abbey. When Abbey entered the room, she could see the anticipation in their eyes. Sister Abbey spent a few hours with them in the office getting to know them better. She wanted to be sure they were good people. It seemed as though they were both very prepared for a baby. The man was short and thin. He dressed very professionally. He was a business man who was working in the automobile industry. This was a good industry. It was a new prospering field. More and more people were purchasing these vehicles. He was quite successful. The wife was a home maker and so desired to have a baby. Unfortunately she had already miscarried two babies early on in her pregnancies. They were both quite anxious to meet the new babies in the convent. Abbey felt confident in the couple. She explained to both of them they were twins and quite beautiful. The excitement was building in both of them. They wanted desperately to see the babies. Abbey directed them from her office into the nursery where Serena and Annabelle were sleeping. When the couple walked up to the crib and saw the two babies the man immediately had a cross look in his face. He looked over at Sister Abbey very disturbingly. "There is a latin baby in here," he stated very crossly at Abbey. The wife had a disappointed look in her eyes. Sister Abbey became very concerned. Unfortunately there are many prejudices in the world and this would make it very difficult for poor Annabelle. Serena carried a beautiful milky color skin and her hair was slightly lighter then Annabelle. Abbey immediately responded in the most positive light that she could in defense of Annabelle. "She is a very beautiful, sweet baby. At least pick her up and hold her." The man was very disturbed by the color of the babies skin. "No... my family will not accept that. Nor will they accept the relation of a spik. I can't have that. We have a good reputation you know." The woman had already picked up Serena and held her up for her husband to see her. "She is beautiful look at her. Please can we have this one?" She spoke about the babies as if they were property and not human beings. Sister Abbey was disgusted by the attitude, but the dilemma was that unfortunately Annabelle would be met with this horrible reality. Abbey was determined to keep the girls together. Abbey spoke up with a disdainful tone. "These babies are very special. I won't have you coming here and speaking with such disrespect because of her color. I'm sorry, but this simply will not work...

please leave." The woman started to whimper as she placed Serena down in the crib. The husband grabbed hold of his wife's arm as he led her out the door. He was very irritated and had no interest in continuing the conversation.

Abbey struggled for a few months with the problem they faced. Poor Annabelle was just not the baby people wanted. Her dark skin turned most of the couples off to the idea of adoption. By keeping the babies together in the crib the couples would know the latin relation. Abbey finally decided to separate the two babies. She placed Annabelle in another room in a separate crib. When the next couple came in and saw Serena they immediately fell in love with her. They had no idea of the history behind Serena, so there was no longer a prejudice. The couple was immediately interested in taking her home. Sister Abbey went into her office to get the paperwork together for them. She had to re-create a birth certificate. Richard forced his hand on stating that Jenines baby was born dead. She had the papers drawn up and ready. This was Serena's only chance of a family. She hated separating them, but she couldn't see not giving at least one of them a chance at a family.

Everything was drawn up and signed. The couple was ready to take their baby home. Sister Abbey held Serena one last time before she handed her over to the new parents. She had a pit in her stomach over separating the girls. She said a prayer over little Serena and kissed her forehead goodbye. As the couple walked out Abbey could suddenly hear little Annabelle starting to cry from the room in the back. She headed right to her. She picked her up and walked over to the window. She watched the couple climbing in their fancy car and drive away. Little

Annabelle cried so loud it was almost as if she knew her sister was taken away. Sister Abbey wanted to feel joy for Serena, but she felt so much despair for little Annabelle. She could feel the pain in little Annabelle's heart. The rest of the evening Abbey stayed with Annabelle and tried her best to console the baby. It was a very difficult night. As Abbey rocked little Annabelle she admired the little nighty she was wearing. The little button that was sewn onto it was very pretty. Sister Abbey remembered when Jenine placed this pretty nighty on her. Her prayers continued on throughout the night for Annabelle. Many months had passed and not one couple was interested in adopting her. The only thing that rested baby Annabelle at night was the blanky that she used to nestle between the two babies. Sister Abbey often wondered if Annabelle could smell her sister's scent on the blanky. She chose to never wash it, so Annabelle would still feel some sence of closeness to her sister.

One of the nuns came in one morning and delivered the letter Jenine had written for sister Abbey. When she read it she pondered on the thought wether or not Salvador would want Annabelle in his life. She prayed about it for many days and nights. Sister Abbey hadn't been feeling well for quite some time. She thought to herself, *when I'm gone what will become of this sweet child. I have to try for Annabelle.* She had a meeting with the other nuns and they all discussed the idea of talking to Salvador. He would no longer be on Richard's farm and surely far enough away that Richard would never know. They could pose the question to Salvador, as to if he would want the baby. It was a long and stressful discussion with all the nuns.

They finally came to the conclusion that this would be for the best. It was worth a try for the sake of baby Annabelle.

Salvador and Phyllix had spent a lot of time getting their new farm ready to bring Jessica and the children home. There were much needed repairs to be done before Salvador could move them. They had worked for many months on all the repairs. They arrived at Richards and Jenines dairy to pick up the family. Jessica and the girls were so excited for the first time in a very long time. Jessica was actually smiling. She was many months pregnant at this time as well. Phyllix had borrowed a friend's car as to make the move quicker and easier on all of them. What little they owned was placed in the vehicle and everyone was ready to go. Phyllix walked up to Richard and Jenines house to say goodbye. Richard had already started out the door. He shook hands with Phyllix and waved goodbye to the rest of the family. Jenine watched intently from her window. She didn't even have the desire to say anything to anyone. She just watched quietly. What little emotion left in her was sucked away when she had to leave her babies. She was pale and thin. She spoke very little. Salvador often wondered if she was going to be ok. He knew how desperately she wanted a baby. For her to have done the things she did to just have the baby die. He was sad for her and for his lost child. He knew he needed to move forward and salvage his family. He had to try to re-build his relationship with his wife Jessica. He saw her in the window and when Jessica wasn't watching he waved in Jenines direction. He wanted to say goodbye without drawing attention to himself, or her. Jenine saw him and gently placed her hand on the window. She couldn't even bring herself to smile. She just held her hand there as if to touch his face from a distance. He climbed into the passenger seat and Phyllix got into the driver seat. Jessica was busy getting the girls in the car and herself. As they drove away a tear climbed down Jenines cheek. Her silent sadness was a dark place for her. She lost all desire for anything and had nothing left. She simply existed from day to day. Then she came to a sad realization in her mind. She sighed to herself, *well I guess my evil ways.. my heartless self... I guess my punishment is here to stay.*

The girls held on to Roscoe in the back seat and giggled to each other. They have such high hopes in coming to their new home. Of course Louisa had to ask, "Pappa does this mean we can get another pet pig?" They all laughed together as soon as she asked them the question. It was almost as if they all felt a sense of complete freedom and joy. Salvador reaches back to Louisa to touch her knee. He pats her lightly while he's laughing. "We will most definitely get you girls a new pet pig." Even Jessica laughed. She felt so relieved to finally have a normal life again. She had baby Manuel in her arms. He was sleeping peacefully on the trip. He was much bigger now, but still only about one year and a half old. Maria had been a big help with baby Manuel. She has certainly grown to be quite the responsible child. Little Louisa was still the fun loving carefree person. Salvador would call her the dreamer. It reminded him often of himself. As they finally reached the Cardoza ranch Salvador announced, "were here, were here." The girls and Jessica looked out the window. They were anxiously awaiting to get out of the car. Even Roscoe was jumping around in the back ready to get out of the car.

Phyllix pulled up and they all quickly climbed out. They were all looking in amazement at this beautiful two story home. It was large with two porches. Maria quickly let Roscoe out of the car and started helping her mom with Manuel. Jessica knelt down and handed Manuel to Maria. She turned around and saw the miles of beautiful green grass that seemed to go on forever around them. Louisa was jumping up and down, "can we go in pappa, can we, can we, I wanna see?" She was so excited she could barely stay still. Salvador laughed, "c'mon let's go in, of course Louisa lets go." Jessica started walking up the front porch steps as she admired the beautiful double doors in front of her. She was so pleased with what she saw. Salvador could see the joy in her eyes. For the first time, they met eyes looking across the patio at each other. Salvador reached over and caressed her cheek as he use to do all the time. Jessica let a single tear go down her face. She was still angry, but she wanted so much for them to have a new start. She was willing to finally give him a smile. Maria had known for a long time that things were not good with her mom and dad. In that moment she saw them showing affection again. it made her so happy. She whispered down to her brother, "I think were gonna be ok Manuel." Even she felt some joy, more then she has for a while. She allowed the burden of her parents pain affect her on some levels. That moment seeing them walking on the porch of their new home Maria finally felt some relief as well. Little Louisa was still too young to understand what had been going on. She was busy dancing across the porch as excited as a child who just got a new pony. Phyllix headed over to the dairy barn. He wanted to check on things and give the family time to boast in their new home.

The house was in beautiful condition. It was a Dutch Colonial home. It looked like a large two story barn with two large porches. There where big double doors at the main entrance and windows everywhere. The porches carried large round pedestals and the framing around all the windows were big beautiful black shutters. The entire house was white with black trimming and black shutters. There were planters under both the big front windows for big beautiful plants. You could see lacy white curtains through all the windows. Lucas had left the curtains behind. His mother had made them special for that house. He couldn't see taking them down. As Jessica opened the big double doors you could almost see the entire downstairs floor plan from the front door. It was a big open space from beginning to end. A stairway was on the left side. Big steps with a railing that lead all the way up the stairs to the second floor. The railing was a wood color and shiny. The curves in the rail were intricate in design. The flooring was all natural wood floors. You could see the kitchen from the door. Jessica stood there in awe of what she was looking at. From were she was standing she could look acrossed and see the same beautiful big doors. Salvador was so excited he couldn't stand to wait. He kept pulling at Jessica to come further in the house to look around. He grabbed her hand like a child in a candy store ready to go shopping. "C'mon Jessica, come look at your kitchen." She followed willingly smiling and almost giggling. As they entered the kitchen Jessica was shocked. She loved everything she saw. A large butcher block table was placed in the center of the kitchen. There were cabinets everywhere. A wood stove was located on the back wall by all the cabinets. The same natural woods went from end to end. There was a pump in the sink for water. You could pump it right in your own kitchen. Jessica walked over to this large brick fireplace that was in between the living room space and the kitchen space. It was so big you could fit five loafs of bread in it. "This will keep us very warm in the winter time won't it Salvador?" Jessica spoke with pride and honor. She felt so good to know that Salvador and Phyllix worked so hard to achieve this for them. The girls were so excited they wanted to go looking up the stairs as well. Maria handed Manuel to Jessica, "can we please go look up stairs mamma?" Maria asked in anticipation. "Of course go, look go." Just as Jessica uttered the words the girls took off running to the stairs. "Slow down girls. You are going to fall. Be careful, my goodness meha's slow down." Both the girls halted and started to giggle and walk more gently. Salvador started to laugh. His smile lit up the room. Jessica covered her mouth as if to be serious, but couldn't help to giggle as well.

Phyllix came walking in as he saw both of them standing in the kitchen area. "So what do you think Jessica. Isn't it great?" He patted the wall like a carpenter who just built a home. Jessica smiled and handed Manuel to Salvador for the first time. Salvador was pleasantly surprised. He reacted immediately to grab onto Manuel from her hands. Suddenly Jessica started to cry, but they were happy tears. "I'm so proud of both of you. Thank you so much for making this happen for us, thank you." Phyllix walked over and gave Jessica a gentle hug and patted her back. Salvador walked over as well to be closer to her. He was mesmerized holding his son for the first time. "Things are going to be good for us. We are going to be ok," Salvador said proudly as he coddled his son in his arms. Maria had started down the stairs excited to tell her mom what she had seen. She leaned down to look at where everyone was. She could see her pappa holding Manuel and her momma wiping her eyes of tears. Maria decided to sit at the stairs and just allow her parents the time. Just as she sat down Louisa came running down the stairs. Maria grabbed her arm, "wait Louisa look." Maria pointed her sister to her parents. She wanted her to see the closeness. She wanted Louisa to be aware of the bonding that was happening in that moment. "Everybody will be happy again sissy. Wait here for just a moment. Give them a moment." Louisa sat next to her sister quietly. Louisa didn't really understand the strain that had been on the family, but she knew to listen to her sister.

Chapter 10

Back at Jenine and Richards ranch everything seemed to be running smoothly and successfully. Suzy would tend to their garden, while Richard continued to work with the dairy and his employees. Jenine was lost in the mix of that home. She had lost a lot of weight and was becoming increasingly depressed. It seemed Richard just ignored her and would constantly tell Suzy to stay away from her. She actually was starting to feel guilty for being a part of her turmoil. One evening Suzy snuck up to Jenines room when Richard was busy in the dining room with a business associate. He was also setting up new deals to make more money and prosper further. When Suzy reached Jenines door she tapped on it ever so quietly. She didn't want Richard to know she was up there. Jenine was lying in her bed coddled in a ball with a blanket covering her. She didn't get out of bed much. She would cry periodically then just sleep. She never even responded to the knock on her door. Suzy entered the room very slowly as she spoke, "Jenine, is it alright for me to enter please?" Jenine slowly turned in the direction of her door. She still didn't bother to respond. Suzy knelt down to Jenine's bed side and started to caress her hair. "Jenine you look as though you haven't even cleaned your hair in months. I know this situation hasn't turned out well. I'm very sorry for this, but you need to eat. You need to come back out into the world." Jenine still had nothing to say. She just laid there with emptiness in her eyes. Suzy started to wonder if a doctor should be called in to take a look at her. If she attempted to suggest that to Richard he would probably get irritated. She felt compelled to ask him anyway. She stood up from the bed and quietly exits the room.

She headed down the stairwell and could hear Richard deep in conversation with one of the town's people. They were smoking pipes and having drinks. It wasn't polite for any woman to interrupt him. He was very adamant on that subject, but Suzy felt it was time to give attention to Jenine. *This wouldn't look good for him either.* Suzy thought in her mind. If she was truly ill and he just allowed that to continue, people in town would start to question Richards true intentions. He has a reputation of being a good solid religious man. They also saw him as a good husband and provider to his wife. If he just allowed her to get ill and do nothing, that could tarnish his good name. She entered the dining room and Richard immediately turned his pleasant look on his face, to a bit of disgust. He felt it was rude of Suzy to interrupt his meeting. The man sitting in his chair stood up out of respect, as soon as Suzy came in. He nodded to her, "hello this fine evening Miss Suzy. I haven't see you since the wedding. How is Miss

Jenine doing?" Just as he said it, Suzy felt a bit of relief. She knew by him mentioning Jenine it would enable her to bring up Jenine's condition. She desperately wanted to get Jenine proper medical attention. "Well hello sir, nice to see you also. Actually since you mentioned it, Jenine is my reason for coming in. I needed to make Richard aware that Jenine is not well. We need to hail for a doctor tonight." The man had a bit of confusion on his face and looked over at Richard. "Well Richard, maybe I should go then? We wouldn't want to oversight Miss Jenine's health, over business. We can continue this later if you like?" Richard was extremely annoyed that Suzy cornered him like this, but he had no choice at this point. Richard looked over at Suzy and shook his head. "Well sir, I suppose I should head out then. To hail a doctor this evening." Richard said irritatedly in Suzy's direction. "We can continue this tomorrow evening. Is that good for you?" "Yes, yes, of course no problem. You must let me know how she is doing then." "Suzy please let this gentleman to the door. I will head out also." Suzy leads the man out as Richard reaches for his hat and coat. Richard lingered at the door waiting for the man to drive away. He was anxious to address Suzy, before he headed out. He wanted to be sure the man was gone before he spoke to her.

Just as he drove away, Richard turns to Suzy. He grabs her shoulder, pulling her aggressively towards him. "How dare you corner me like that. If you ever do that again, your face will look like her's did when we arrived back from the last trip. Do you understand me?" Suzy was surprised at how horrible he became in that moment. It truly scared her. She knew he was capable and willing to do such harm to her. She remembered what Jenine looked like when Richard had hit her. It truly startled her. Suzy had always believed that Richard loved her and would never hurt her in that way. Now she is coming to the realization that anyone who crosses him, or gets in his way he will hurt. It does not matter if it is a woman, or not there was no stopping him. "I will be heading out to get a doctor, but it is a waste of time. She is not ill. She's drowning in her pitiful sorrows, over those spik babies she created. Quite frankly I don't care. Now that you made it publicly known. I am forced to take action for my reputation sake. He stormed out the door angry and flustered. Suzy felt relieved he just left and it ended there. She headed over to the kitchen to make tea for Jenine. She was hoping to at least get something warm in her system. Suzy reflected on what Richard had said. In that moment she became confused. She realized what Richard had said before when he brought Jenine home. It wasn't making sence to what he just said at the door. It was all starting to go over in her mind. *Oh my goodness, she had twins. He said babies. Did they both die?"* She quickly got together a tray with a tea cup and tea. She headed up the stairs to speak to Jenine once more. She didn't bother to knock this time. She knew Jenine wouldn't answer her anyway. As soon as she entered she placed the tray down on the dresser and knelt down to Jenine. "Tell me what happened Jenine. Did you have twins and they both died? Please tell me. Richard is not being honest and I want to help you." Jenine quickly rolled back over facing the wall once again and started to cry. She actually spoke for the first time. The only thing she could muster out was, "Annabelle and Serena." Jenine wanted so badly to tell Suzy they weren't dead. She wanted to share her pain. She knew if Richard found out it would be bad for both of them. She just continued to cry. Suzy put both her hands on her mouth in shock and felt the despair of Jenine in that moment. She wasn't given anymore information so she assumed they both had died. Suzy sat up on the bed by Jenine pulling her close to her. This way Jenine could at least cry on Suzy's shoulder. Suzy wanted her to have someone hugging her. She didn't want Jenine to feel completely alone. Eventually Jenine fell to sleep again. Suzy left the room. She wanted to give her some peace and quiet. After a few hours Richard came up the driveway with the doctor. As soon as they entered, Richard pointed him up to Jenines room.

Suzy was downstairs in the kitchen and Richard walked in his study. Suzy decided to stay close to the bottom of the stairs and wait to see what the doctor might say. It took the doctor about an hour before he came down the stairs. Suzy immediately walked towards the doctor. He was shaking his head and clasped his hands together. "Well shall I discuss this with Mr. Richards, or with you Miss Suzy?" "Richard is in his study and doesn't want to be disturbed. Please share with me what is going on with her?" "Well Miss Suzy, she is going through severe depression with the loss of her child." As soon as he said child Suzy knew Jenine did not tell the doctor everything. She had to be careful not to share information that could cause questions in anyone's minds. "Yes well doctor what can we do? She's not eating?" "I have a tea that is a calming tea. You should prepare her a broth so that she is getting something in her system. Unfortunately I don't believe that she will bounce back for a while. The best thing for her is that she is given space and the proper time to heal. If she doesn't improve within a few weeks I would suggest possibly bringing her into the hospital. Maybe we can provide her more care." Suzy was disappointed that there wasn't much the doctor could do for her. "Well thank you doctor for your time then. I will walk you to the door."

After a few weeks while Suzy was tending to the garden. She had noticed Jenine walking out the back door, onto the patio. She was quite surprised to see her out of her room. It was refreshing. Suzy felt that maybe she is feeling better. She decided to leave Jenine alone and allow her the space she needed. She simply continued her work in the garden. Suzy smiled and waved in Jenine's direction, but it seemed Jenine wasn't even paying attention. She just kept walking out towards the old trail Salvador use to go down everyday. It was early morning and everyone was busy working the dairy. Nobody even noticed Jenine. Jenine had lost so much weight her clothes were very loose on her. The shoulders of her dress were slipping off and Jenine had to keep pulling them up. At this point Jenine couldn't cry anymore. She didn't have the strength for even that. She stumbled through the trail as she was so weak and lifeless in her journey. She reached the tree Salvador used to lean on when he looked out into the ravine. There was a small bridge going across to the other side. She leaned back onto the tree as if to emulate how Salvador once stood. Her dress was stained and torn in some areas. Jenine hadn't been taking very good care of herself, or her appearance. She looked as if she was wilting away. Her hair was stringy and tangled. She didn't even bother to braid it. She had dark circles under her eyes and her mouth was dry. At this point she was severely dehydrated. She walked over to the ravine. It was shallow and rocky. There was a fast current running through the rocks. It was slightly deeper under the bridge, but not by much. It maybe ran about four feet high under the bridge. Jenine walked over the bridge and stood there for a moment holding the rails. She looked up to the sky and simply said, "Lord forgive me, for I am not strong." Then she suddenly dove head first into the ravine. As soon as she landed in the water her head hit a large rock below. She was immediately knocked unconscious and went deep into the bottom of the ravine. Blood started to stream through the waters. This was truly the end of Jenines journey in her life. She had ended her suffering forever. Her lifeless body started to float away, when her dress became caught up on a large sharp rock. The water simply continued to flow across her body as if nothing had occurred.

Many hours had passed since Suzy saw jenine walk down the trail. It was dinner time and Suzy was starting to worry. Richard was at the dinner table. Suzy decided it was time to go looking for her. She entered the dining area, "Richard I'm concerned, Jenine left the house hours ago. This is the first time she has gone outside in a very long time and she still hasn't returned." Once again Richard showed his total discourteous attitude for Jenine, but he didn't want her wondering around at night. That would make people think she was crazy, or something. He couldn't have that reputation. "Well I guess we better get our lanterns and go see what the problem is. She's probably out by the water feeling sorry for herself." Suzy was surprised that he was willing to be a part of the search, but she was glad since she didn't care to walk out there alone. They took the trail and started yelling out for Jenine in hopes she might let them know where she was. It was quite dark out and even with the lanterns it was difficult to maneuver through the trail. When they reached the end, both of them were surprised that she was nowhere to be found. Suzy became increasingly concerned. Even Richard was starting to worry. He didn't much care for her, but if she took off that would raise many questions from the town's people. "Would she cross that bridge Richard?" Richard thought that might be possible. However that wasn't common for her to go out that far. They both headed over the bridge, just as they crossed the center of the bridge Suzy saw a glimmer of blue cloth off Jenines dress through the water. She had to take a second look with the lantern closer in. She leaned forward and Richard grabbed Suzy by the arm. "Woah, woah..... What are you doing Suzy? That's a high current down there, be careful." Suzy gasped and clenched both her hands to her mouth in shock. She couldn't believe what she saw. "Oh my God... oh my god... lord in heaven." Suzy fell to her knees and started to cry. Richard still did not know what Suzy saw. "What on earth is wrong with you Suzy? What are you looking at?" He couldn't possibly imagine such a thing as what Jenine had done. Suzy pointed into the water. Her lantern placed closer to Jenines silhouette deep under the rocks. Richard looked down where Suzy was pointing. He squinted his eyes trying to focus in the water to see. Suddenly he saw what Suzy was frantically pointing at. There she was. Her face bobbing to the surface with blood across her eye and her cheek. The rock she hit her head on cracked her skull. The blood was everywhere floating through the water and across her face. Her long hair was just draping through the water. Her dress sprawled around her. Richard was immediately startled and almost lost his footing on the bridge. Suzy quickly grabbed his leg and he grabbed the rail. For a few moments Richard didn't even have words to say. He was completely shocked. Part of Jenine's dress was still tightly bound onto the sharp rock. It kept her body in place under the water. "We have to go get some help Richard. We have to get her out of there!" Suzy was so upset. She was practically yelling at Richard. She was angry at him for doing nothing to help her. He allowed this to happen to her in Suzys mind. "Why, oh why... Jenine!" Suzy was still so upset. She could barely think straight. "Stay here Suzy, I will be back." Richard took off running back down the trail back to the dairy. He quickly gathered up some of the men who stayed on the farm to come help him. He sent one of them to town to get the police and the town doctor. He knew the doctor wouldn't be able to revive her at this point, but he had to be sure that the proper people were made aware of what had occurred. The men were instructed to get a large blanket and some rope. None of them were sure what had happened, but they knew it was bad. Richard told them Miss Jenine took her own life. They all quickly started back down the trail. Everyone worked together to get her out of the current safely. They had to be careful not to fall in themselves. When they got her to the other side they placed her on the ground and Richard had them cover her up with the blanket. It was very difficult for any of them to look at her. She had been in the water for so long it was a dismal sight for anyone. Her lips were blue and her face was white. Suzy couldn't bare to look anymore. She wondered away and sat next to the tree and just cried in disbelief.

After a while the doctor and the police officers came to the sight with their lanterns. They walked across the bridge and started looking at the scene. The doctor kneeled closer to her body and took off the blanket to get a closer look. He checked her pulse and of course deemed her dead on site. He investigated the cut on her head and saw that the injury to her head was so extreme that she most likely died the moment she hit her head. The doctor explained his findings to the police. They turned over to Richard and started asking him several questions. Even the police knew they had to step cautiously at their tone with Richard. He had a lot of power in that town. They did not want to insult him in any way while doing this investigation. The doctor remembered seeing Jenine a few weeks earlier. He explained to the police the level of depression Jenine was going through over the loss of her child. Just as Suzy heard what the doctor was saying she leered over at Richard. At this point Suzy was seething anger from her eyes to his. They wrapped Jenine's body in the blanket. The men all carried her back to the house in complete silence. Suzy went in the house long before they had completed the investigation. She went into the kitchen and managed to find herself some liqueur. She didn't normally drink, but she suddenly found herself not caring about etiquette anymore. She just couldn't wrap her mind around what had happened. Richard made arrangements with the doctor to set up a burial place and time. There was a graveyard in town and the doctor made sure to take care of the details for Richard. By the time everyone was finished it was extremely late. Richard came in the back door to find Suzy passed out drunk on a chair in the formal room. He didn't quite know how to deal with what had happened either. He decided to leave Suzy there. He went into his room and sat down on his bed. He was exhausted and very unsure how things would unfold in the eyes of the town. He rubbed his face and just kept shaking his head.

The next day the doctor gave word that everything was arranged. Richard can plan a funeral in the next few days. Word traveled across town quickly. It seemed everyone simply accepted that Jenine had committed suicide from severe depression. They all believed she could not get over the death of her baby. No one questioned Richard any further on the subject. There was an out poor of sympathetic towns people. They were all sending flowers in to Richard for the funeral. The dairy workers were allowed to attend the up coming funeral. They had known Jenine for so many years. Many of them didn't care for Jenine since she was such a cruel person. They had all come to the realization at how fragile she became. When she lost her baby. They saw her slip away in so much despair. Many of them felt sorry for her. They didn't want to see her go in such a tragic way. Suzy chose not to speak to Richard. She was so angry at him that she didn't even want to look at him. She knew the truth about him more then anyone did. At least she thought she knew the truth. She never found out that neither of Jenines children where dead and Richard forced Jenine to leave them behind. Phyllix had been in town for a while when he overhead the talk in town about Jenines suicide. When he returned to the Cardoza Ranch he pulled Salvador aside. Far away from the house. He didn't want Jessica to hear what they were talking about. Phyllix knew that there was more to the relationship with Jenine and Salvador. He had figured out long ago that the baby Jenine was carrying was Salvador's. Jessica always sensed that as well. She had heard the rumors that the baby died. This made Jessica feel she could push the bad memories aside. She never wanted to think about the affair again."Salvador something has happened that I think you would want to know." Salvador stepped forward with curiosity in his eyes. "What is it Phyllix? Is something wrong at the farm?" "No, no nothing like that.... it's Jenine." He paused in grief.... "There saying... in town she committed suicide at the bridge on the Dairy." Phyllix could barely hold back the tears. "The funeral is in a couple of days." Salvador stepped back startled at what Phyllix just told him. He had almost a blank look on his face. "Whaa... whaat, why? I don't understand." Phyllix didn't even have a chance to respond. Salvador turned and walked away almost in a daze. Phyllix often wondered if a part of Salvador grew some twisted form of love towards her. Phyllix quickly followed Salvador and stood in front of him to stop him from walking away. "You can't do this Salvador. You can't show Jessica that you feel any emotion for this woman. You will crush her. Snap out of it Salvador. You have to!" Salvador stopped and looked at Phyllix realizing what he was saying was true. He lowered his head for a moment and lifted back up. "I know.... I just need a minute ok.... Just let me walk." Salvador was struggling keeping the tears from falling. His heart was torn in pieces. Phyllix moved out of his way and let him go. Jessica was on the deck shaking out some rugs and hitting them with a stick to get the dirt out. She looked over and saw Salvador walking towards their new garden. She could tell something wasn't right with him and had a curious look in his eyes. She decided to dismiss it since she was so busy. She went on with her work never to see the realization of Salvador's pain for another woman.

Salvador wandered out into the large field as far as he could. He wanted to be sure Jessica could not see him. He fell to his knees and began to bawl uncontrollably. He realized in that moment that he had fallen in love with Jenine. Some twisted thing happened inside him that he can never understand. He allowed himself time to grieve before he returned back towards the house. The funeral had started and Salvador stayed clear of it. He knew he needed to just move forward. He prayed for her soul and felt that it was time to move on. For his wife's sake he chose not to linger in his emotions. He wanted so desperately to have happiness with his family. Many people in town attended Jenines funeral out of respect for Richard. Suzy chose not to attend. She had so many disturbing feelings at this point for Richard. She didn't want to be a part of any of it. Richard played the sad mourning husband well. None of the town's people questioned the situation. They were all very supportive and brought flowers and prayers for Richard. Even the doctor and the police who where at the scene attended the funeral. The preacher mentioned Jenines struggles with the loss of her child. He gave a soothing sermon. The nuns at the convent had heard about Jenines suicide. Sister Abbey was struggling knowing the truth of Jenines true issues. She knew why it drove Jenine to this suicide. She chose to attend the funeral and stayed in the back. She prayed for Jenine's soul and cried for her. Sister Abbey had to leave the funeral before it ended. She worried of any questions that may come her way. She knew Richard would not be pleased to see her there.

Chapter 11

Now that this has happened sister Abbey has decided now more then ever that it was the right decision to bring Annabelle to Salvador. She began putting together the arrangements for the trip. She already knew where Salvador was living at this point. She had recieved the letter from Jenine earlier on and had done her research. People in town were already talking about the newly named ranch. The Cardoza Ranch. Salvador and Phyllix had been working hard on the dairy. They had some employees and had things running quite nicely. Jessica and the girls were putting together a beautiful garden of vegetables. It was large enough to feed three families. They weren't financially well off, or anything. It did help to be farmers. They could fend for themselves on many things. Jessica was very handy with sewing. Salvador and Phyllix would purchase feed sacks then Jessica would take the emptied sacks and put together a dress, or shirt. Something someone needed in the family. She would make curtains, socks, clothes, etc.. She used every bit of the material. It had become a common thing for the stores that sold the feed to bag it in different designed sacks. The store owners became very aware that woman used them for clothing and other household needs. It compelled farmers to buy more, just so their wive's had more material to work with. Everything they did was done with care and nothing was ever wasted. Phyllix slept in the barn. They had set up an area there for him. He would eat with the family every evening. He was quite happy with that arrangement since he had no wife. He felt that was appropriate. Jessica had finally had her fourth child and named her Rose.

Salvador and Phyllix did a wonderful job getting the farm running smoothly. The girls had many chores. They had a chicken coop for the chickens and the eggs. They used the manure for the garden. The girls didn't care for that job, but they had to do it. The garden had tomatoes, beans, peas, turnips and many other things. Jessica was already planning for the harvest once everything matured. She was going to can as much as she could for winter use. Jessica taught both the girls how to churn butter. They had a big old barrel churn. They would put about five gallons of cream at a time and both girls helped each other crank it. They couldn't do it too fast. They had to make it thump as it went down so it would work. Everyone was working on this particular day and had so many things yet to do to prepare before winter came. Salvador was busy harvesting their wheat and oats. He and his workers would separate the grain from the stalk. They called that thrashing. Phyllix was working in the dairy all morning. Later that day Jessica could hear a car coming up the drive way. It wasn't too often they had visitors out there. That was a bit of a surprise to her. The girls became quite excited. They hadn't seen many cars as they were becoming more popular in the towns. The farmers took a lot longer to reform to this new way of transportation.

As the car drove up Salvador looked over and saw the vehicle. The girls put down their buckets of seed and started to run towards the up coming vehicle. Jessica yells out at them, "girls where are you going?" Louisa turns to her. "We just want to see who it is madra please." She tilts her head and gives Jessica a sweet smile. Jessica giggles, "go, go you two little miss noseys go." The girls run over to the end of the driveway and wait. Salvador heads over that way as well. Jessica just continues to work on her garden. It was a peaceful place for her. She enjoyed it and didn't have much interest in who it was. She got use to the idea that Salvador and Phyllix had business people come over once in while. People who may have been interested in some livestock, or possibly milk produced on the dairy. It seemed boring and uninteresting to her. She loved their changed life, but left the details to her husband and cousin. As the vehicle stopped someone came out of the rear door. It was Sister Abbey. She had baby Annabelle wrapped up in a blanket. Abbey was holding Annabelle close in her arms. Louisa points to Sister Abbey. "Maria it's a nun. She has a baby in her arms. Look at that Maria. Maybe she needs help, or something?" In that moment Maria gets a terrible feeling in her gut. She remembers back what things had happened when Manuel was born. She may have been young, but she knows Jenine had gotten pregnant soon after all those events that took place. A part of her even sensed this can't be good. Salvador can see from a distance that a nun came out of the vehicle. He walks closer and can see that she has a baby in her arms. Abbey remains close to the car as she waits for Salvador to walk closer to her. Abbey instructs the driver, "please wait here for a moment." Just as Salvador gets close enough Abbey walks towards him. "You are Salvador I assume?" Salvador gulps and can see she's holding a baby. "Yes, yes I am?" He has this very confused look on his face. Louisa approaches Salvador, "pappa look at the baby." Louisa is so innocent. She doesn't understand what is about to unfold. Maria however is starting to put it all together. She gets extremely angry and scowls in Salvador's direction. "Your going to ruin our life pappa. Mama will never, ever forgive you!" Maria is so angry she screams at him and turns and runs away. Louisa is completely confused. She stays close by to see the baby. Sister Abbey explains very little, but enough for Salvador to realize this child is his. "I don't understand. I thought Jenine lost her baby? I just don't understand?" The only thing Sister Abbey can safely tell him is that this child, this beautiful child is his. She points him to the button on the babies nightgown. The very button Jenine sewed on Annabelle's nighty. As soon as Salvador saw the button he knew it was true. He starts to cry and looks deep into the beautiful eyes of Annabelle. "She needs a home Salvador. Can you please love her and care for her?" Salvador was completely in the moment. He wasn't even looking behind him to see that Jessica was standing there watching. She had gotten up and walked over without Salvador, or sister Abbey even noticing her.

Jessica became angry and she knew exactly who this

child was. She began to scowl in Salvador's direction. No words could even come out. Sister Abbey knew this was going to be a difficult situation, but this is truly Annabelle's only chance for a family. Salvador looks over at Jessica. He was prepared to plead with her. Before he could even speak Jessica put her hand up in front of his face. "Don't speak to me. Don't touch me. Just stay away from me. Do you understand? I hate you!!!!" She turns away and runs into the house. While she is stomping away, she is uttering her portugese language in every unkind word she can come up with. She couldn't even bring herself to cry. She was too angry to even shed a tear. Maria had ran into the cornfield as far away as she could go. Louisa became scared and confused. "Padre why is everyone so angry? She is so pretty." Salvador takes Annabelle from sister Abbey. He had already decided this is his daughter. He will not turn his back on her. "I will love her. I promise you this." He delicately caresses Annabelle's face as he speaks to Abbey. He looks closely at the button in awe. Abbey smiles, "I know this will be difficult for your family, but I can see you will love her. I must go now." She climbs back into the car and sits. Louisa comes closer to Salvador to see Annabelle. He kneels down to her to show her how pretty the baby is. Just as the driver is pulling out, Sister Abbey taps him on the shoulder. "Wait, just a moment." The driver stops. Sister Abbey puts her head out of the window to speak once more to Salvador. "I must tell you one thing, but no one must know. Do you understand?" Salvador tilts his head in confusion, "of course, yes what." Abbey looks down on the floor board of the car. She even questions herself before she speaks. She feels in her heart he should know. "I just... I feel you need to know the truth."

She begins pulling at her sleeve feeling so uncomfortable. She knows in her heart she has to tell him. "THEIR WAS A TWIN...." Just as she said it, she taps the driver. "I must go now. Drive please." She states in an impatient tone. She was worried Salvador would have more questions. She knew she would not be able to answer them. Abbey has no idea that at that moment Salvador is thinking, *it must have been the twin that died.* He jumps up hurriedly and starts to run towards the car. "Wait... wait... I don't understand please wait." Sister Abbey yells out of the car. "Her name is Serena! That is all I can say!" The car roars away from him. He stops there for a moment to reflect on everything. He's still holding Annabelle in his arms. He looks back at his house and his daughter Louisa is standing there with confusion on her face.

He walks back towards Louisa with the baby in his arms. He kneels down to Louisa so she can get a closer look. She gently rubs baby Annabelle's face. "Pappa can I hold her?" Salvador loves the innocence of Louisa. He knows she does not grasp what is going on around them. "Louisa this baby is your baby sister. Do you understand?" She gets a puzzled look in her face. Then she turns and looks deep into Annabelle's eyes. "She looks like you pappa." He smiles, "yes, yes she does, doesn't she. I will let you hold her, but you must be very careful ok?" Louisa holds out her arms to grab the baby. She had held Manuel and Rose several times already. She was use to holding a baby. "I'm a big sister pappa." Louisa smiles with pride. "I must go speak with mama. Will you sit on the porch with Annabelle for me please?" "She follows her pappa to the porch and sits with the baby.

He enters the house and finds Jessica sitting in the kitchen. "Jessica we have to talk about this." She jumps up from her chair. "No we don't. We don't have to talk about anything. I understand completely. You are a lyer. I understand you loved Jenine, didn't you? Tell me the truth" Salvador lowers his head to the ground. He looks back up at her ashamed. "I don't know. I just don't know how I feel." Jessica becomes even more angry. "This baby was suppose to be dead." She screams and starts to spur out her native Portuguese. She begins waving her hands frantically at Salvador. Her anger just seemed to unfold uncontrollably. Salvador becomes angry and lashes back at her. He became assertive with Jessica. His frustration took over. "Jessica stop this now. This child is mine. Do you understand? This is no longer a choice. This conversation is done. Jenine committed suicide. Annabelle has nobody. You will take care of her, as you would your own children. That's it!!! I'm her father!!!" He slams his fist down on the table. Jessica was startled by his aggressive outburst. She stepped back and said nothing. Salvador had become so outraged, he threw the bowl sitting on the table across the room. He leaves the house and storms passed Louisa as she's coddling the baby in her arms. Phyllix had heard the shouting and came back towards the house. Jessica stepped outside to the porch and watched Salvador walking away. Phyllix saw the baby in Louisa's arms and looks up confused at Jessica. He chuckles not realizing how bad the situation had become. Then innocently asked Jessica, "whose baby is this?" Jessica looks over at Phyllix and scowls. "That is **SALVADOR'S DAUGHTER!!!!**" She angrily storms back into the house.

There was no more tender love between Salvador and Jessica. Jessica did her wifely duties in the day and at night, but lost complete respect for Salvador. At every opportunity Jessica would have Maria care for Annabelle. She became almost like the surrogate mother of Annabelle. Maria became so disgusted with her pappa. She rarely even acknowledged him anymore. She would stay away from him as much as possible. Maria simply took on the duty of caring for her little sister Annabelle. She accepted that this was her sister and never blamed Annabelle for her fathers bad choices. Louisa would help her mama with the other children, along with her chores. Maria simply took care of little Annabelle. Every time Salvador would show attention to baby Annabelle it would almost clear the room. Jessica didn't want to watch and Maria didn't want to be present. Phyllix always tried his best to bring them together, but it was hopeless. He had figured out how the baby came to be. He understood this family was torn and may never come back together again. Jessica would never introduce Annabelle in any other way. When neighbors came to visit she would inform them that Annabelle was **Salvador's daughter**. Nobody questioned what she was saying. Nor did they understand the meaning. Most of them assumed it was her baby, but she would make it clear in her way. Since Manuel was so close to the same age as Annabelle they grew up together very close. Maria felt a certain obligation to Annabelle. She was given the majority of the responsibility for her. Jessica never bonded with Annabelle. She tried respecting Salvador's wishes. Unfortunately it was the bare minimum effort. She never liked the situation. Jessica harbored resentment for a long time.

As time went on. The years passed. The Cardoza family created a system that worked well for them. The dairy was producing enough to support the family and the workers. Annabelle's birthday is today. She is nine years old. Manuel was only about a year older by a few months. He loved playing with his little sister. He became very close to her and always watched over her. Maria still took care of her as if she were her child. Maria carried her anger with her father throughout the many years that passed. Eventually she sat down with her pappa and they worked through it. Maria decided to forgive him. In her heart she will always feel fear to trust him. This day was very special to Maria. She wanted it to be a happy celebration for Annabelle's birthday. Manuel was anxious to help with the preparations. Louisa has grown to almost sixteen years old at this point. She was maturing and a very pretty young lady. She was a hard worker in the gardens and all the many chores the girls had. Maria now almost nineteen she was interested in finding someone for herself to marry. She had high hopes for the up coming festival they will be joining very soon. It is a traditional festival called the Chamarita. She wanted to find a good man that would never do to her what her father did to her mother. Maria had serious trust issues at this point in her life. She did not make friends very well and kept to herself mostly. Maria had learned some baking techniques from her mother. She picked enough berries to make a pie in celebration of Annabelle's birthday. Manuel and Salvador were in the barn covering up Annabelle's gift and preparing for the surprise. Jessica now pregnant with their fifth child, just continued with her daily duties. She stayed in the kitchen paying no special attention to the birthday celebration.

Salvador was not entirely sure what the exact date of Annabelle's birth was. He just narrowed it down to the approximate month and picked the day. That's the day they celebrated from then on. It was January 21, 1921. Jessica ended up simply serving her husband's needs in the bedroom, but her love was gone for him. She remained very disconnected with Salvador. She simply continued life as if she was just going with the motions.

Annabelle was so excited she was sitting on the porch singing while she put together pretty arrangements of wild flowers. She picked them in the fields. She absolutely loved flowers and gardens. She had a voice of angels. Even when the workers heard her sing they couldn't help, but pause for a moment and listen. She would sing a song she learned from church. They were a catholic family and every once in a while they would be able to attend church in town. That's when Annabelle heard the songs. It was a song the nuns would sing in the back of the church. She perked up her back to really get good control of her voice in harmony. "I come to the garden alone...while the dew is still on the rosessss..." You could always see Salvador in Annabelle's eyes. She had large almond shaped dark brown eyes. Her eyelashes were long and thick. She had long, thick, dark brown hair. It had a bit of wave in it. The hair cascaded down to the middle of her back. She loved wearing a big thick satin bow in her hair. It was red and soft. Something Maria had made for her many years earlier. Her bangs were long and hung to the side of her face. She could never quite get the bow to hold all her hair together, but most of it stayed in it well. She had such a tiny frame and everything on her was tiny. Little hands, little feet, she was like a cupid doll. Her skin was a beautiful shade of beige, soft and perfect. Her lips were a shade of peach, plump and pretty. It was like she was born into perfection. She had talents at such a young age. She picked up many languages early on. At the help of her sister Maria. She loved to dance, sing and draw. Jessica disliked how perfect she seemed. For her she felt she could never compete. She wanted to hate her, but it wasn't within Jessica to hate a child. She hated how it all came to be. She simply kept her distance without being mean, or hateful towards her. Her focus was on taking care of the gardening and her home chores.

On this particular day Jessica had all the girls dresses washed and ready for the big festival coming in the evening hours. The time was coming for everyone to get ready for the festival. She was looking forward to this festival. It brought many of the towns people and the farmers together to celebrate the Holy Ghost. It was an exciting time. The Chamarita was always very colorful, full of music and food. They danced and came together hand in hand. There was a young girl who was selected to be queen at the party. It was mostly symbolic, but always beautifully put together. So much of the Portuguese history would be put into this festival, but everyone was invited to join in on the celebration. Annabelle and Louisa had the same style dress on. Jessica used one particular feed sack to make both of their dresses. They were beige with splashes of red flowers printed through the dress. Jessica was able to get some red silk ribbon. She lined them across from the front and tied them into bows in the back on both dresses. She lined the ribbon across the bottom of the dresses like a seam. This would bring all the pretty red colors together. Fortunately Annabelle had the beautiful red ribbon in her hair Maria had made for her. It matched the dress beautifully. The dresses went just below their knees. Of course Louisa being much older then Annabelle it made Louisa feel a little silly wearing a matching dress to Annabelle. She was happy to have the pretty dress anyway. Jessica also made a dress for Rose in different colors.

Maria had learned how to sew quite well by watching her mama through the years. She put together her own dress with the same beige material. Her dress was much more sophisticated and no ribbon was lined through it. She kept it simple, but very pretty just the same. It was longer and covered her more. That was more appropriate for her matured shapely body. Salvador would not have approved it to be shorter. Jessica used a very different fabric. It was from a neighbor who shared some pretty purple and white fabric she had. It was mostly white with lavender flowers. She sewed the lining with the lavender flowers as the pattern of the lining on all the edges of the dress. She made long sleeves that hugged her arms, but made the shoulders just a little loose and showed a little more of her neck. Had the lining of the lavender flowers draping across the top and a very little V shape, near her breast line. It was very modest, but quite pretty. The dress hugged her shape down to just above her waist line. Then it bloomed outward some, to give a little movement in the dress. It was very long and draped down to her ankles. For most farmers the woman as they matured didn't show a lot of skin. It was a modest time, but on this particular festival the Portuguese woman definitely brought out more colors and just a little more skin. Jessica's hair was up in a bun, done loosely with some flowers placed in it. She still loved putting flowers in her hair. She made a simple dress for Rosie to match hers. She had the front of the dress go straight across and little ruffle sleeves, with a short waistline. She put rose's hair up also and put a few little flowers in her hair. She hadn't been close to Salvador in a very long time, but a part of her wished for some closure with the pain they had gone through. She wanted to be close to him again, but struggled so much with her anger towards him. Life hardened her in so many ways. Salvador still had his typical farmer pants on with his suspenders. He had a few button down shirts and Jessica made sure to place out a nice white shirt for him that wasn't too stained from being used as a work shirt. Phyllix also was anxious for the festival. He still hadn't found a wife. He was looking forward to the fun of joining others together and dancing. First before they were to head out. It was time to bring everyone together and give Annabelle her surprise birthday present that Salvador was working on.

Salvador called everyone together just as Maria and Louisa joined Annabelle on the porch. Manuel was already with Salvador helping him carry out Annabelle's gift. Jessica had been getting cleaned up, as she had worked in the garden most of the day. Just as Salvador called out for them she came out the front door. Everyone thought Jessica looked so pretty. She had strands of grey throughout her hair and small wrinkles that started forming across her face. She was still very radiant and beautiful. Salvador was almost speechless. He still adored her greatly and never quite knew how to close the gap of pain in their relationship. Salvador looked up at her, smiling modestly.

Jessica looked down to the ground. It was like she didn't know how to accept his admirations. Louisa immediately spoke, "you look so pretty mama." Jessica giggled like a school girl. "Come on now we have a festival to attend lets get on with this." It was hard for Jessica to allow any attention to herself. Salvador had pulled out the covered surprise from the barn to show Annabelle. Manuel was anxious to help. Annabelle stood up. She was a very happy little girl. She craved more love from Jessica, but in her mind that was her mama. She never quite understood why there was such a line drawn with her. Nobody would ever discuss how Annabelle came to be. Salvador was very insistent of that. He never wanted Annabelle to feel like she didn't belong. As Salvador and Manuel brought the surprise out, Annabelle became anxious jumping for joy. It was a bike. Just the right size for Annabelle. It was a cute little yellow bike. It looked a little banged up. Salvador picked it up from a family neighbor who no longer had use for it. Their children had grown. They were kind enough to allow Salvador to buy it for a very small token price. Annabelle was suprised. She flew down from the porch and screamed excitedly. "Wow pappa!! Oh thank you, wow it's so pretty." She was jumping up and down ready to just jump on and ride. Manuel even laughed. He thought it was so funny how gitty she became. Manuel immediately jumped in, "Woah... sis, woah... we have to show you how to ride the bike." Manuel knew a thing or two on how to ride a bike. Some of the neighbors kids had them. They would let Manuel ride with them on their bikes sometimes. Everyone laughed as they watched little Annabelle making her attempts at the bike. Everyone except Jessica of course. She just simply sat on the porch and watched emotionless.

Maria could even appreciate the joy Annabelle was experiencing. Jessica just wanted to move forward and join the up coming festival. She patiently sat and watched as Manuel made his attempts to teach Little Annabelle how to ride.

Maria went in and got the pie and started cutting it into pieces and placing it on plates. After a while she ran out to the porch and announced it was ready for everyone. Annabelle wanted to keep trying, but the pie sounded good too. She jumped off her bike and they all headed in to the kitchen. Jessica was quiet through most of the celebration. Salvador always noticed her reactions. He appreciated that she at least said nothing and just allowed Annabelle to be a part of the family. Salvador adored Annabelle. There was always a special place in his heart for her.

Chapter 12

As the family was finishing up their pie Maria was placing the plates in the sink. They were all very anxious to get going and join in on the Chamarita celebration. Annabelle approached Salvador, "pappa can I please take my bike? Please, por favor papa?" Salvador laughed, he was so happy with his little Annabelle. Every time he looked into her eyes he could see himself. Phyllix had managed to borrow one of the neighbor's trucks. The whole family could quickly get into town for the Chamarita. "Well Annabelle, I suppose we could fit it in." They all headed out the door and started climbing into the back of the truck. Salvador loaded the bike after everyone was in. They went down the road and Annabelle started to sing a fun song. One that everyone could join in and sing together. They all clapped and sang excitedly. Phyllix and Salvador sat inside the truck while Phyllix drove.

The Chamarita was being held in Half Moon Bay. The festival is rooted in religion and Portuguese culture. In the

14th century, several violent earthquakes struck the Azores leaving a famine to sweep across the islands. Queen Isabel of Portugal, known for her charitable works and devotion to God, relieved the famine by sending provisions to the suffering. With this, she began a tradition of feeding and honoring the poor that is still practiced by Portuguese communities throughout the globe.

Now, the queens of Half Moon Bay and surrounding Bay Area communities walk the parade route as a reminder to care for all in the community, regardless of social status or income. This is such an important celebration to the community. At this time the communities are suffering from a great depression that had started early on in the year. The stock market has been declining. By bringing everyone together in this Chamarita it shows promise that a miracle could come. Fortunately for most farmers they have been able to keep a good selection of canned goods from their gardens. They also have farm animals for meat, milk and eggs. They sustain themselves fairly well even in such hard times, but it has affected everyone in many ways.

After their long drive they pull in to a large parking area that was designated for all the visitors for the festival. Jessica stands up, "come now Meninas (girls)." She helps all the girls down from the truck. Salvador and Phyllix come to the rear of the truck to help. Salvador climbs in after the girls come down. He grabs Annabelle's bicycle and pulls it down. Manuel helps little Annabelle climb onto her bike. There was a small park near by where they were holding the parade. They were a little early before the festivities were to begin. Manuel walks the bike over to

Salvador. "Pappa may I please, (Por Favor) take Annabelle to the park for now since we are early?" Salvador was happy Manuel was so protective and caring for his sister. "Sim, (yes) just watch out for her. I will whistle for you later." So Manuel and Annabelle head over towards the park area. It's a small grassy area with a few trees. There were some benches for people to sit and rest after an afternoon stroll. Manuel worked with her for a while helping her to balance herself on the bike. Manuel was getting tired so he sat down on the grass and told Annabelle to keep trying. He wanted to sit for a while.

Annabelle started to push herself down a trail. The trail went through a group of trees. She managed to get herself going for a moment then she got nervous. She started to fall and threw her feet down into the spoke area of her bike. She got her dress caught up in the spokes and fell down. She was a little farther away from Manuel then she intended. He didn't see her fall. Just as she hit the ground she started to whimper and tried getting her dress out of the spokes. She was lying under the bike. She couldn't quite get her arms around to the wheel to get herself unstuck. Just as she started to panic she suddenly heard a voice from above her. "Are you ok?" Annabelle was startled. She looked up into the tree and saw a boy. He was hanging upside down on one of the tree limbs. He had his legs clasped on and hanging his arms down like a monkey. He looked so silly to Annabelle. She almost forgot she was stuck. "Como te llamas?" (whats your name) The boy asked in his silly tone. Annabelle was shy, but she was in an awkward situation. Her legs were starting to hurt from the bike laying on her. "I speak english you silly boy. I speak Portuguese also. Do you understand me? Ow... ow... my legs... ooh it hurts." Annabelle was struggling to get her dress free and her legs free. She was so embarrassed and very stuck. The boy jumped down from the tree flat on his two feet like an acrobat. "I speak English. I wasn't sure what language you spoke. Can I help you with that bike?" Annabelle looked onward at this boy in a bit of awe. *He was so cute,* Annabelle thought. He stood tall, with dark brown hair. It was a little long passed his ears and flowing wavy hair. He had big dark eyes, but one of his eyes was different. Almost like he was winking. It was a lazy eye. She had never seen that before. She thought it was almost endearing. His pants were slightly torn and he has suspenders on. He was a little dirty on his face. *Probably from climbing trees*, Annabelle assumed in her head. He was very thin. For such a young boy. He had a little muscle in his arms. Annabelle was so embarrassed in that moment, but she was in such a precarious situation. "If you could please help me? This bike is heavy and my dress is stuck." The boy reached over and knelt down to get a closer look. He managed to unravel her dress through the spokes. He then grabbed hold of the bike and lifted it up off Annabelle like it was as light as a feather. Annabelle was developing a bit of a crush. She thought in her mind, *he was a strong boy.* He sat the bike against one of the trees and put his hand out to Annabelle to help her get up. She grabbed for his hand and stood up with a bit of a limp. She had hurt her leg in the fall. Her knee was bleeding a bit and it was sore. "Ooh," the boy sais, "maybe we should get some water and clean that up for you?" Annabelle was turning red. She was so shy and had never really met such a cute boy. "I'm ok, really thank you." She looked down to her feet in embarrassment. The boy also took quick notice of how very beautiful Annabelle was. He loved her red ribbon in her hair. He was struck in his heart by how very sweet and tiny she was. He seemed to be a very confident boy, so he immediately went back to the introduction. "My name is William. What is your name?" "Annabelle," she announced. They both stood there awkwardly not knowing where to go from there. Just then Annabelle realized Manuel was waiting for her to swing back around with her bike. She never quite made it. "Umm my brother, he is waiting for me over there. Do you want to come meet him?" William was happy to go with her. He wanted to know more about this mysterious beautiful girl. "I would love to." So William grabbed Annabelle's bike for her, as to be a gentleman. Annabelle blushes once again, but allows him to be kind.

As they both are walking back towards Manuel were he would be waiting, Annabelle is able to muster up some conversation. "Why were you hanging on that tree?" William laughs, "why not?" He said. "Don't you like to play in trees?" Annabelle laughs, "well I don't know. I don't play in trees." Annabelle was always a very clean girl. Getting dirty wasn't one of her choices of play. William stops for a moment and turns to Annabelle. "Well maybe you should try it some time? It's quite fun." Then William goes on to talk about what he likes to do and where he is from. As they get closer to Manuel they become more comfortable chatting up a storm. William was only about a year older then Annabelle. They seemed to be enjoying each other. Manuel could see from a distance that Annabelle was walking with a boy. Manuel immediately stands up from his spot and peers over at the boy. He is very protective of Annabelle. He starts walking towards both of them. As soon as he meets them, he approaches William with a suspicious eye. "What are you doing?" William could see that Annabelle's brother was protective. "No worries she fell down. I just gave her a hand up." William spoke with such ease and poise. It was hard to be too suspicious of him. Manuel looked at William closely as if he was measuring him up. It was actually quite comical, even Annabelle had to giggle. "Ok, ok Manuel that's good enough. Look, I need water. My knee is bleeding. I guess I'm not quite getting this bike riding thing so well." Manuel looked over and saw her knee. He had a scarf in his right pocket, so he pulled it out and spit on it. Then reached down and started wiping off her knee. Annabelle cringed, "ooh icky Manuel your spit icky." Manuel continued wiping, "stop acting like such a baby geez belle." William laughed. "Can I help teach her to ride?" Manuel didn't like the thought of that much, but he didn't have a lot of friends so he was open to giving him a chance. As the day went on William and Manuel helped Annabelle. She eventually was able to keep her bike up and ride without the help of the boys.

Salvador decided it was time to get the kids together for the parade. He headed towards the park and let out a big loud whistle. Manuel heard it first. "Annabelle pappa is whistling for us. It's time to go." Annabelle was almost sad to stop. She really liked William and didn't want it to end. "Can William come with us Manuel? Do you think pappa would mind?" "Well we could ask." Manuel looks over at William, "are you going to the parade also?" Manuel tilts his head while he questioned him. William was excited to spend more time with Annabelle. He was developing his own crush on her himself. "I would love to go with you, but yes I was going to the parade." They all head towards the family. When they reached Salvador, Manuel approached his father with the question. "Pappa may our new friend William celebrate with us?" Salvador looks down at the young boy. "Where are your parent's menino (boy)." William respectfully answers. "I'm here with my Uncle. He wouldn't mind, if you don't sir?" It wasn't uncommon to see children running a muck throughout the festivities. Everyone was like family when they were together in the Chamarita. Salvador was fine with him joining them. They all found there place to sit and wait for the parade to begin. Annabelle, Manuel and William found a good spot on the grass and they all sat. William of course made sure he was right by Annabelle. Maria noticed the boy seemed smitten by Annabelle. She snuck her way over to the other side of Annabelle to chat with her. She started whispering in her ear. "Belle, I think this boy likes you." Belle started to giggle and whispers back, "he's so cute. Look at his adorable winking eye." Both the girls innocently giggle and continue to whisper things back and forth.

The festival was so colorful. The queen and her maidens were dressed so pretty. As they crossed past Annabelle and William. Annabelle looks in admiration. "Ooh such pretty dresses. I wish I could look like that." William quietly tells Belle, "your much prettier then any of those girls." Belle blushes as he said it. Maria heard him and nudges Belle and giggles. Once the parade finally came to an end it was time for everyone to head in to the building. Beef had been prepared for days for the visitors. Inside they had wonderful variations of music playing and everyone clapping and dancing. William decides this is his opportunity to get closer to Belle. He quietly walks over to Salvador and respectfully asked him, "Sir may I ask your daughter to dance?" Just then Salvador realizes this boy has a crush on little Belle. He knew there was no harm in a dance since he is watching. He gives William permission to ask Belle. William walks up to Belle. Maria and Manuel are standing right next to her. As he is approaching her Maria already knew what he was going to ask. She tried to be casual and looks the other way. Belle didn't seem to even realize what he was doing. When he approaches her and puts his hand out and smiles Belle becomes terribly embarrassed and very shy. She turned red again. William was a little nervous, but anxious to hold her hand. "Belle would you d-a-n-c-e w-i-t-h um me?" Belle starts to giggle uncontrollably. Maria quickly helps her regain herself and whispers to Belle, "put your hand out Belle, he's a sweet boy." She even grabs hold of Belles hand and helps her put it forward towards William. Just as their hands touch suddenly Belle is entranced in her own fairy tale. William grabs her hand and glides her across the floor like a princess. As they join in on the traditional dance they clap and swing in circles. Put their hands in the air and keep gliding across the floor as they grab hands again and again. Belle starts to become in a trance looking into Williams's eyes. He is even mesmerized by her pretty face. As the night moves on they danced many dances together. William took every opportunity he could to hold her hand. When they got tired they sat and talked and laughed. When it got too hot in the building they would step outside to cool off. Eventually they were standing just outside and there was a big tree behind the building where the party was being held.

William decided it was time to get Belle to try something new. "Hey Belle, want to climb a tree with me?" She laughed, "no silly." William pointed Belle in the direction of the moon. "Look Belle see the moon. It's so bright tonight. If you climb up there with me, you could see it even more. Come with me. I will even help you." The music was still playing loudly. They could hear it outside. Everyone was having such a good time inside they didn't even notice Belle and William stepped out. Belle finally decided to climb the tree after all. Some how he made her feel adventurous. William grabbed the first branch and pulled himself up, then reached down for Belle. She reached up and he pulled her up with complete ease. He was so strong she loved that. As they continued up the tree Belle was becoming nervous the higher they got. William could see that in her face. "No worries Belle. I would never let you fall." Somehow she could feel in her heart that he meant that. They were so high up in the tree they could see the moon as if they were standing on top of it. Annabelle was mesmerized once again. She loved how adventurous William was. William looked at Belle more closely and loved how the moon shined off the side of her face. They held hands innocently. This moment was so special to both of them. Somehow they both felt connected. William started to feel some fear and asked, "Belle will I ever see you again? We have to stay friends me and you." Belle giggled, "I would like that, but how? I live so far away and you are just visiting your Uncle." William scootches closer to Belle, "I will write you every day. Will you write me back?" "Yes of course, yes we should do that." They both stayed in the tree for a while holding hands. Then suddenly they become startled by Maria down below. Maria could see them up there. Before pappa saw them, she thought it would be wise for them to come down. Maria shouts up at them, "were leaving soon Belle!!" Annabelle and William make there way back down. Once they reach the bottom William tells Belle to wait there for him. He runs in to the building to get some paper and a pencil. He writes down an address for Annabelle and brings it out to her. Then he hands her a paper so she can write her address down for him. They both fold their papers delicately and put them away in a safe place so nobody knows. Maria headed back in as she saw them both coming down the tree. William knew his time with Belle was almost over so he decided he wanted a kiss. This would be his first kiss. As well as Belles first kiss. She could tell he was coming closer to her and became embarrassed and shy. She put her head down. William pulls back and decides maybe it's better to ask. "Annabelle can I please kiss you?" She looks up at him and closes her eyes and puckers her beautiful peach lips. William smiles and giggles to himself at how sweet she is. He comes closer to her face and places his young lips on hers. As they connect their lips for the first time they both feel a sudden warmth within themselves. It was a quick kiss, but the best first kiss. They would both remember forever.

Suddenly Williams Uncle calls out for William. He pulls away from Annabelle holding her hand. He looks into her eyes and whispers, "don't forget me Belle." He then lets go and runs to his Uncle before he could see that he was with a girl. Annabelle just stood there for a moment holding her hands together. She realizes he placed something in her hand. it was a beautiful flower he picked from the ground. She grasped it closely to her heart and sat on the ground. She closes her eyes again trying to hold on to her very special moments with William. Maria saw that William was leaving with his Uncle, but she didn't see Annabelle come back. She decided to go to the back of the building to see if she was still there. She walked up and saw her sitting on the ground. "What are you doing sis?" "Oh Maria, he was so wonderful." Maria sat down with her, "tell me all about it." So Annabelle shared everything with her sister. Maria was excited for her. She hadn't even had her first kiss yet. "What was it like? The kiss what did it feel like?" Annabelle shared so poetically every detail. Then the girls shared their dreams of some day having the perfect husband and becoming mothers themselves some day. They giggled and talked for hours. Salvador and Jessica came out. Salvador let out his big whistle once again. Maria stood up and helped her sister up so they could head back. Annabelle slipped her very special flower in her dress pocket with the address William gave her. Her flower broke apart and the pedals were loose in her pocket, but she didn't care. She vowed to keep every pedal. They stepped back into the building and Salvador pointed out to Maria, "I think your sister has found a friend." When he said it Maria became scared. She thought perhaps pappa figured out Annabelle and William were together. Then she realized he was referring to her other sister Louisa. He pointed in the direction of Louisa and there she was dancing with someone. She was smiling and seemed to be enjoying herself. Louisa seemed smitten with a boy that night herself. Annabelle didn't even take notice. She was so wrapped up in all her wonderful thoughts of William. The man Louisa was dancing with was much older. He was probably in his twenties and he was known quite well in town as a business man. This interested Louisa. It was very different from her pappa's occupation. He dressed very different then what Louisa was accustomed. He was a blonde, blue eyed, tall, slender man. Dressed in business attire. He had taken his jacket off as it had gotten very hot with all the dancing. He seemed to be interested in Louisa and she wasn't turning away his interest. As the night was coming to an end it was time for everyone to start heading home. Salvador had noticed Louisa was exchanging information with this man so he decided to intervene. He walked up and just as Louisa was handing the man a piece of paper Salvador grabbed it out of Louisa's hands. She was extremely embarrassed. She looked over at him. "Pappa," she states with disgust at his interruption. "No worries Louisa, I just think it appropriate he introduces himself to me before you share personal information." He states with a firm tone towards the man. The man turns to Salvadore, "yes of course sir, how rude of me. My name is Billy Proctor." Salvador puts his hand out to shake it. "That's not a Portuguese name? You don't look Portuguese to me?" Billy nods his head agreeing, "yes, you are correct. I'm not Portuguese." Salvador becomes disgruntled. He wants his daughters involved in their same nationality and heritage. He wasn't about to approve for it to go any further then a dance. Louisa becomes horrified and embarrassed at her fathers intruding. "Pappa stop, oh my gosh pappa." Salvador instructs Louisa to get back to the truck. "It's time to go." Louisa storms off to the truck in complete horror of her father's involvement. Billy simply backs up a few steps apologetically and Salvador walks away. "Have a good night," he states. He gets into the passenger side of the truck. All the girls were already in the back and Phyllix was ready to drive off. Louisa was so angry and embarrassed. She curled up in a ball in the back of the truck and crossed her arms. She had nothing to say to anyone. Salvador was unaware Billy already knew that Louisa was from the Cardoza Ranch. He had every intention of seeking out Louisa. He knew exactly where she lived.

Chapter 13

Manuel had been working on the chicken coop for his pappa. It needed some repairs so he was hammering away on the back side of the coop. Annabelle came up to talk with him. She had already written William his very first letter and a very sweet poem. She knew her pappa would not like the idea of her writing a boy. Annabelle slipped the letter into an envelope and it was ready to be mailed. She had placed it securely in one of her pockets in her little apron. Annabelle wanted Manuel's help desperately. She started off her conversation by offering to help him on the coop. "Manuel do you need any help out here?" She smiled innocently at her brother. "Your silly Belle, girls don't hammer." Manuel laughs. Annabelle didn't care for that comment much. "I can do just the same as you, so what I'm a girl." Manuel rolls his eyes, "ok, ok you can hand me those nails. That would be a great help," he laughed as he said it. Annabelle plops down on the ground where the nails are. She starts grabbing handfuls while she's grumbling at the thought that girls can't hammer. She hands him one nail at a time. Annabelle had to think hard how to approach the question in her mind to her brother. "So Manuel, umm do you remember that boy William? The one we played with." Manuel remembers quite well, "yeah what of it?" Annabelle steps lightly in her mind. "Well umm, you liked him right?" Manuel could see she liked him. He knew she liked him a long time back when they all met. "Sis get to the point, what's wrong?" Annabelle started fidgeting with her dress. "Well he gave me his address so I could write him. You know pappa wouldn't be ok with that. So I figured maybe if you wrote him too and we just put the letters together pappa don't have to know... you know." She gives Manuel her cute big eye's and tilts her head in a sweet manner. She is hoping he would help her. Manuel didn't much like the idea of her writing a boy either. He was very protective of his sister. He was also a push over. He wanted his sister to be happy too. "Just letters sis right?" He holds his hammer up in a scolding manner towards Belle. "Yes, yes of course. Just letters please, oh please Manuel?" She clasped her hands together in a begging motion. "Well... I guess so. You really liked that kid huh sis?" Belle suddenly put her hands by her face in a dreaming motion. Her eyes looking up at the sky. "Oh yes I do, I really, really do." Manuel shakes his head, "ick sis stop that geez. I get it already." Belle jumps up dropping all the nails excited and happy. "Oh thank you so much brother, thank you." She runs over to him and gives him such a big hug he almost drops the hammer to the ground. "Geez sis alright, stop, cmon geez." He knew he made her happy. The hug didn't really bug him that much. He had to act like it did. Being her brother and all. "Ok let go now, go on. I got work to do."

She lets go of him pulling the letter out of her pocket to hand to him. "Well you already had the letter ready? How did you know I would say yes huh?" Annabelle knew her brother quite well. He would do almost anything for his sister Annabelle. They were so close. She hands him the letter and starts to giggle. "Thanks Manuel," she skips off and starts to sing as she heads back to the house. Manuel just shakes his head. He puts the letter in his pants and starts hammering away again. Manuel already figured he would have to write William. He will need to let him know to address the letters back to him and not his sister. She would get into trouble if pappa found out. As time went on the letters were being mailed every few weeks. Eventually William was able to get one mailed back to Belle as well. As soon as Manuel got it he hid it in his pocket and found the right moment to give it to his sister when pappa wasn't watching. William was kind enough to write Manuel a letter as well. Manuel actually kind of liked getting a letter. He sat down and read his first before he gave Belle her letter. William was very kind and told Manuel all about his adventures and the fun things they did where he lived. William told him about all the horses they had and how he was allowed to ride sometimes. He stated in the letter how much fun he had. Manuel got so wrapped up in his letter, he didn't even notice his sister Belle was walking up to him. "Hey Manuel, did I get a letter?" She started to nudge him, "hey." Manuel stopped and realized he was ignoring Annabelle. "Oops sorry sis yeah, yeah here." He hands her the letter he had bundled up in his pocket. Belle quickly grabs it from him and takes off running to her private spot by a tree out in the field.

Annabelle loved her spot. It had a big beautiful tree full of branches rounded at the top. It completely shaded anyone sitting below. The tree sitting all by itself way out in the middle of the corn field. Annabelle would always say the tree is lonely out there by itself. So she decided to keep her tree company and make it her very own private spot. She called it her thinking spot. She even decided to carve her initials on the tree and later added William's initials as well. In her heart he was so special he deserved to have his initials on her tree as well. She did the initials low enough on the tree so her pappa would never see it. She put W.O. and A.C., for William Oros and Annabelle Cardoza. She was definitely crushing big time for the boy who gave her the very first kiss she has ever had. He was such a care free boy. She loved that about him. She slowly opened her letter as if to treasure every moment. She got nestled in to her spot spreading her dress out over her legs. She crosses her legs and leans back on the tree. The first line she seen was, To My Dearest Belle.... oh how sweet she thought in her mind. He called me his dearest. She holds the letter close to her body as if she was hugging the letter. As she reads on slowly to savor every word William talks about how close he felt to her and how he wants to be with her so badly. Every word was so sweet and caring for Annabelle. Even at the end of the letter he tells her, *P.S. I'm sending 100 kisses to you in my heart.* Annabelle just melts inside. She holds the letter close to her and reads it over and over several times. She then realizes she has to hide this letter somehow in a safe place. She finds a really big stick and digs deep down. Right in the middle of the roots growing. She had a little metal box she had planned on placing her letter in. She pulls the box out of her pocket and places her letter inside. First kisses her letter. Then she placed the box into her deep hole by the tree. She buries it. Then covers the hole with branches off the tree and leaves. She hopes nobody ever looks there. Just as she finishes Manuel starts approaching Annabelle. "Hey sis, what you up to over there?" He hadn't seen what she was doing, but he knew she was doing something. Annabelle quickly retreats to the other side of the tree. She pokes her head over. "Hello Manuel how was your letter?" She asked quickly to change the subject. Manuel laughs he knows she's hiding something. He figured it had something to do with her letter so he didn't impose further. "My letter was great. Do you want to read it?" Belle got excited to be able to read yet another letter William wrote. She loved that idea. "Oh yes please Manuel, I would love that." As she read his letter she realized it contained more information about William. Who he was and what he liked. She loved that she could actually get to know him by reading her brothers letter. So it became a routine for both of them. When the letters did come Manuel would always share his letter for Annabelle to read. She continued to hide all her letters away in her hidden spot. She learned more and more about him as time went on. He would talk about Spain and their heritage. His brothers and sisters. How they all helped their father with so many chores. How much William has learned about cattle ranching. Eventually in one of his letters he informed both Manuel and Annabelle how they would be returning for a visit again soon. Annabelle was so excited. She could barely contain herself. It didn't say when, but just knowing he would be returning again gave her something to look forward to.

Louisa had been sneaking out of the house to meet Billy. She knew her pappa did not want her seeing him, but she really liked him. She made this decision on her own. One night Jessica caught Louisa sneaking out. She had been in the kitchen late one night. She wasn't feeling well. She heard the door creaking in the front and peaked around the corner. She saw Louisa walking out. "Louisa, Louisa what are you doing?" Louisa was startled to hear her mom so late at night. She turned around and froze in position. Jessica approaches her, "what's going on?" Louisa started to stumble at first unsure what to say. Then as she thought about it she decided she just didn't care. "Mama I'm going to see Billy." She said it almost proudly. Jessica knew Salvadore didn't want Louisa seeing that boy. He wanted his girls to marry portugese men. "Oh no Louisa, what are you thinking?" "Mama I don't care what pappa wants. I love him. Do you understand? Pappa don't understand what that means." She states in a rebellious tone. Jessica was still angry with Salvador, but she still loved him some where deep in her heart. She knew she couldn't go against him on this. "Louisa you must not speak this way. Your pappa loves you." Louisa again stood her ground. "I'm going and your not going to stop me mama." Louisa bolts out the door quickly. She ran out to the road and met Billy. Billy was waiting patiently for her. Jessica just stood there in disbelief. She knew in her heart that she would be losing her youngest daughter soon and there was nothing she could do. She decided to close the door and say nothing. If she told Salvador he would not react well. She acted as if she saw nothing and went back to the kitchen. The time had come after a few months and Jessica bore her fifth child naming her Francis. Salvador was hoping for a son. He desperately wanted the opportunity to have his namesake carried on. He had lost that privilege when Manuel was born. Their newest baby girl was beautiful. Salvador decided in his mind he was just going to keep trying. He hoped the next pregnancy may be his next son. If him and his wife Jessica's relationship improved he prayed she would honor him with carrying on the name.

Everyone was busy doing their daily chores one morning when Salvador walks up to Jessica in the garden. She was busy pulling weeds and picking some vegetables throwing them in a bucket. He kneels down to her looking distressed on his face. "Jessica were losing customers for our dairy. The stock market is really hurting our bottom line." People in town are losing money and it was causing a lot of farms to lose customers. This ultimately hurt their profits. They were able to keep up on their own food supply and needs, but his workers were getting less hours and less pay. They didn't have as much demand as they had before. Since it was affecting their profits it also made it difficult to pay Lucus his desired shares. Jessica was concerned about their situation as well. She could see that things were getting more complicating. "I have a lot of canned goods. I could go to the local market and offer to sell more. Also to our neighbors, or maybe more towns people in need. I could offer to sell to them also." Salvador rubbed his chin thinking about her proposal. "That's a good idea, do that it will help." Salvador was admiring the beauty of his wife while he was near her. He reached his arm over and touched her hand as she was getting ready to pull another weed. She stopped and looked up at him. He smiled at her and she decided to reciprocate his affection and she smiled back. Suddenly you could hear the dog barking and someone pulling up in the driveway. They both looked over to see who was coming. Salvador looked back over at Jessica, "I better check it out. Remember this moment." He smiles at her again. She giggles quietly to herself.

Salvador walks over to see who was coming. He could see a nice looking car pulling up. He wasn't expecting any customers today so he was surprised. The car stops and someone climbs out. Just as the man turns his head Salvador could see who it was. "Billy what are you doing here?" Salvador remembered him from the Chamarita. It had been quite a few months. He wasn't glad to see him. Billy was nervous, but you could tell he was on a mission. He walked right up to Salvador and put out his hand for a hand shake. Salvador reciprocated, but hesitantly. "Well sir, we need to talk. I was hoping you might have a few moments?" Salvador guided Billy into the house. Just as they entered Louisa was inside doing some work. She saw them both enter. Louisa put her hands in front of her face surprised and unsure as to what was about to unfold. She stood up and Salvador immediately instructed her, "Louisa you need to head outside for a bit." Louisa quickly grabbed her apron and headed out the door. She gave Billy a quick grin of nervousness before she left. She had no idea of Billy's plans to speak to her pappa. Both Salvador and Billy took a seat as Salvador motioned to Billy to sit. Billy's hands started to sweat as he clasped them together rubbing his palms. He was so nervous that Salvador would not understand how much he loved Louisa. Salvador was becoming inpatient. "Well son, what do you have to say?" Billy rubbed his legs in anticipation. "Well sir, the thing is...well... I'm in love with your daughter. I would like your permission to marry her? I understand that you would prefer to keep your girls within their heritage. However a man can't help his feelings. I can provide a good home for her. I make a good living. She will never go without her needs." Salvador stood up. He was angry of the notion of Louisa marrying outside of their portugese heritage. "Look son, I am not about to forbid this idiocy. This is absolutely against what I want for my daughters." Salvador began to pace in the room. He could hardly contain himself. He knew if Louisa was truly in love with this man she may rebel against him. She may do it with, or without his support. Him and Louisa didn't exactly have a good relationship at this point. She has been rebelling for some time now. Then it occured to Salvador, "how is it you love her when you only had one single dance with her many months ago? Is their something your not telling me?" Billy became anxious. He knew he would have to devulge more information to Salvador. He would never believe that he fell in love with her just from that day. "Well sir, I will be honest only to persuade you. I know you will not approve of what I am about to tell you. I have been seeing Louisa and courting her ever since the Chamarita. I know this is terribly dishonest of me. I am truly sorry for the deception I have caused. Please work with me and understand my intentions where honorable." Salvador became more angry as he heard what has been going on without his knowledge. He paced into the kitchen and kicked a chair in frustration. "This is my house, this is unnacceptable. How could you dishoner me and my daughter in this manner." In that moment Billy realized Salvador was assuming that he had sexual relations with her. He immediately jumped up from the chair. "Oh no, no sir....I would never do that sir. I have the utmost respect. I would never... no sir... nothing like that. I give you my word. Your daughter is still pure sir." Billy knew if he could not convince Salvador immediately that it could create a physical altercation between them. Billie waved his hands in every attempt to convince Salvador. He had not done anything to disrespect his daughters honor. Salvador started to calm down. He walked over to the door and called Louisa in to the house. Both men sat and waited for Louisa to enter the room. When Louisa came in she was a bit shaken. She feared her father would forbid her from marrying the man she loved so very much.

Jessica had noticed everyone had been in the house for quite some time. She decided it was time for her to go into the house as well. She wanted to know what was going on. Salvador instructed Loisa to sit down and tell him herself how she felt about Billy. Louisa was scared, but she wanted her fathers approval. Even with their problems between them. He is still her father. "Pappa please understand. I cannot control my feelings. I am in love with Billy and I want your approval to be with him." Just as Louisa was explaining her feelings to him Jessica walked into the house. She overheard Louisa pleading with Salvador. He was more angry that Louisa had been hiding this relationship from him. He felt totally betrayed. He raised his daughters to be honest with him and always respect him. Jessica could see the disgruntled look in Salvador's eyes. She decided it was time for her to speak up on Louisa's behalf. Jessica cleared her throat in anticipation. She did not want to say the wrong thing to upset the situation further. "Um...

ahem..." gulping through her words. "May I say something for a moment please Salvador?" Salvador was startled at her entrance and that she wanted to speak on this matter. "Salvador you must remember we were once young also. Falling in love was a blessing by god. Who are we to dictate where are hearts fall? He seems to be a responsible young man and will provide well for our daughter. What more could we ask for, but for her to be in love with him as well. It is a true blessing. Don't you think?" As she asked the question she stepped back in case Salvador was angry at her intrusion to the conversation. Salvador stood up and glanced around the room. He had noticed that all three of them were tencely glaring in his direction awaiting his answer. He put his hand on his chin. He was lightly swaying his fingers in a circuler motion looking down at the floor. He started to grin ever so slightly. Almost to a quiet chuckle. "Well... I guess I have been slightly out numbered here hmmm." He put his hand out towards Billy and proudly states to him. "Well son, I guess the votes are in and you seem to have taken my daughters heart. I will give you my blessing." Billy and Salvador shook hands. Louisa claps her hands together in pure joy smiling almost to a point of giggling herself. Jessica steps forward again as she smiles towards Louisa. She was happy for her joy she is experiencing in that moment. Just as Salvador was shaking Billys hand he pulls Billy a little closer to him and whispers towards Billy. "Understand this though, if you dishonor my daughter, or hurt her in any way... I will hurt you. Do you understand me young man?" Billy straightens up his back and gulps, "yeh, yeh, yes of course sir, yes."

After many months of planning Jessica arranged a

special engagement party celebration. She had borrowed some extra tables from the neighbors and set them outside. She picked several flowers and placed them in vases on all of the tables. She had four tables total. That seated about eight people per table. She put beautiful table cloths over each table that she had made specifically for the event. She had several bowls of freshly picked mixed fruits. Salvador had a big bonfire going in the back yard area and had been de-feathering chickens most of the morning. Fortunately they had a nice flock of chickens availalbe to ready for the party. He stuck four at a time through a large metal pole. He prepared for use to cook the chickens over the fire. Jessica had made up a wonderful sauce with tomatoes and fresh seasonings along with some other secret family ingredients. She brought a large bowl of the sauce over and a brush for Salvador to season the chickens. Jessica had plenty of vegetables to prepare for the party. Louisa was upstairs putting on her best dress and placing a pretty large ribbon in her beautiful thick hair. She rubbed some water across her eye lashes as to make them look brighter and longer. She rubbed her cheeks and patted them to get a little rosey look on each side. She giggled as she looked at herself in the mirror. Mary and Annabelle were silently watching as Louisa was getting prepared for the party. Both the girls were happy for Louisa, but they both admired her and felt a little jealous. They admired her great fortune to be getting married to someone. They both had a million questions for Louisa. So much neither of them completely yet understood. Annabelle fantasized that it was her with William some day. Through all the letters he had sent. She felt so close to him. She knew in her heart that she and William will be together some day.

Salvador's Daughter

Salvador and Jessica invited a lot of their regular customers from town. Most of the employees and some family were invited. Unfortunately most of the family resided quite far from their home. There was no time and little money for most to be able to make a trip for this celebration. As they have lived there they have made many friends and felt close to them. They were happy to celebrate with them. The guests started arriving. Everyone could smell the chicken. It smelled absolutely delicious. A few of the employees could play guitar and violin so they decided to keep some solemn music going during the party. Jessica did most of the greeting while Salvador continued to monitor the chickens and turn them frequently around the fire. Most of the men joined Salvador in conversation while they helped him watch the fire. Some had cigars and spoke of hunting expeditions. Billy had arrived with his mother, Aunt and Uncle. They started introducing them immediately. Maria and Annabelle followed Louisa down the stairs as she was to make her entrance on the patio. Manuel didn't seem to be involved in much that was happening. He seemed to pretty much stay to himself. He hung out behind the chicken coop with his knife and small piece of stick. Carving away at it to make yet another gadget of some kind. He liked wearing this old cowboy hat he found a long time ago. It was quite dirty and limp with it's worn out brown leather. It was his favorite hat and only hat. He loved his suspenders and usually wore no shirt. He always had a hankerchief hanging out of one of his back pockets. He used that as a sweat rag, or anything else he might need it for. Rose had a tendency to just roam aimlessly around the yard. She would bounce from Salvador's side to Jessica, to Manuel, or anyone she felt inclined to harass at the moment. She was going in circles around the chicken coop. She would see Manuel sitting there and stick her tongue out at him. Manuel paid no special attention. He became very use to her antics.

Louisa, Maria and Annabelle entered the porch area. As soon as everyone saw that it was Louisa they quietly clapped in honor of her engagement. Many of the woman friends of Jessicas giggled and laughed in joy for their friends daughter. Billy immediately went up the stairs to greet his future bride. Louisa was very happy. He escorted her down the stairs and they started to dance on the yard with the music the guests had been playing. Billy cascaded her around him in circles pulling her closer to him. They glided around the yard together. Jessica had noticed Maria coming down the stairs with Annabelle not far behind. So Jessica proceeded to introduce Maria to Billy's mother and Aunt. "If I may introduce you this is my daughter Maria. Of course that very beautiful girl dancing with your nephew is the newly engaged Louisa and uhhh...." Annabelle crept forward as Jessica started to struggle with the introduction of her. Annabelle had always noticed things were different with her mother, but she was grateful at least Maria was close to her. As Jessica stuttered Billys Aunt tipped her head in question glancing at Jessica, "well dear, yes... this child is ???" "This is uhhh... this is ..." The Aunt was becoming frustrated and interrupted "This is your other daughter... yes???" Jessica became flustered.... She did not want to say those words. She jumped in quickly in correction of what the woman said. "This is Salvador's daughter.... maam..." The aunt was getting more confused. She couldn't make sence of the comment. Wether, or not this was indeed Jessica's daughter. She thought in her mind how strange to introduce your child in this manner. Jessica quickly jumped in again, "my husband have you met him?" She starts to guide both of the women towards the bonfire quickly exiting the area in which Annabelle was standing. She immediately introduces Salvador to them hoping they would disregard her answer as being simply the daughter. It still seemed to be a hard pill to swallow for Jessica.

Annabelle was feeling very sad at that moment. It hurt her the way her mother, or so she thought who was mother, just pushed her aside in the way she did. Annabelle had never been told anything about how she came to be in this family. She only knows that she has been there her entire life. It was forbidden by Salvador for anyone to tell her otherwise. The hard part for her was understanding why she always felt as though her mother kept a distance from her. She was feeling sad. She decided to go to her private tree spot and stay there for a while. She couldn't stomach another odd introduction by her mother. She dug down to find her metal box and read her letters from William. That always seemed to cheer her up. She got a piece of paper out of the box and a pencil. She was readying herself to write to him her feelings. As she started to write... *Dear William*, she felt this urge to cry. Even with all her siblings sometimes she felt completely alone in the world. Some how different, some how not the same. She wiped her eyes and attempted once again. *Dear William, we have only known each other for a short time, but yet I feel closer to you then anyone in my home. You completely accept me and give me love. I wanted to say thank you and I hope*

I can see you soon. Please always be my friend. In her heart she wanted to tell him more then friend, but she wasn't brave enough to say that to him. Just as she was about to write more she heard a rustling coming towards her. She looks up and notices that her sister Maria was coming towards the tree. She quickly placed her things inside the box and threw them in the hole. She sat over the hole so Maria would not see it. Maria started calling out, "Belle are you over there?" Belle quickly rubbed her eyes. "Yes Maria I'm here, over here." Maria stepped closer to Belle and could see something was not quite right. She saw dirt in Annabelles nails and on her hand as if she had been digging. Annabelle didn't realize that since she was crying when she wiped her face with her hand she dug the box out with. She got dirt all over her face. Maria felt badly for her. She could tell she had been crying. She brought a suprise to Annabelle hoping it would cheer her up from that introduction. Even Maria could barely stand it. She sat next to Belle and smiled wiping her face with her dress. "Now little sis everything will be ok. I brought you something special today." Annabelle loved suprises. She perked up and could see that Maria had something hidden behind her. "You brought me something?" She smiled in anticipation.

Maria pulls out a doll behind her back and presents it to her. Maria had made this doll special for Annabelle. It was small and petite with a pretty little yellow dress and poca dots. She placed a tiny little ribbon in the dolls hair. Her hair was brown and long kind of like Annabelle. She had a tiny little pearl necklace around the neck. Her eyes were sparkly and brown. Annabelle was enchanted by such a beautiful gift. Maria hands it over to her with pride. Belle reached her finger close to the dolls face and gently rubs the face and hair in amazement. Maria started to laugh, "silly sis take her, she's yours." Belle was very careful and gentle. It was such a tiny doll. It could almost fit in her apron pocket. "I don't want to break it Maria." Maria laughs, "you silly sis, it will be fine. What fun is a doll that you can't play with?" Belle placed the doll in her lap inspecting everything carefully. While Annabelle was busy admiring her gift, Maria noticed a hole just below her. Where she was sitting. "What is this Belle?" As Maria pushed aside Annabelles dress she could see the metal box in a hole below her. Annabelle quickly moves over to cover the hole. "It's nothing Maria, nothing." Maria always knew when Annabelle was telling stories. "You need to move right now Belle and tell me what is going on?" Annabelle became very worried her sister would not approve of her letters. She knew she had to tell her and that she has gotten caught in her deception. Belle went on to explain the story behind the letters and who it was. She told her about the agreement her and William made to write each other. She also explained how Manuel was helping her with the letters. Maria was actually quite intrigued and happy for Annabelle. Which greatly suprised Belle that Maria would be so supportive and give her blessings. Meanwhile at the party later that evening Billy had done a public proposal in front of all the guests. He announced that they would be getting married in his home state. Jessica and Salvador already knew about those specific arrangements. They wanted to be a part of her wedding, but understood this was how this had to be. Billy originally lived outside of this state. His occupation warranted him leaving town.

As the party drew to an end and most of the guests left, Louisa had a bag packed. Salvador and Jessica said their goodbyes. Of course Jessica cried, but they were happy tears for her daughters future. Salvador still considered it to be against his wishes since his daughters name would become, *Mr's Louisa Proctor.* When he thought of that he shook his head in his mind. He had high hopes to get Maria and Rosie married into the heritage at least. *That terrible american name his eldest daughter would be inheriting well it's just wrong.* Salvador thought in his mind. Jessica knew he wasn't pleased with the outcome of who Louisa chose. She was glad he was kind enough to not stop it from happening for the sake of Louisa's heart.

That evening while Salvador and Jessica were cleaning up Salvador could hear Jessica suddenly laughing. He looked over at her and could see a glimmer of happiness in his wife. Salvador smiled at her. He sat down on one of the picnic tables closer to her. She was gathering up the loose flowers off the table. He leaned inward towards her and peered his eyes noticably in her direction. She giggled, "what are you looking at you old fool?" He smiled, "what are you laughing about?" Jessica smiled, "well it seems we have just watched one of our children fall in love and leave the nest. I guess it's something to be happy about." Salvador thought to himself for a moment. He looked down at the ground and started to snicker. "Well, I would have prefered her to have done that within our geneology. I suppose it's good for her." Jessica waves her hand at him, "oh Salvador for Pete's sake she's happy. He's a good man. He's a good provider. She can make ten babies for him and a good home. They will be very good together." Salvador grins, "well I suppose... Speaking of babies Jessica Amelia. Is there something you need to tell me?" Jessica steps back with a suprised expression. She rubs her stomach fondly for a moment. As she looks up at him, she begins to giggle once more. "Well, Salvador you are right. There is another bundle of joy in here." Salvador jumps up from his seat. "I knew it, oh Jessica another child." He rushes over to her and hugs her closely rubbing her back. Jessica becomes slightly flustered for a moment. She begins pushing on his chest to make space between them. "You know I can't keep making these babies. I'm getting too old for this." She smiles even with her slight sarcasm. She was about three months pregnant at this point. They finish up and head back in for the night. Jessica bore her last child about six months later. This was Salvador's last child to be born. Jessica finally honors her husband in giving the name, Salvador Lawrence Cardoza Jr.

Chapter 14

It took a good six months to a year for everyone to get use to Louisa being gone. She started writing the family as soon as she reached the final destination. Jessica often enjoyed time by the fire after dinner and reading all of Louisa's adventures in her very different life. Seven years has passed and in some of the more recent letters Louisa informed them of two children she has conceived since their marriage. Jessica hoped for the day to come that they may be able to see Louisa again and the children. Since the stock market crash it has been a terrible hardship that has lasted for several years. Back in the late 20's when it started they had been hoping it would have changed, or improved to some degree. It just never seemed to turn around. Many of Salvador's regular customers were moving on to other areas to buy there goods further away for cheaper prices. Salvador tried to drive his price down without hurting his employees getting paid. It was becoming extremely difficult. He had already let quite a few of them go. It finally reached a point that the original agreement between Salvador, Phyllix, and Lucas Danielson was not working out. The original 20% profit just wasn't enough to hire the help they needed to run the dairy. So they had to start dipping into the salary that Lucas was paying them just to cover expenses. They were going broke fast and Lucas had already contacted them earlier in the week. His actual profits have dropped significantly. His frustrations were becoming obvious in the letters he sent in to Salvador and Phyllix. It was apparent even to the children the stress was high for everyone on the farm.

Annabelle now sixteen and blossomed into such a beautiful woman. She has grown a beautiful shapely body. She had absolutely stunning long, thick, dark, hair with waves. She has the most beautiful eyes. Her curved peach lips are full and plump. Her lips are shaped like a perfect heart. She has so many natural talents. She had a spanish friend in school who taught her the spanish language fluently. She also learned how to read and write from her. Her english was perfect with a slight accent of her portugese heritage. When she sang everyone paused to hear her. She had a voice that almost mimicked the beautiful sounds in a catholic church when the nuns up above would sing. Her voice just glided the words like an ocean wave in it's most natural god given beauty. She could write poetry, play piano, even draw and paint. Yet still with all of that she had one passion that meant more to her then any other. That passion was her first true love, William. They had another encounter after the first Chamarita and that was a few years later at yet another Chamarita. They were able to sneak away and spend more time together.

The letters have continued for all these years. The more they wrote each other the closer the words came in saying I love you. William continued to make the promise to protect Annabelle forever. After Annabelle had finished her chores she took a trip out to her special tree with yet another letter in hand. Salvador still had no idea how long Belle has been communicating with William. He knew Manuel and him were good friends. They had developed a very brotherly type friendship through it all. Belle decided to have her hair in a beautiful braid today with the special ribbon Maria had made her so long ago. As she sat next to her favorite tree, butterflies were roaming around her. They were so colorful and free. They were so natural. Belle loved them. Often times they would land on her hand and she would have an idle conversation with them. She would begin to hum a song to the butterflies as they fluttered around her. When they flew away she reached down and pulled her metal box out of her secret hiding spot. She sat comfortably in position. When she opened the box the beautiful doll Maria made her many years ago was sitting on top of the hundreds of letters. She pulled her doll out and sat her on her lap before she opened the letter to read. Once again William starts it out so poetically. *My Dearest sweet Annabelle: How much I long to see you again. I have learned so much about ranching and herding cattle. I will be ready to work hard. Then some day give you a good home and good life. I see us together forever. You have been my shining star placed in my heart forever. I was going to suprise you, but I thought it unfair to hold out such great news. I am coming once more to visit, but this time I believe I can convince my aunt and uncle to allow me to stay. You and I can begin a plan for our future....* "Oh my gosh." Annabelle hugs the letter as soon as she read the last line. She begins to giggle in absolute joy. *She thinks in her mind, now maybe I can share my feelings for William with my father and my mother when he comes?* Maybe now we can really start to talk about our future? It will be so wonderful." Annabelle reads on....*I want you to know my sweet Annabelle that I truly love you and I plan on giving you a good life. I believe we are old enough now, that we can begin to talk about our future together.* Annabelle starts to fantasize herself in a wedding dress walking towards William. He is truly her prince. He has said the words in the letter, *I love you.* Annabelle's heart begins to pound harder. She could hardly believe he finally said the words. She knew her future will bring such happiness. Annabelle begins to talk to her doll as if the doll could communicate back to her. She named her doll Sara. "Oh Sara can you believe it? My prince loves me and we will be together." Annabelle stands up and begins to dance. She sways her Sara doll going in circles around the tree. She sang while flowing her dress about. Then she stops for a moment play acting like she is William. Her Sara doll is Annabelle. She tells Sara, "my sweet Belle, thank you for this dance." Belle curtsies towards her doll and bows. She begins to giggle to herself and sits back down. She puts Sara back in the box and grabs a pencil and paper to reciprocate the words to William. She wants to be sure he understands she loves him too.

Back at the house Maria, now in her mid-twenties has come for a visit. She had married earlier in the year to a local farmer nearby her parents home. She continued to come to her parents home to check on Annabelle regularly. She came to help their mama today since she hadn't been feeling well. She was in the kitchen making some fresh bread for the evening meal. It's a regular work day for the family even Manuel has reached the point of working for his pappa in the dairy. Jessica has spent most the day in bed. She had decided to stay close in the house to keep an eye on her mama. Phyllix had been throwing some wood in his truck to haul to town for a furniture shop. Just as he was throwing the last bushel in, a car drove up the drive way. Salvador had been working with some of the cows too far to notice anyone coming. As soon as Phyllix seen the car he shouted out at Salvador. He was too busy to even hear him. Phyllix waited patiently at the truck to see who was getting out of this mysterious car. It was Lucus, quite a suprise to Phyllix for sure. Now he began to worry. Lucus has never been interested in coming to the dairy. He was generally happy to just get his profits check and stay out of the way. Lucus approched Phyllix and put his hand out for a greeting. Phyllix reciprocated, "well aren't you a long way from home?" Lucus chuckled, "yes, yes I am. I think we have some things we need to talk about. Where might Salvador be?" Phyllix knew this couldn't be good. He gulped and felt a bit of sweat going down his forehead. "Well I can go fetch him. If you would care to wait on the porch for a moment?" Phyllix directed him to the porch where there was a bench for him to sit at. Then headed over to find Salvador. Lucus was now forty five years old. He was still a fairly handsome man. You could see some of the new wrinkles to his face around his mouth and eyes. He had some thin streaks of gray through his light brown hair. He had managed to loose his little gut from earlier years of beer drinking. His character did not change. He was still a swindling man who never cared much for others. He still hasn't been able to clench a deal on a woman. He has spent way too many years looking for the next big deal and not nearly enough trying to make a family for himself. As he waited he pulled a cigar out of his pocket and bit the top off proceeding to light the end. He puffed away at it till it was lit good. He leaned back crossing his legs. He didn't seem to have much of a care in the world. Big puffs of smoke covered the air as he blew out. Phyllix and Salvador began walking back towards the porch. As soon as Salvador saw Lucus he whispers in a low tone to Phyllix. "Did you know he hasn't gotten a good commission check in a few months now?" Phyllix responds without turning his head in an even lower tone, "we better come up with something good cousin." By now Manuel could see there was a visitor on the porch. He managed to sneak away and crept up the backside of the house. He was just close enough so he could listen in on whatever was going on. Salvador approached Lucas with his hand out to greet him. Lucas stood up shook hands and went straight to business. "We need to discuss this dairy. I'm not pleased with the commissions it has been carrying. It seems you don't have much help left around here." Salvador immediately interrupts Lucas in anticipation of salvaging this situation. "Look Lucas you know with the stock market crash and the economy troubles were doing the best we can." Lucas was unimpressed with Salvador's response. The only thing Lucas is ever interested in is his money. Lucas grabs a bundle of papers from his back pocket and pulls them open to show Salvador and Phyllix. "It looks here that we had an agreement and it seems to me

I'm getting the short end of the stick." As lucas points to the written portion of the paper that he is referring. "I'm going to have to cut out your salaries and your going to have to do something to change this situation. I already have a few buyers who have interest in building some manufacturing companies on this property." Salvador and Phyllix become agitated immediately when they here this. Phyllix jumps forward waving his hands. "Now hold on just a minute this is still our property." Lucas becomes angry, "No sir it is not. You simply work this property. You don't own it. As he points to the section on the contract, you see here look right here on this document. You read this fine print." Lucas adamantly points to the section he is referring. Both Salvador and Phyllix look closely at the document in surprise. They had no idea Lucas had swindled them out of any real ownership. Salvador becomes angry, "what kind of business man are you? You can't do this to us." Lucas laughs in his evil manner, "Oh but I can and I will." Manuel could hear the conversation and became very worried for his family.

Annabelle had finished her letter and was heading back towards the house. Skipping joyously she had such a beautiful glow about her. She had a pure hearted love in her eyes. She was singing quietly as she was approaching. Lucas happened to glance over and see her. Salvador and Phyllix had not even noticed Lucas wondered away from them for a moment on the other side of the porch. They were busy looking over the document together. Desperately trying to figure out how they could have missed what was written on the agreement. Lucas became mesmerized by the sight of Annabelle. He watched as her dress glided while she moved. The closer she became the more he watched her. He started to rub his chin enchanted by her beauty. He took one last puff of his cigar and peered over at the men looking over the document. He suddenly reached an idea that might just solve this little problem of the property. He waited for Annabelle to reach the porch standing there holding the rail. He speaks out towards her. "Hey there pretty girl. What's your name?" Manuel got a sick feeling in his stomach in that very moment. He stepped out and immediately scorned something at Lucas. "That's my sister. You have no business talking to her." Salvador noticed the reprehensible tone of Manuel. Salvador looked over and saw that Manuel was on the side of the house. "What are you doing Manuel? Get back to the dairy. Do not speak to guests that way!" Salvador had no idea what Lucas was conspiring in his mind, nor did he know why Manuel spoke to him in that way. Manuel became angry and stormed off towards Annabelle. He tried to grab her arm and guide her away from the porch. Belle didn't understand what was happening. She became agitated and pulled away from Manuel. Manuel tried to grab at her again. Belle yelled at him, "stop it Manuel. What are you doing?" Manuel tells her, "you need to get out of here. Come on trust me Belle." Just as this was happening Lucas shouts out, "now hold it right there." He walks down the stairs off the porch approaching Manuel and Belle. Lucas gets a closer look at Annabelle. He begins to stroke her face with his hand ever so gently. "Tell me your name," he states in an eery tone to her. Annabelle so innocent appreciates the attention not realizing this man was very evil. She nervously giggles and states, "my name is Annabelle." Manuel becomes more angry and protective of his sister. He jumps between Lucas and Belle. "It doesn't matter what her name is you dirty old man." Now Salvador realizes this could be trouble. He quickly runs down the stairs towards Manuel without knowing what Lucas was doing, or why Manuel was reacting in this way. "Manuel stop it. What are you doing?" Salvador was more concerned about Lucas taking the property and leaving them homeless, then trying to understand why Manuel was acting this way. Salvador grabbed Manuel and pulled him away and began to scold him. "Get back to the dairy right now!!!" Manuel became angry and stormed away. He looked at his sister first and at the man. He knew this was a bad situation and was angry that his own father couldn't even see it. Belle became concerned. She looked down for a moment. Lucas was so enchanted by her he began to speak softly in her direction. This time he Intended for Salvador to hear him. "I think it is possible Salvador. We can work something out here. Something to make us both happy..... ohhh soooo happy yes." You could hear the disgusting tone in his voice as he mentally was removing Belle's clothing right off of her. Belle became uncomfortable and started to walk away from Lucas as she nervously sais, "I should go." Lucas grabs her arm not allowing her to move. Belle attempts to pull away from him and starts to screech in a panic. Salvador finally realizes what was going on in Lucas's head. "Now hold on just a minute. Wait, hold on just a minute. Lucas, you can't be serious. My daughter is only sixteen years old." Finally Lucas lets go of Annabelle. She runs into the house. Phyllix can see the situation turning very badly. Lucas turns to Salvador, "I'm only going to explain this once, so listen good. This property you will both lose. I will sell it. That little girl over there can remedy our situation. I want her that's it, no negotiations. You give me her. I will sell the property to you hook line, and sinker. I can sweeten the deal for you as well. I will loan you both a little ernest money to help you get back on track. Really Salvador would it be so bad? I'm a business man. I can take care of her. One less mouth for you to feed and you could see her once in a while. Besides I heard your wife is sick. Do you got the money to get her a doctor? How sick is she? Sometimes we just gotta make sacrifices after all." Lucas chuckles and Salvador gets ill to his stomach at this proposal. Lucas throws his cigar on the ground and stomps it out heading back to his car. "You got two days to figure this out. Both of you, or I'm selling. I will be back. He gets in his car and drives away. Manuel was still within ear shot of the conversation. He heard what the man was suggesting. Manuel became so angry he bawled up his fist and slammed it into the nearest tree. Leaving his fingers bleeding.

Phyllix walked down from the porch over to Salvador shaking his head. "What are we going to do?" Salvador looks down and starts kicking rocks in frustration. "I can't believe were back in this situation once again. Do you really think Jessica is going to accept losing yet another home? Honestly Phyllix, Jessica and I are finally getting along better. This could break us. I mean literally break us." Phyllix becomes adamantly serious looking directly at Salvador. "You can't seriously be suggesting letting him take Annabelle?" Salvador starts shaking his head again. "I don't know.... I mean look... after all you know as well as I do.. Jessica hasn't exactly warmed up to Annabelle. She has just gone with the situation, but if she finds out that we lost this place because I wasn't willing to give up Annabelle. She may never forgive me." Phyllix becomes stunned at the suggestion. "It's not like I don't love her, she is my daughter. Hey it's not so crazy a lot of people marry their daughters off these days. He would be able to take care of her right?" Phyllix lowers his head and walks away in disgust. "I'm not having this conversation with you Salvador, I'm just not." Manuel had heard what his pappa was saying and approaches Salvador. His hand was bleeding, but it was as if Manuel couldn't even feel it. He was so wrapped up in emotion. The only thing he cared about was stopping this insanity. "Pappa you cannot be serious? You will break Annabelle's heart." Manuel knew Belle was very much in love with William and he was in love with her. He knew what her hopes and dreams were. His pappa was about to break and destroy it all. Salvador became angry at Manuel's constant intrusion's. "You are being disrespectful. I'm not having it. Do you understand Manuel? There are some things you don't understand about life." Manuel couldn't control his anger any longer. He thrusted forward at Salvador with his right hand clenched in a fist. He socked Salvador in the face. Salvador grabbed a hold of Manuels arm and pushed him down on the ground. He jumped on top of Manuel punching him in the gut. Salvador pulls his right arm back ready to throw another fist in his face. He screamed out, "you want to fight like a man, you take it like a man." Just then Jessica had heard the yelling from her bed and ran outside still in her nightgown. She had been in bed most of the day. She came running down the porch to Salvador screaming at them..... "stop.... stop... what are you doing... stop!!!" Maria wasn't far behind. She was mortified to see her husband and her son hitting each other. Maria soon joined the madness. She ran out behind her mother. She stood there with her hands across her mouth in astonishment. Annabelle peeking around Maria to see what was happening. Jessica screamed out for Phyllix to come back and seperate them. Phyllix came running over and pulled Salvador off Manuel. Manuel jumped up from the ground spitting blood out of his mouth towards Salvador. "If you do this pappa, I will leave!! I will never speak to you again!! You will no longer be my father!!" He spits more blood out of his mouth and storms away towards the field. Jessica shocked looks towards Salvador. "What's going on? What just happened?" Salvador pushes Phyllix away from him in disgust. Jessica walks up to Salvador attempting to wipe some of the blood off his face with her hands. Salvador pushes Jessica away and storms into the house.

That evening the dinner table was bare. Manuel and Phyllix stayed away. Maria and Annabelle stayed quiet. As did Jessica and Salvador. The only thing you could here in the room was the clanking of bowls being handed around the table, so they could each serve each other. As to break the silence Maria speaks up and announces, "mama is looking much better today. Wouldn't you say pappa?" The room still silent. Everyone just continues to eat. Annabelle still had no idea what was happening. She didn't know why Manuel had hit pappa. Jessica decides to offer some kind of conversation. "Thanks Maria for keeping things up around the house. Thank you for taking care of things during my illness." Maria offers a slight nod in mama's direction, a little smile. Salvador finally decides to enter the conversation. "Yes.. yes... thank you

Maria." He continues to shove food in his mouth. The level of discomfort in the room was very obvious. Annabelle still concerned about the situation. She looks over at the two empty chairs where Manuel and Uncle Phyllix usually were. She decides to ask the question. "Pappa why is Manuel so mad? Why is Uncle Phyllix not here either pappa?" Just as she sais it the tension comes right back into the room. Salvador slams his fist on the table without saying a word. Annabelle jumps back from him. Jessica immediately interrupts looking right at Salvador, "that's enough." She waves her hand towards Salvador, then waves her hand at Annabelle. "We won't speak of this Belle just eat." Everyone just simply goes back to eating. Later after the kitchen is cleaned up the girls go to their room, as did Jessica and Salvador. Jessica begins brushing her hair in the mirror as Salvador enters the room. He sits on the side of the bed speechless. He knew he had to tell her what happened. He grabs part of the blanket hanging on the side of the bed. Fumbling around with the fringe he wanders into deep thought. Trying to come up with a way to tell her what was about to unfold before them. Jessica looks at the reflection of him through the mirror. "So are you going to just sit there and fumble with my afghan, or are you going to tell me what is going on with you and Manuel?" He proceeds to explain the details of the day and how it came to this point. Jessica eventually turns to look directly at Salvador while she listens intently to every word. When he finished Jessica was almost unable to contain herself. She thought in her mind. *I could finally rid myself of this horrible past of Salvador's daughter. I could have my family back.* She was defninitely selfish in the moment. She almost wanted to smile. Jessica is not an evil person, but the pain Salvador caused her with his infidelity. Then this child she has had to raise as if it were hers. It was sometimes almost unbareable. To her this was an opportunity to move forward. She rationalized in her mind, *lots of people found sooters for their daughters. It's not so terrible.* Salvador could see a slight grin on Jessica's face. He knew this would be something she would want. He loved his daughter, yet somehow even he managed to rationalize this situation. The only thing Salvador kept thinking about was, they cannot lose their home again. He couldn't risk losing Jessica's love. He just couldn't handle the thought of that yet again. Jessica turns back towards the mirror brushing her hair looking at Salvador's reflection. The two of them spend many hours that evening discussing what to do. Salvador tossed and turned throughout the night. He knew what he had to do, but it haunted him. He rationalized within himself logic behind it. *For the sake of my marriage. For our home.* He continued to mutter the words in his mind till he drifted into sleep.

After a few days Lucas made good on his word and showed up at the dairy. Salvador didn't even give him the opportunity to get out of his vehicle. He did not want the kids to hear what was going on. He kept Lucas in his vehicle. Phyllix had already been told that Salvador intended on giving this man his daughter. He didn't like it, nor agree with the decision. Phyllix didn't want to lose the property either. He simply let Salvador do whatever he chose with Belle. He stayed out of it all. It did hinder the relationship with Phyllix. He was sickened by the whole idea. Salvador approached Lucas at the vehicle. "Stay here please we need to keep this private." Lucas simply sat back in his seat interested in what Salvador had to say. "Look we can make a deal here that will work, but first you need to draw up the agreement. Let me look it over. No tricks Lucas I mean it. Everything better be legit this time do you understand?" Lucas grinned, "so are you saying?" Lucas couldn't finish his sentence when Salvador interupted him. Lucas was shocked he didn't realize Salvador was really gonna give him his daughter. "You undertstand you will be honerable in how you do this as well. This will be a wedding. You will marry my daughter and treat her as your wife. Your not just taking her and doing as you please. You have to honor me and my daughter. Do you understand?" Lucas shook his head, "yes, yes of course... however Mr. Cardoza this won't be any kind of wedding with you walking her down the isle and all that business. It will just be a simple ceremony with a judge that's it. I'm not making this all fancy and crazy." Salvador was not liking what Lucas suggested. "No your not going to dishonor my family. We are Catholics, she is to marry with a priest. She will be given a proper wedding." Lucas shakes his head again, "you are asking too much at this point. We have to come to some kind of compromise here." As they continue to discuss the details Manuel could see his pappa having a conversation at the car with this Lucas person. Suddenly Salvador shakes hands with Lucas and he drives away yelling out, "we will get back together in a week or so with the final papers!!" He waves as he drives away. Manuel gasp's.... it occurs to him. *Oh My God... he didn't*".... he realizes pappa just did it. He made a deal with this man. He is actually going to give him Annabelle. Manuel starts to run towards his father. "Pappa tell me that wasn't what

I think that was?" Salvador turns to Manuel, "son there are things you just don't understand." "That's bullshit pappa... damn it you cannot do this to her!" Salvador gets annoyed at his constant challenges. He waves him away. "Just go to work and mind yourself boy." At that point Manuel has had it. "That's it... you son of a bitch!" He spits at his father, "I'm done, I'm leaving. I won't stand around and watch this for another second." He throws down his hammer and stomps out to the field to talk to Annabelle.

Salvador just dismisses his words and heads back to the dairy. Annabelle had been sitting by her tree writing yet another letter to William when Manuel approached. Manuel paused for a second watching his sister as she writes. He wanted to tell her what was about to happen in her life, but he could hardly bring himself to hurt her. She looked so happy and peaceful sitting there. He had brushed his foot across a branch, and it snapped. Just then Belle looked up to see who it was. "Manuel you silly, what are you doing over there?" She smiles at him so innocently. Manuel walks closer to her, "I was just...Uhh just..." He thought for a moment, *I can't tell her this, I just can't.* "I was just checking in on you Belle." He approached and sat beside her. Belle became excited and wanted to share with him what William had said. "Oh Manuel... I wanted to tell you, he's coming to see us again. Can you believe it? Isn't that wonderful?" She smiled wide while reaching her hand out to a butterfly on the tree. Manuel became sick to his stomach. He attempted to smile for her as much as he could muster. "That's...great sis... that's just...great." He looks down. Belle could see something was wrong. "What is it?" She reaches her hand over to his chin and motions his head back up. He just clams up frustrated he stands. "I gotta go sis, I love you." He runs in the other direction of the house, as far away as he can. Belle stands and watches him go confused and concerned. "But wait... Manuel wait whaa...." Over the next few weeks Annabelle becomes anxious for Williams visit. Maria was aware that William was coming. She offered to drive Belle to him. Her Uncle Phyllix let her use the truck once in a while to go into town. Maria had already agreed to take Annabelle to town as soon as she heard William was coming. Word traveled fast whenever there were visitors from out of the area. Maria had already pre planned an excuse to take Annabelle. She had told her Uncle Phyllix she was needing to go in to town and pick up some supplies for her house. Nobody even questioned her. Not even their pappa. Annabelle was so happy and ready to go. Maria laughed at Belle.. "cmon Belle.. stop being so obvious that smile on your face looks painted on you permanently," she laughs. "Let's go Maria, cmon lets go." Belle knew exactly where William would be. His aunt and uncle had a fruit and vegetable store in town. William usually helped them out when he came to visit. As soon as they drove up Belle stayed patiently in the car while Maria went in to see if William was there. William had already stepped out to see if he could help. He was thinking they were some new customers out front. When he looked over he could see Belle sitting in the truck. Maria smiled and motioned William to the passenger side of the truck where Belle was sitting. Annabelle didn't even know he was standing by the door. William was so excited to hug her he didn't even bother to surprise her. He just spoke right up. "Annabelle your here." Annabelle was startled, but just as excited. She jumped out of the truck and ran right into his arms. They hugged so tight you couldn't get a crow bar in between them. Just as she was pulling away William could see how absolutely beautiful she still is. And as time has passed he could see that she has many new features of a young woman. A beautiful curvy slim shape. Her hair so long and thick. Her lips always seem to get plumper every year. The most beautiful big brown eyes he's ever seen. At that very moment William realized he is completely and totally in love with her. Annabelle stood back from him in her shy like manner looking up at William. Maria could see that they needed some privacy so she spoke up. "Well um Belle, I guess I have some shopping to do for mama... so I will leave you two, to catch up." She chuckled as she walked away. William decided they needed privacy so he thought of the perfect solution. "Lets go to the park where we met. Belle what do you think?" Annabelle loved his idea. She put her hand out to him so they could be close as they walked together.

Annabelle was chatting away telling William all about her sister Louisa and her children. She talked about her brother Manuel and what he's been up to. William could hardly get a word in edge wise. Belle had learned a lot in school that year also. She wanted to share about the books she had been reading. She loved reading. She was learning so much about history and some science. Annabelle was so well rounded. She could pick up talents so well. She could draw the most amazing pictures of wildlife and roses. She mastered the most beautiful butterflies. She had brought one of her pictures for William and handed it to him so he could keep something personal from her. As William opened up the paper that was carefully folded he saw a grand picture of three butterflies. The colors in them were so unique and blended so nicely. She had drawn them all sitting on a large branch with hundreds of green leaves coming off it. The details were most amazing. William smiled and Annabelle started to explain to him that the butterflies are a symbol of peace and harmony, safety and freedom. He absolutely loved it when she became so dreamy. She had the most rich imagination. William smiled and reached for her hands and held them together in his hands while looking in her face. "You know Belle you are my peace and harmony." He reached for her face and lightly brushed his hand across her beautiful profile. He leaned in and kissed her lips so tenderly. Annabelle started to lightly kiss him back then pulled back from him. She giggled. Her youth and innocence shined through. William laughed with her and smiled. They continued walking and William shared with Annabelle about his life in Mexico. He was also excited to tell her about his newest adventure moving there and helping his Aunt and Uncle with their farm. "I want you to know Annabelle. I want us to be together." Belle giggled again not realizing what he meant. "Well we are together silly." "No Annabelle I mean...well I mean...I want to take care of you Belle..I want you to be mine." William looked down at the ground feeling vulnerable for a moment. Annabelle smiled and whispered to him. "I want to be yours to." Unfortunately they didn't have much more time. Maria had to get back with the truck. She had been yelling out for Annabelle, but neither of them heard her. They both sat under a tree and held hands. William decided to take one last opportunity to kiss her. This time Annabelle wanted to kiss him and didn't feel as shy about it. This was the most intence kiss the two of them had ever had. Now that they were both older and in their teen years they were feeling so many new things. Kissing each other was bringing that out. Just then Belle whispers again to him. "I want to be with you forever William." She starts to kiss him more. Williams heart was pounding so hard. He knew this was going to be his wife some day and he didn't want to let go of her. They were both so wrapped up into each other, neither one of them noticed Maria coming up the trail in the park. She could see that they were kissing. She tried not to sound intrusive. She really did have to get that truck back. "Uhhh... ahem." Just as Maria made that noise Annabelle got startled and William pulled back. He looked over seeing Maria coming. Belle became embarassed and looked down. Then she pulled herself to her feet, "sorry sis... um yeah... we can go." William chuckled and pulled himself up to his feet. He made sure to be extra polite to Maria since after all she was the one nice enough to bring Belle to see him. "So sorry Maria for taking up too much time." Maria smiled, "no worries William, I understand. I really do got to get going." She looks over at Annabelle, "are you ready?" Annabelle nodded sadly. She hugged William and almost started to cry. William touched her lips. "No tears now Belle. I will be in town for a little bit ok. Maybe I can come see Manuel?" Belle smiled, "yes oh that would be so great." Maria grabbed Belle's hand, "lets go sis." William watched them as they both walked back towards the truck. He was thinking how great life will be. He had already been making plans on a job and putting together enough money to marry Annabelle. He knew she would be his wife someday. He knew in his heart they were meant for each other.

After a few days had passed Annabelle was growing impatient she had no inclination as to when William would be coming. She was constantly watching the driveway waiting for his arrival. She had already told Manuel that he would be visiting soon. So Manuel gave his pappa heads up and reminded him who William was. Salvador remembered it stayed fresh in his mind since so many letters were coming so often for Manuel. Of course he still had no indication of the relationship between William and Annabelle. Jessica still had very little interest in what Annabelle was up to. She was kind to her, but still that motherly connection had never happened. Maria has played the role for so long with Annabelle that everyone just accepted it that way. Sometimes Annabelle would question that gap in her relationship with her mother. She could never quite understand why. Since Salvador forbid anyone to tell her the truth. Annabelle was never really made to understand the awkwardness of her relationship with Jessica. Still every once in a while you would here that same style introduction Jessica would make. She always made it a point to say, "Salvador's daughter." Maria knew some of the story behind Annabelle's past, but it was never discussed. Manuel still had no idea of the truth behind it all. It was difficult for Maria to know this information. She had lost so much respect for her pappa and it definitely caused some tension for Maria with her pappa. Annabelle was always doing things to try to gain her mothers love. She would go out of her way and make special drawings for her, or put together beautiful flower arrangements. She would cook special meals, or write beautiful poems dedicated to her mother. Nothing Annabelle ever did really worked. It was very frustrating for her at times. Annabelle refused to give up. On this particular day Rosie and Belle were scrubbing the household laundry on their wash board. As Belle would finish scrubbing a piece of laundry Rosie would then rinse it out and ring it out. Then took it over to the clothes line and hung the laundry on the line. The two girls had to handle a lot of the household chores for a few months now since Jessica had been so ill. Their youngest sister was very spoiled unlike them. They had always had to participate in the chores, but not their youngest sister. She seemed to just float around and get into mischief. Francis was just dancing and gallivanting around them while they both worked hard on the laundry.

As Rosie was hanging something up she shouts out at her, "Meha go play over there. Go on go... stop it!" As Rosie slaps her hands together at Francis in a parental manner. Little Francis giggles and runs off towards the dairy. Annabelle smiles and laughs. "Honestly that girl won't be able to take care of any man. You know she has learned so little." She chuckles as she speaks. Rosie just rolls her eyes.. "I know," in agreement with a sigh. You could suddenly hear the rumbling of a vehicle coming down the drive way. Belle got butterflies in her stomach. She became so excited and jumps up to go see who is coming. Rosie smiles she could tell from the trip to town they made how close Belle has become to William. Rosie was happy for Annabelle. She knew in her heart that Annabelle was in love. As Annabelle reaches the driveway she stays back a little behind the porch as to not look to obvious to pappa. She had to remain very discreet so he wouldn't find out of there relations. Manuel happened to be heading toward the house when he saw Belle peaking over the porch. "Belle what are you doing?" Annabelle waves

Manuel over to her. He promptly walks over to her. "Look, look brother. I think William is coming down the driveway." It just so happened she was right. William had borrowed his uncles truck to make a special trip out to see Belle and Manuel. Just as he pulled up and exits the truck Belle could see it was him. Salvador heard the vehicle and stepped away from the dairy to see who was there. Manuel immediately stepped out from behind the porch and told Belle to go in the house and then come back out acting suprised so pappa doesn't get suspicious. Annabelle did as Manuel said. As Manuel walked out towards William, he approached him with a big smile. "Hey there William. I'm so glad you could stop by and see us." They both shook hands and smiled while Manuel threw a wink his way as to hint to him that pappa was heading over. William knew Annabelle's pappa would not approve of any relations just yet. Salvador walked over and greeted William. "So William how is your Uncle's farm coming along?" William grinned, "fine, fine sir just fine." His nerves started to creep up on him. Just then Annabelle walks out of the house acting surprised to see William there. She walks over to the boys. "Hey pappa so I guess William is here for a visit? Shall I get some lemonade?" She casually smiles over to William. Salvador was very busy that day which was a huge benefit to Annabelle and William. He simply nods his head, "yeah... yeah sure you all have things to do, but a short visit would be fine." As Salvador is speaking he's walking back towards the dairy. "I have a lot of work to do today William so please excuse me. Have a good day and tell your Uncle I said hello." Willaim nods back to him, "yes sir, of course sir." Just then William turns his face directly to Annabelle with a big smile. Of course Annabelle smiling just as big. Manuel starts to laugh, "you two are so funny. Look at you man. Can you be more discreet," he states sarcastically. Manuel still didn't much care what his pappas opinion was or what he thought. He was trying to keep a positive outlook for Annabelles sake. He is still praying in his heart that Salvador will not follow through with his plan. Annabelle runs into the house to put together some lemonade for them. Manuel directs William up to the porch as they both sit down to chat. Manuel pulls out his jacks as he sits down. He casually throws the jacks down and bounces his ball. As he picks up jacks. It was a great way to pass time. He could play the game while he talked without even thinking about what he was doing. William laughs out loud. "Your pretty good at that," as he smiles and laughs. It didn't take long for Annabelle to get the refreshements together and bring them out. She walks out onto the porch and hands WIlliam and Manuel a glass. William notices that Annabelle didn't bring herself a glass. "Belle aren't you going to join us?" Belle giggles, "no, no I'm fine really." Annabelle instantly and excitedly announces, "Manuel I would love to show William my special tree. Let's take him out there?" Manuel grabs up his jacks and ball and stands, "sure why not. I could take a walk let's go." William proceeds to follow both of them. Just as they were heading down the trail Annabelle looks back to be sure they are far enough away to reach out her hand for Williams. They casually rub their hands as they walk side by side and suddenly William grabs hold of her hand and squeezes. Annabelle smiles as she walks.

The closer they got to the tree the more William could see this massive beautiful bountiful tree out in the middle of the field. It was standing alone amongst the entire field of yellow daisies and grass. As soon as they get there Manuel grabs a stick he had been widdling and left by the tree to come back to. The stick was partially shaved off and shaped like a whistle. William was impressed with his work. Manuel sits down next to the tree and pulls his knife out to get busy. He wanted to give Annabelle and William some private time. Annabelle pulls on Williams arm. "Cmon now, I want to show you my secret spot." She pulls him over to the other side of the tree. Manuel laughs as he widdles. She sits down next to her hidden hole under the tree pulling William down to sit in front of her. He immediately noticed the initials carved in the tree A.C + W.O, (Annabelle Cardoza + William Oros). He smiles and Annabelle begins to turn a little red realizing he is seeing her very vulnerable side. He runs his fingers acrossed the initials. He bites down on his bottom lip in deep thought of his dreams for their future together. Annabelle touches his hand on the tree and lightly rubs his fingers. They catch each other face to face and William leans forward to kiss her. He was always so gentle with Belle and remained a gentleman. Though even with his respectful ways he made Annabelle feel like she was floating. Suddenly Manuel pops his head over the tree, "now... now... William." Manuel still remaining very protective of his sister. William pulls away and looks over at Manuel, "of course, of course." William smiles over at Manuel in a cunning sort of way. William was only able to spend a few short hours with Belle, but he didn't leave without telling her he was heading back to Mexico for a short while. Then he will be back permanently in the area and hopes for a long future with Annabelle. Belle was so excited. She was happy to know that soon she will be with him. They will have a wonderful life together.

All the while Manuel knew that their father had different plans for Annabelle. He was very angry at the prospect of what was to come, but he didn't know what to do about it. He prayed their father would change his mind. He thought this man Lucas was surely not going to base a sale of property on ownership of his sister. It just didn't seem real in his mind.

Chapter 15

As a few weeks pass Lucas had set up a meeting with Salvador. He planned to come to the house to speak with Jessica Amelia and Salvador about the details. Jessica made sure that they would be alone in the house with no interruptions. She had Phyllix take the children on a litte road trip to town. Lucas was sitting at the table with a pile of papers. He went on to explain how this agreement will play out. The compromise was that there would be a small get together at the Catholic church. The only ones involved would be Annabelles father. He was fine with Annabelle wearing a dress, but Salvador would simply be there as witness to sign the marriage certificate. Lucus had a lot of power in that town the priest couldn't have any say in how this played out either. lucus was at least willing to allow their religious ceremony with the church. With this agreement came full ownership of the property for Salvador and Phyllix. He was also extending a loan with a small interest rate of repayment on the loan. This will help them bring more stability to the business with supplies and hired help. The other condition to this agreement was that Lucas will continue to earn a percentage of profit on the total earnings of the dairy. Salvador was not pleased with that part of the agreement. He felt he was ambushed into the majority of this contract any way you looked at it. Lucas wanted a continued profit of 20% for life. His way of explaining that was it's a guarantee income. No matter where he is he was guarnteed that money for life. He did however allow a six month grace period before any profit earnings were to come to him. Salvador proceeded to sign the contract. Phyllix had already signed earlier under the condition that Salvador agreed to the terms. The plan was for the very next day to meet up at the church with Annabelle. Lucas felt that the sooner the better and it's better not to give Annabelle too much time to think about what was happening. Lucas left and Salvador remained sitting at the table with Jessica. He muttered, "she will never understand, or forgive me." Jessica looked up at him pleased at what he had done. She felt that he finally took a step forward for her. It was truly a sad moment for Salvador, but he felt he had to do this. Phyllix finally came home with everyone. They all walked in the house. They saw their pappa sitting at the table and all joined them. Jessica suggested to Rose to take Francis to the porch since they needed to talk. Baby Salvador Jr. was napping. Just as everyone was seated at the table it became silent in the room. Phyllix felt very uncomfortable as he knew what they were about to reveal. Phyllis looks over at Salvador, "should I stay, or should I go?" Salvador nodded promptly to Phyllix to remain in the room. Manuel and Annabelle were patiently awaiting as to why everyone was so quiet.

Maria had showed up to check on her family. She walked in the house and saw everyone in the kitchen. She walks in looking around with a confused expression. Looking over at her pappa he was sweating. Maria became impatient, "Pappa what's going on?" Salvador announces to all of them in such a matter of fact way as if nobody would challenge what he was saying. As he rolled the words off his tongue in Annabelles direction. "We have arranged a marriage for you Annabelle, with Lucas. You will be wed in the morrow, (manana meha)."

Manuel immediately jumps from his chair. He was so angry the chair went flying and hit the wall breaking in two. Manuel started waving his fist as if this was the fight of his life. "You cannot do this to Annabelle, I will kill you." Manuel lunges forward immediately ready to fight. Phyllix quickly reacts and grabs Manuel just before he reaches his pappa. Manuel kicks and screams throwing his arms around like a crazy person ready to charge anyone in his path. Jessica jumps up, "stop it Manuel!! stop!! You must stop!!" Phyllix and Manuel end up wrestling each other to the ground. As Phyllix pins Manuel down, Annabelle and Maria start to cry. Maria quickly huddles around Annabelle, holding her close. Salvador stands over Manuel, "this is it Manuel..! You will not dis-respect me in my home..!" Manuel becomes even more enraged and suddenly gains an immence amount of strength. Thrusting his legs so hard he pushes Phyllix off of him. Manuel stands face to face with Salvador. He throws a punch so hard and hit's Salvador directly in his face. It caused Salvador to lose balance and hit the floor. Just then Phyllix redeems himself enough to grab Manuel holding both of his arms behind his back. "You are not my father. You disgust me. Go to hell!!!!" Manuel scorns to Salvador while spitting at him. Salvador gets back to his feet charging Manuel. Phyllix no longer able to hold Manuel he breaks free. Both Salvador and Manuel are in a full fledge fist fight. Thrusting their fists so hard at each other with such rage you could hear the pounding of each hit. Finally Salvador hit him so hard Manuel fell to the floor knocked unconscious for a moment. Manuel manages to shake it off. He pulls himself up from the floor and runs to Annabelle giving her a huge hug and crying. "Sister I love you so much, but I can't stay here." Annabelle starts crying uncontrollably as she utters out to him in despair. "No Manuel please, (por favor... por favor...) don't go." Manuel sais goodbye and turns towards Salvador resuming his disgust at him. "I'm leaving," he storms out the door. Salvador reaches up to his face to wipe the blood from his lip. He yells out to Manuel, "your damn straight your leaving." He charges over to the door grabbing the broken chair pieces and throwing them out at Manuel. He turns to Annabelle in anger, "this is it Annabelle... You will marry this man. You will not dispute this!!" Unfortunately during these times woman had very little say. Maria and Annabelle knew this. Salvador was somehow able to completely dismiss Manuel as a son. The reality of Manuel leaving and never coming back somehow didn't matter to either Salvador, or Jessica Amelia. Salvador felt that Manuel was not acting a proper son so he completely wiped out anymore emotion for him. Phyllix decided it was time for him to leave. He was equally frustrated at the situation. It saddened him that his cousin made such terrible decisions. He quietly walked out without saying a word. Maria was clenching

Annabelle close in her arms crying with her. They both felt in that moment they didn't know their father anymore. Annabelle held her arms out wide to pappa in desperation. Through her broken words she spoke, "pappa please why? I don't understand please." Salvador shut himself down at that point and barked back at her. "Discussion is over!" He stated sharply. Then abrubtly walks out the door slamming it behind him.

The very next morning Maria was instructed to come to the house and get her little sister ready. The child that Maria practically raised. She was instructed to dress her appropriate for the coming encounter to wed Lucas. This broke Maria's heart, but she knew somehow she had to tell Annabelle the truth about her past. She was brushing Belle's hair and rolling it up into a bun leaving some strands to her sides hanging wavy and long. She placed some tiny white flowers in the bun. Tears rolling down Marias face. While she was working on her hair she decided this might be the time. She knew pappa couldn't hear the conversation. "There is something I need to talk to you about Annabelle." Annabelle was already crying and could barely grasp what was happening to her. Maria shouts out to Salvador, "pappa can I please take Annabelle in the field for a few moments?" Salvador wasn't completely heartless so he agreed to allow her to take her for a few moments. Just then Maria grabs Annabelles hand guiding her outside down the trail for the very last time. She took Annabelle to her spot by the tree. Annabelle started to cry even more as she saw the initials on the tree knowing that she may never see William again. Maria quickly dug up Annabelle's box. "What are you doing Maria? This makes me hurt more," she cries. Maria pulls the little tiny doll out of the box and hands it to Annabelle. "Belle everytime you are sad, or lonely. I want you to hug this doll I made for you. Remember it's my heart in this doll ok?" Maria spoke with her lips wimpering. She could barely get the words out without the tears falling down her face. Maria pushes the doll into Annabelle's arms clenching Annabelles arms against herself forcing her to hold the doll close to her heart. "I love you Annabelle. You are so very special and precious to me always know that in your heart." Maria could hardly speak her words through the tears and pain she felt. She knew looking into Annabelle's eyes that Belle felt like the one parent her father, she believed loved her. For some reason is throwing her away. It was so difficult for Maria to compose herself, but she knew she had to tell Annabelle the truth about her life. She was only able to get a few more words out saying, "Annabelle you need to know the truth." Belle looked up at her confused. "Belle you have a twin sister and ...." Just as Maria was about to continue Salvador came down the trail. He could hear the words, "sister." He immediately interupted bluntly. "Belle it's time to go." He grabs Annabelle by her arm pulling her up to her feet. As soon as he see's the doll he grabs it out of her hands. "What is this you can't be sporting this around. Your about to marry a man?" He tosses the doll to the ground, just then Maria runs and grabs it up. "Pappa you don't understand." Salvador had a bag in his arms full of some things for Annabelle to take with her. He ignores Maria and practically drags Annabelle back to the house, pulling her up to her feet. Annabelle tries with all her strength to stand, but is so stricken with pain of never seeing who she truly loves again. Her life, pappa, sisters, brothers. Her life about to change so drastically. She has difficulty bringing her legs up to stand firm and walk with Salvador. They get to the truck and Salvador throws the bag in the back. He turns to Phyllix to tell him something and just as he turns Maria quickly stuffs the doll into Annabelle's bag. Belle could see what she did, but said nothing. Salvador decideds to have Phyllix go with them. Salvador instructs Annabelle to get in. Maria runs over to Belle one last time in tears hugging her little sister goodbye. She didn't want to let go. Maria is holding Belle so tight it almost hurt Belles arms. Annabelle was crying sucking each tear in her mouth as it fell to her lips. Her nose was running as she puttered out a painful cry. "I love you sister so much. I don't want to go." Maria starts nodding her head at her. "I know.... I know... I wish.. I could do something." She felt helpless in saving her sister from this. Finally Salvador peels them apart. "Enough of this. Everything will be fine. You will still see her Maria. She's just getting married." Maria looks up at her pappa in horror. She still can't wrap her head around this horrible thing. She cries to him in anger and sadness. "Why Pappa... why.. are you doing this? It's wrong... you know it's wrong." Salvador becomes angry at her disprespectful way towards him. Maria continues holding on to Annabelles hand as Salvador begins to pull Maria away. Maria wasn't strong enough to hold on. The girls begin screaming and crying reaching their hands towards each other. Salvador manages to take Maria in the house as he lifts her up with complete ease and tosses her in and shuts the front door behind him. He walks over to the truck and picks up Annabelle tossing her in the back as if to *toss her out like garbage*. Annabelle thought while she cried.

On the ride to the church Annabelle starts to quiet down finally after a while. She rubs her sleeves of her dress across her face to dry it. Belle starts to recap her thoughts on what Maria had said. *What did she mean, I HAD a twin sister?* They pull up to the church and grab Belle's bag and headed in. Lucas was already there waiting in one of the pews. He heard them coming and looked back to see his bride. There she stood. She had a white and yellow dress on. That was the best dress Maria could come up with. They were limited on choices since this wasn't a planned wedding. The dress was originally all yellow, but Maria had to make a few changes to it in order to be sure Belle showed white in her dress. She was after all still an innocent proper girl. It was a fairly simple dress that went down to her knees. The fabric was motionless since most of their clothes were made with flour sacks. It was entirely yellow on the dress portion. The upper portion of the dress except for the white collar in front covered her chest all the way to her neck. The sleeves of the dress had white collar's folded up. Maria added a white apron style to put over the top of the dress and tied it to Belles waist. Her hair was up and honestly she simply looked like an innocent child with her teenage shapely body hiding under it all. Salvador had her bag in his arms and sat it down on one of the pew seats of the church. Lucas was happy to see everything coming together and was ready to simply move forward with the ceremony. The priest was waiting at the front. They all proceeded forward Lucas stood to the left of the priest and Phyllix to the right. Just before Salvador went forward he pulled Annabelle aside for a moment. He whispered to her, "Annabelle I need you to know that I do love you. Maybe some day you will understand that I had to do this." He kisses her on the cheek and in that moment Annabelle pulls her face away from him. He knew she would be angry, but there was one more thing. He reaches in his pocket and pulls out a string with a button hanging from it. The very button that Jenine sewed onto her wedding dress so many years ago. The button that belonged once to Salvador when Jessica Amelia sewed it into his shirt. The very button that Jenine sewed onto Annabelle's baby clothes. This button that has followed in Belles life journey. "I need to give this to you and you must keep it. I promise some day you will understand what it means" He puts the string around her neck and tucks the button under her top. He grabs her arm and pulls her forward to Lucas placing her hand in his. Annabelle became disgusted. She never wanted to share her hand with anyone except William. She has absolutely no control of what was happening to her. The priest begins with prayer. Then moves into the marital words of ceremony. Annabelle just stared forward at the walls of the church. She couldn't even hear the priest as he continued. When he finally asked Annabelle do you take this man. Salvador had to nudge Annabelle to get her to answer as she wasn't even paying attention anymore. Since Annabelle had no interest in even answering Salvador answered for her. "She does." The priest wasn't pleased with the arrangement. He knew he couldn't get involved anymore then he was. Lucas was a large contributor to the church. The politics behind it wouldn't allow the Priest to object. As it all ended Lucas quickly grabs her arm and pulls her back down the aisle towards the exit door. She barely has time to grab her bag from the pew as he drags her out with him. Salvador just stood there hopeless. Even

Phyllix was disgusted and didn't care to talk to Salvador while they headed back home.

Lucas had his own ranch with a large home so when they drove up at first glance Annabelle was stuck in this maze of confusion. She felt completely lost. It was early evening by this time the sun was setting. She was clueless as to what was to come on this evening of her life. Phyllix didn't even attempt to be gentle with Annabelle. He just knew what he wanted. He was getting exactly what he wanted. He grabbed hold of Annabelle by the arm forcing her to drop her bag and dragged her up this long stairway. Everything looked so fancy and it was easy to tell he was a man with money. When they reached the top of the stairs she could see the entrance to a large bedroom in front of her. The bed in the room was the largest Annabelle had ever seen. A heavy suede bergundy blanket draped over the top mattress. Wood pedastals framed the bed with sheer fabric draped across and hung down the sides. The entire bed was covered with different size pillows as a decoration. Lucas dragged her in the room and tossed her onto the bed. He didn't even talk to her other then to command what he wanted. He hated the bun in her hair. He immediately grabbed hold of her head and twisted her to the side so he could pull the pins out. She was mortified and frozen in fear. She was so young and innocent and has never truly been with a man. Her closest encounter had only been the wonderful loving kisses of her one true love William. Now she lies with this old man putting his hands all over her and there is nothing she can do. She was shaking so badly Lucas could feel it as he ran his hands down her arms. Lucas honestly didn't care. In some ways he liked knowing that he was going to be her first sexual encounter. As he attempted to kiss her lips Annabelle rejected him and turned her head away. Lucas became angry and grabbed her face pushing it back to his lips. He stuck his tongue in her mouth attempting to kiss her sloppily. She clenched her mouth trying to keep him from accomplishing this task. This made him even more angry with her. He jumped on top of her straddling her to the bed making it impossible for her to get out from under him. He pulled her head back and looked at her square in her face. "Listen up little Belle, you are my wife now. You have a duty to comply with me and my needs. Either you comply or this will become even more uncomfortable for you. Do you understand me? Are we clear?" She could see nothing behind his eyes. It was like looking at a black hole. She felt like she was falling. There was absolutely nothing for her to grab hold of to stop her from falling deep into this endless pit. Suddenly Belle screatches out with one tear strolling down her face, "Please stop?" She wanted so badly to fight him with all her strength, but for some reason she couldn't bring herself to fight. He was very strong and she was so tiny framed. She bacame angry at herself that she couldn't retaliate against him. Lucas was losing his patience with her very quickly. He put his hand around her neck and began to squeeze. He had no intentions of strangling her, but he wanted to dominate her stopping her from fighting him. He then uttered the words, "you are not a child anymore. You are a wife. This is it, this is where your life is now." Then he said words she never expected to hear, but these were the words that forced her to stop fighting. "Your not Salvador's daughter anymore. Your my wife." Annabelle started to bite her tongue and cry out loud. She could not control her painful emotions anymore. It hit her like a stone rock to her heart. He proceeded to do his business with her. She clenched her hands so tight her tiny nails on her fingers drew blood as she pressed her fingers into her hands. He stripped away her dignity that night until there was no fight left in her. The whole experience was so painful and crudely forced on her. By the time he was finished sweet Annabelle had completely sunk into the deep dark black hole. She just laid there looking straight up at the ceiling. The tears had dried on her face and she was motionless. It stripped away a piece of her forever. Lucas rolled over off her and fell asleep. He was satisfied and done with her for now. She could smell his sweat on her. It made her want to throw up. But she was afraid to move. She eventually grabbed hold of a piece of the sheets that were russled at the bottom of the bed. She pulled them up wrapping them around her as if it would somehow embrace her body and hide the shame of what had just happened to her.

As several months past on Lucas had managed to gain the control of Annabelle. Enough that she did all her wifely duties as he expected. Everything her mother and Maria had taught her. She now did in this home. So much was changing in Annabelle. When you looked into her eyes now she doesn't seem to be in there anymore. She has turned into this shallow empty hole. She simply just went with the motion of life. With no real care. No real desires. Her dreamy and creative personality was now lost in a sea of endlessness. She had no one. Not even a friend. She would speak to her little doll Maria had made for her so many years earlier. She always hid the doll deep in a closet where Lucas would never find it. Lucas made several trips out of town leaving her alone. He had some servants that were also hired to keep control of Annabelle to be sure she stays in line. Whenever he would return he always had one major expectation and that was for her to service him. So everytime that happened. She generally would just lay there and let him do his business. The only time it became an issue was when he would try to kiss her. It was the one and only thing she wanted to hold onto for herself. "The kiss." She treasured her kisses with William and she desperately faught to not have to give this man her lips. She wanted to treasure them and protect them. She felt like it was the only innocent thing she had left. Finally one evening Lucas became agitated that she would not allow him to kiss her. He grew tired of her fighting him on that. She was folding the blankets on the bed back and plumping the pillows. Lucas approached her from behind and swirled her around facing him. Annabelle immediately put her face down to avoid his lips once more. Lucas had made up his mind that he wasn't going to allow her to fight him on that anymore. His anger came at her full force pulling his arm back and smacking her in the face so hard she flew backwards. Banging her head on the bed frame and blood started to flow from her forehead and across her face. Where she was smacked was turning purple and swelling almost instantly. Lucas didn't care. He reached down on the ground for her pulling her back to her feet. He grabbed her face and forced her lips on his once more. Lucas had not hit her before so she was so terrified. She didn't have it in her to fight him. But the entire time he kissed her sloppily, tears streamed down her face. This man actually managed to take away from her the one and only final thing she had left to treasure for herself. Her head was pounding from the hard blow when she hit the bed frame. She even felt dizzy and unable to stand steadily. Annabelle no longer dreamed of any future. She no longer felt William would ever want her now. There was nothing left for her to offer William. She felt dirty and inproper. Unworthy of his love. Annabelle has become an empty shell. She hated this man with everything in her. After every encounter she would run to the creek on the property and jump in the water. She would attempt to wash her body with the sand under the water. Scrubbing herself as hard as she can trying to wash away the nasty smell of Lucas on her body. She use to cry all the time, but suddenly one day there were no more tears left in her. She was an emotionless zombie just simply existing for this man. One evening she was dishing food onto Lucas's plate and accidentally dropped some of the stew onto his pant leg. He became angry once more and proceeded to stand and smack her. As she lost her footing and was about to fall he grabbed her arm and yanked her down to the floor. He squeezed her arms so hard she felt like he was going to brake it. The only thing Annabelle could bring herself to say was, "please.... please... I'm sorry please." He finally let go and sat back down and wiped his pants off. He then proceeded to eat his stew. As Annabelle attempted to stand Lucas yelled, "no you stay there, your not eating!" So Annabelle sat quietly until he permitted her to get up later that evening. Annabelle was reduced to nothing more then a dog and this was the hand dealt to her.

William had finally made what he thought would be his last journey from home. He traveled back to California to propose to his Annabelle. He was so excited for his future with her. He had no inclination of the marriage that was forced on her. He came up the driveway expecting to see Annabelle pop out from the house excited to see him. On this particular day the only people that were home was Salvador, Phyllix and some of the workers. Salvador walked over to see who was coming and saw that it was William. William stepped out and approached Salvador shaking his hand. By this time Annabelle would be seventeen and William felt it was time to ask Salvador permission to marry Annabelle. He wanted to come clean with him about their relationship. William had noticed that Annabelle hadn't sent him any letters since the last time he was there visiting. It concerned him, but he still never questioned the relationship. He believed in his heart she still loved him. He thought maybe she was angry that he took longer to come back then he originally planned. He hoped she would forgive that and they would still be able to go forward together. He had sent several letters explaining why it was taking longer. He hoped she received them. While all along Salvador would get the mail he would see the letters addressed to Manuel so Salvador simply threw them away. Since Manuel never returned home after the fight. Salvador wanted nothing to do with Manuel and only recognized his namesake son Salvador Lawrence Jr. William opened the conversation with Salvador immediately. He was so excited to move forward. "I need to speak with you regarding Annabelle." Just as William was readying himself to continue Salvador jumped in the conversation. "Annabelle, oh well you must not have heard son?" William stepped back for a moment with a confused look on his face. Salvador was not very honest, but didn't realize William had carried a torch for Annabelle. "We found her a perfect suitor and arranged her marriage to someone who can take very good care of her." Salvador did his best to convince himself that he did something good. Without realizing the terror of a life he condemned his own daughter into. William stepped back in shock and horror. "What are saying!!!! What do you mean?" Salvador suddenly realized, *why the sudden interest in Annabelle with William?* "She's married son. Has been for quite a while now. Is something wrong?" William felt his heart fall into his stomach as soon as he heard the words, *she's married.* He started to become angry and confused. He was so blindsided with this information. He didn't even know how to react. "She was meant to be mine!" Salvador suddenly realized William was in love with Annabelle. It simply never occured to him. Now he stands before a young man who was in love with his daughter. He thought about it for a moment and realized he has to squash this connection. Since he has a contractual agreement with Lucas he does not want any friction or issues coming from this young man. "Now see here son my daughter is married. In the eyes of god you have no business involving yourself. You need to move on and forget about her. You understand me? I don't want any trouble." William became frustrated and started to pace and kicked a rock angry. He jumped in his truck and slammed the door driving away. Salvador shouts out to him, "no trouble, you hear!! I mean it!!" William just continued onto the road. He drove around for hours trying desperately to make sence of it all. Salvador never made it clear to him that this was not Annabelle's wishes at all. So William could only assume that for whatever reason Annabelle didn't want to be with him. She chose another man over him. He was so angry he went to a local bar and drank himself into his misery and heart break. Many days later Williams Uncle had mercy on Williams heartache. He suggested William go help his family make their move to Arizona. Hoping that might help him keep his mind clear of this situation. So William finally brushed himself off and headed to Arizona.

Lucas had made another trip out of town and Annabelle was sitting on the floor by her closet talking to her doll. She had taken the button her father placed around her neck on a string and decided to find a place to conceal the button. She had sewn a pocket on her dolls dress and placed the button inside with the string. She then sewed the pocket shut so nobody would know what was inside. And nobody could take it away. Since she couldn't talk to her sister anymore she spoke to her doll as if it was her sister. Belle heard a noise downstairs and quickly hid her doll in the closet behind some boxes. She stood up grabbing her broom and proceeded to sweep. Suddenly she heard the noice again. She realized it was rocks, small rocks hitting the door. So she went down the stairs and peeked out to see if someone was outside. As she leaned forward she could see the bushes moving. Belle yells out, "who's out there?" Just then Manuel whispers from inside the bush. "It's me sis, Manuel." Annabelle suddenly becomes fearful. If one of the servants find out he is there, or if Lucas comes home and see's Manuel he will surely beat her senseless. Annabelle looks behind her in the kitchen to see if anyone is near and can see whats going on. Fortunately they were all too busy to realize Belle even has a visitor. She quickly directs him to the side of the house showing him to kneel down so nobody can see him. "What are you doing here? Don't you realize how much trouble I can get into?" She was so happy to see him. She couldn't help but hug him, as she tells him he has to go. Manuel could see that his sister was pale and her hair was a mess. Even her clothes were dirty and barely fit her correctly. "I want you to know. I am trying to save money. I want to get you out of here and take care of you sis." Annabelle suddenly became very fearful. She knew Lucas would never let her go. The only thing she could think about was how powerful he was. He could hurt her brother. He had no idea what she has endured this entire year. "Look Manuel you must not come back here please. It will only make this worse. You must go and be well." Manuel became deflated in his motivation to help her, "but Belle"? "No... you must stop this. Now please Manuel go now." Annabelle feels herself wanting to beg him to get her out of there. In her heart she is so afraid of getting caught and him hurting her. She can't bring herself to run. She thinks in her mind, *what would I even be running too? I'm used goods now. William wouldn't have me anyway?* Manuel frowns and hugs her goodbye, "sis I will always be close by...ok...always know that." Annabelle nods as Manuel sneaks through the bushes out to the road waving sadly to Belle. Just as he is out of sight one of the servants call out for Annabelle. She quickly retreats in the direction they are calling from, but not without one last look towards that road. For a moment she wonders, *could I ever get out of here?* Then turns and runs back towards the front door of the house.

Chapter 16

Annabelle spent many days thinking about the words Maria had said to her about having a twin sister. This was eating away at her curiosity. If only she could talk to Maria again and find out more. It made Annabelle wonder and question so many things about her life. *What happened to this sister and where is she?* Belle thought to herself. The majority of Annabelle's days were filled with chores. One of the female servants actually took mercy on Belle. She was an older woman in her late fifties who was spanish and generally handled the cooking and laundry. Her name was Martha Patricia Rodriguez. She was a very short chubby woman, but so short she sometimes had to inquire to the other servants to reach things in the kitchen for her. She spoke mostly spanish, but knew just enough english to get employment. Martha had never been married, nor had any children. She took to englishmen in need for her room and board. She worked for a roof over her head and food in her belly. Annabelle could understand her language most of the time. Fortunately Annabelle had been raised by so many spanish people since her father employed many of the spanish as well as the portugese. He always use to say we have to look out for our own kind. The english out numbered us. Annabelle was so smart she could pick up on the languages very easily. If Belle was struggling with a container of water to carry in the house it was Martha who always ran to her aid to help her. On one particular occasion Martha could hear Belles cries in their room after Lucas had been in with her. He took off shortly after and headed to town. Martha peeked her head in the door inquiring to Annabelle if she was ok. When she peeked in she could see the bruises on her arms. Annabelle just laid there in the bed motionless while staring up at the ceiling. Martha could see that this poor girls spirit had been stripped away from her. Martha decided to enter the room and brought compassion to Annabelle. She sat on the side of the bed with her and simply stroked her hair. In those moments words weren't even required. It did help Annabelle feel she had someone on her side. Lucas was not aware of Martha's kindess to Annabelle and he probably would not have approved. Annabelle would be turning eighteen in a few months and Manuel had decided he needed to check on her once more. He was so worried about her. He felt so terrible that their father made her marry this awful man. He made it his mission to watch over her. He was planning a trip to their house soon.

Today Annabelle has been hanging clothes on the line. The sun was shining bright and it was a very hot California day. Belle had braided her hair as to stay as cool as possible. She had a long dress on that covered her from her neck to her ankles. She was extemely hot. She kept taking breaks and walking over to the water well and pulling up a bucket of water to drink. She was sweating through her clothes and became extremely uncomfortable. She finally decided she had enough. She walked into the house and found a pair of sheers cutting the sleeves of her dress to be much shorter and reveal her arms. She then grabbed the bottom of the dress and cut it up to her knees. Then she became very courageous and walked back to the water well pouring a bucket of water over her head. There were some men on the property that were hired by Lucas to tend to his ranch. One of them happened to look over and see what Annabelle was doing. He watched and couldn't help but notice that she was an incredibly beautiful woman. Annabelle had no idea someone was admiring her. She innocently went back to hanging the clothes. She felt so much better and cooled off. This man admiring her did not even realize how obvious he was being. He actually became entranced by her beauty. Lucas noticed this man peering at Annabelle and became extremely angry. He walked over to him and socked him square in the face. He then proceeded to kick him violently. The other men just cleared out of his way. Nobody ever stood up to Lucas. The man was bleeding from his face from the blows with Lucas's shoes. He started apologizing immediately, but it was already too late. Lucas fired him and sent him on his way. Lucas looked over at two of his workers demanding they escort him off the property. "Get him the hell out of here now, or I will kill him myself." Lucas threw a rock at him hitting him in his back as he tried to stand. The man finally got to his feet and hurriedly away as the other two men pushed him towards the driveway. Unfortunately

Lucas wasn't finished with his rage. He stomped quickly towards Annabelle. She didn't even know what had just happened. She was hanging an item of clothing. Just as she clipped the other end of a blanket onto the line Lucas had grabbed her braid and yanked her down. It was done so violently that she was completely startled. He pulled her backwards and down to the ground. He stared her square in the face as he noticed she had cut her dress. Her arms and legs were revealed. He could also feel that her braid was wet. "What do you think you are doing?" Annabelle was completely suprised and didn't realize what he was angry at her for. She was so scared in that moment she started to stutter trying to speak. "I d..o..n't un..d..e..r..stand." Lucas grabbed her sleeves of her dress. "This Annabelle... and this... Annabelle!!" He shouted at her as he grabbed each section of her dress that she cut. "I was sooo hot... I nee..d..ed to c..o..ol off." Lucas became even more angry and pulled back his arm and violently slapped her across her face. Martha could see what was happening from inside the kitchen. She became frightened for Annabelle and ran out the back door. She remained on the back patio, but watched in horror. She put her hands over her mouth restraining herself from screaming at Lucas. She wanted so badly to go save Belle. Belle had grabbed the side of her face Lucas hit and quietly cried as she held her face. Lucas then grabbed her dress, "what are you a hussy? You don't show skin around these men. They are horny animals and nobody is allowed to look at my wife EVER!!! You want to show your body off you tart?" He grabs her dress and rips it off her. Annabelle quickly grabs the dress off the ground and covers herself crying hysterically. While she is lying on the ground below Lucas. "Are you cooled off now!!!!" He storms away back towards the field. He yells back to Belle, "go in the house and get some appropriate clothes on right now!!!!" Annabelle tries to pull herself up from the ground, but by this point she is weak and hurting from his abuse. Martha rushes to her aid as soon as she can see that Lucas is out of sight. She pulls Annabelle up from the ground and assist's her back into the house. Once Martha gets her in her room she quickly finds another dress to cover her complete body again. While Martha is helping her she can see Annabelle's face turning purple and swelling. Belles arms and legs had cuts and bruises from him violently tearing her dress off her. Martha quickly retreats to her room to get some salve to treat her cuts with. Martha just kept saying. "Oh Annabelle... sweet little Annabelle" then Maria repeats it in spanish with so much despair for her. "(Oh Annabelle... dolce Annabelle)" In her very big accent, "poor, poor Senora," (pobres, pobres Annabelle). Even Martha couldn't hold back from crying. She cared for her and it hurt her to see this happen to Annabelle. Once Martha gets her dressed Belle sits on the bed in a trance holding the bed post leaning her head. She was emotionally and physicall exhausted trying to do everything right as to not anger Lucas. It just seemed no matter what Belle did. He would find a reason to abuse her. Martha pulled Annabelles braid out since it became a mess after everything that happened. She started to re-braid her hair for her. Annabelle spoke no words she just sat there in a trance.

Martha was eventually able to get Annabelle to go back to her chores as to not anger Lucas again. She carefully picked up another item to hang on the line she was in pain and sweating in her clothes, but she was too emotinally lost to even care. Suddenly you could see in her face that she was no longer sweet little Annabelle. That girl is long lost. She just sunk into this deep depression. Everything that made Annabelle what she was. Her creative nature of drawing and painting. The beautiful poetry she once wrote for William. The beautiful music she could play easily on a piano. Or her angel voice that glided with the wind as she sang. All was gone. All was lost. She no longer even had fight in her to dream. It was just an existence. That's it... just simply an existence. Her vibrant shine in her face has turned into a dark place. Even Martha could see that she was just gone at this point. Martha couldn't reach her anymore. She was just lost in a never ending labrynth. A maze that went absolutely nowhere.

Manuel had made his way over to Lucas's house. He snuck through the bushes once more. He could see that Belle was out back hanging clothes. As he snuck closer to her side he was able to see the bruising on her face. Manuel was completely dumbstruck in that moment. He became angry and pushed his way through the bushes. He bravely walked right to Annabelle. As soon as Belle saw him she became frightened. "Manuel," she whispers as she looks over her shoulder to be sure Lucas doesn't see him. "What are doing? You cannot be here." Manuel arches his shoulders up as he can see even closer her hands bruised as well. "What the hell is going on here? What is he doing to you?" Lucas heard the voice and immediately turned and started walking toward the house again. He then saw Manuel standing before Annabelle. He starts to walk even faster remembering this was the meddling brother. "What the hell are you doing here!!!!" Lucas yelled, get off my property!" Manuel storms towards Lucas. At this point Manuel is so angry he is seeing red. Their is no controlling him and nobody to stop him from retaliating for his sister's sake. Manuel storms at him so quickly he throws the hardest punch he can muster and clocks Lucas square in the face. Belle winces in fear. She starts to scream, "no Manuel please don't!!!" It was too late he hit him. Lucas was a very strong man and Manuels hit was just not hard enough to even unstable Lucas. It will leave a mark, but it won't stop him. Lucas pulls back his arm and throws a punch right back at Manuel. The blow was so hard it threw him down to the ground. Manuel quickly gets back up and storms right back at him. Lucas was able to grab his arms and wrestle him down to the ground. He pushes his face into the grass. Lucas was able to hold him down there with all his strength. There was no getting out of this for Manuel. Since Manuel had such a temper he still continued yelling out of the side of his mouth. "Who the hell do you think you are hurting my sister you asshole!!!!!!!" As he's spitting blood out of his mouth and grass. Lucas laughs, "boy even with all your might you will never over power me." Annabelle comes to the aid of her brother kneeled on ther ground she begins to beg. "Please Lucas... please let my brother go.... I beg you." Lucas found it amusing that Manuel thought he could over take him. Lucas completely disregarded Annabelle's pleads. He called out for his workers to come over to him. Two of the men immediately walk over. Lucas instructs them to pick Manuel up and toss him off his property. So as Lucas stands both the men grab hold of each arm and take him away. Manuel still spouting out as he's spitting, "you aren't gonna get away with this Lucas." Lucas looks over at Annabelle once more and demands she go back to work. Belle does as she's told, but still looking back as they take Manuel away. Lucas shouts out to Manuel, "you ever come near my property again, I will contact the sherriff. You will be arrested or shot for tresspassing." Manuel shouts out to Annabelle, "I love you Belle!! I'm so sorry Belle!" A tear forms in his eye as he felt defeated and scared for his sister.

What Lucas didn't know is that Manuel had no plans on giving up. Manuel had been living with some neighbors of Salvador's since the fight. He never returned. He worked the field in order to have room and board. The people never asked as to the circumstances that Manuel didn't want to go home. They were just happy to have the help on their property. He was pacing back and forth on the road trying desperately to come up with a plan. He decided to go pay Maria a visit and tell her what he discovered. Maria was still on Salvadors property living with her husband. They had their own house far enough away from Salvador that nobody would know Manuel paid her a visit. He walked with Maria to the old tree that Annabelle loved so much once upon a time. Maria was sad to go there. It wasn't so bright and beautiful there anymore without Annabelles presence. They sat in her spot under the tree and Manuel proceeded to tell Maria what he had discovered with Annabelle. "He's hurting her. Bruises on her face and hands. She had cuts and scrapes. He's hurting her Maria." Maria was shocked and scared for her sister. Manuel went on to tell her what happened when him and lucas fought. "I can't take him Maria. I'm not strong enough, but I can't do nothing. I have to get her out of there." Maria pondered for a moment. "If pappa found out you got involved he will be very angry. It could jeopardize them having this property Manuel." Manuel started to bite on his lip in frustration. "I understand that, but Maria is this damn property worth her life?" Maria immediately shook her head, "no of course not. Do you think it's that bad? Do you think he would hurt her that way?" Manuel starts kicking at the tree. "If you saw how bad her face looked and her hands I can only imagine how the rest of her body is. I don't want to imagine that and I'm not gonna wait to find out if he would kill her." Maria adamantly agrees. "What are you going to do? How are you going to get her out? Then where will you take her? Lucas would surely hunt you down and put you in jail. Then he would just end up with her again. This is a serious crime taking someones wife Manuel." He stands and leans on the tree with his head in deep thought trying to come up with an answer. With his head facing down towards the ground he then see's the corner of Annabelles secret box sticking up from the ground. Thus reminding him of all the letters and poems written back and forth from Belle to William. He then gets an idea. "Maria what ever happened to William? I mean where is he? Does he know?" Maria had been told about Williams visit almost two years ago by Jessica. "Yes when William came he wanted to marry Belle, but pappa told him Belle got married. I heard William was angry and left. The talk in town was that he went to Arizona to help his family move there." Manuel got flustered, "so what does that mean? Does he know she had no choice, or does he think she was in love with Lucas?" Maria got a puzzled look on her face. "I don't know," as she pondered the thought. "I do know his Uncle still sells fruits and vegetables in town." Manuel was starting to form an idea. "You have to take me there. I think if I can find William maybe he will help me figure this out. I know he really loved her." So the plan was set in motion. Manuel and Maria quickly head to town together. As they pull up to Williams aunt and uncles shop they head in. Both of them were so nervous, but anxious to get help for their sister. Maria approached the woman first hoping she could appeal to her kindness. The aunt seemed hesitant to give any information at all. The uncle was in the back room and could hear the conversation. Maria began to plead, "please you don't understand. My sister was forced to marry this man. He's absolutely horrible. She needs help. We believe William would want to help her." The uncle comes into the room and interrupts before the aunt even had a chance to answer. "My nephew was in a lot of pain over that girl. What kind of business are you trying to get him involved in here?" Manuel was startled, but still stood up to speak. "I believe when you love somebody you go far and wide to protect them. I believe William would want to know the truth. My sister did not choose to marry this man. She loved William." Just as he said it he pulled out a handful of the many letters and poems exchanged between Annabelle and William through the years. He handed them over to the uncle so he could read the words. There were so many of them the uncle was a little flustered. He fingered through them quickly and shook his head. "I guess I have no right to intrude or decide for William what to do. I will get a hold of William. It will take some time, but I will try to get him here by next month the soonest I can. You come back here." He set up a date for them to return promising to try and bring William back to the area. They left and both the aunt and uncle look over at each other. The uncle shaking his head, "I sure hope I'm not getting him involved in something that will turn to disaster." The aunt smiles, "por nada if they in love all will be ok. You did good. The boy needs hope you know." In her broken english. She keeps waving her hands. She goes back to the paper work she was dealing with before the interruption, "por nada it be ok." William's aunt and uncle were of spanish descent they spoke mostly spanish. William was fluent in spanish, but also knew some portugese as well as english. Maria and Manuel headed back home anxious for Williams return. Manuel couldn't rest easy until he could get his sister out of this situation.

As the month progressed Manuel and Maria were becoming increasingly nervous. When the day finally arrived for them to re-visit William's uncle. They were more then ready to go. As they pulled up to the uncles shop they didn't notice any other vehicles in the parking lot area. They walked back in and almost immediately out came William from the back store room. He went right up to Maria and gave her a big hug. Maria was so happy to see him there. Manuel was ready to move forward on a plan to help his sister. "William we have to go sit down and talk about what is going on." William noticed how stressed Manuel looked and he immediately became concerned. Williams uncle joined them as did the aunt. His aunt changed their sign on the window to closed. They all walked to the back room. Manuel proceeded to explain what was happening, but then Maria interrupted him. "Wait Manuel there is something William needs to know first and foremost." She looks over at William, "my sister never stopped loving you. She was forced to marry this man and she didn't go willingly." William was extremely relieved to hear that, but then became very concerned. "Wait.... are you saying Annabelle had no choice?" Maria and Manuel shook their heads. Manuel realized he needed to explain further. "Look William this marriage almost two years ago was arranged by my father. As soon as I was made aware of what they were doing I became angry. My father and I got into a fist fight. It is tradition for the portugese families to do arranged marriages, but this man is a complete creep. He is a very bad man." "Wait... what do you mean he is a bad man?" William was becoming angry and realized his sweet Annabelle is being hurt. Now knowing she didn't even love this man he is ready to get her back the way it was intended. "What is this man doing to her? Tell me now." Manuel further explained the abuse. The bruises he found on her hands and face. The more William heard the angrier he became. The uncle knew William would have to save her. He also knew the legal risk he was taking. The uncle knew who Lucas was and he was well aware of the financial power he carried. "You could very well end up in jail the lot of you. Taking another mans wife. Do you understand this?" They all shook their heads yes, but didn't seem to care. "We need a plan to carry this through. She will need a place to go and hide." The uncle spoke as if he had an idea. William was prepared for anything at this point. He stood tall again as he once did. "She will stay with me there is no question about that." They all spent the entire evening discussing the plan and all agreed to keep it amongst themselves.

Williams uncle owned a very large portion of land in the country it was such a large portion that it would take many, many days to comb through the property. As long as Lucas has no clue of his involvement. It would be easy to hide Belle there with William. The uncle turned to Manuel, "you know Manuel, since you have already had an altercation with Lucas he will immediately suspect you. Manuel nodded his head, "yes I know I thought of that. You know maybe that's a good thing. It will throw him off track and he will never know it had anything to do with William. He will spend so much time on me that it will allow Belle and William to get away far enough he won't ever find them." The uncle and aunt agreed the thought of that scared Maria though. "Manuel I don't want you to end up in jail" she cried to him. "That would be terrible." Manuel shook his head, "no it's fine... it's fine.. I can sit in jail knowing my sister is no longer in harms way." William patted Manuel on the shoulder with so much pride. "You are a good brother Manuel and I will forever be in debt to you for what you are doing. The sacrifice your making." Manuel trying to remain manly goes to shake Williams hand and William throws a half hug to Manuel. "So tomorow night we meet in the back of Maria's house you and me. Maria will have two horses tied up for us back there. After we get Annabelle we split up. You go to the place that not even I will know about. Only your uncle, you and Belle will know where you are. Maria won't even know. At least not for a good few years. Till it's safe again for them to come out." Everyone listend adamantly to Manuel's instructions. Maria then interrupts, "wait you said you and William are splitting up and that they are going some where. Where are you going?" Manuel looks down for a moment and sighs. "Well sis... I'm going to the local pub to have a few drinks in celebration. I'm sure within no time Lucas will be out hunting for me. So I may as well enjoy my time till he has me picked up by the law," he chuckles. "It's alright.... cuz I would rather he waste time on me... then actually know where to look. It gives William time to properly hide Annabelle and be sure she is safe." Maria gulps not feeling too confident about her own brother getting into trouble. She knew in her heart there were not many choices.

Chapter 17

The very next evening Maria had the horses ready and waiting out back for William and Manuel. Both the men were on time. They each picked their horse and jumped on. Manuel guided William in the right direction towards Lucas's home. It would take a few hours to get there by horse, but it seemed the best way to sneak up that late at night. A vehicle would be far too loud. As they drew closer Manuel raised his hand back to William to get his attention. He motioned he heard something so he stopped. He then motioned to William to head over towards the trees on the other side. They trotted the horses as quietly as possible. They tied the horses off and decided to go the remainder of the way by foot. As Manuel got closer his stomach felt hollow and his nerves were at it's highest level. Manuel knew this man was serious about shooting on sight. William held it together so well he seemed so calm to Manuel. He couldn't believe the posture William carried. It made Manuel proud to know him. As they crouched down into the bushes they slowly approach as close as possible without being seen. They stayed in position and at that point Manuel wasn't real sure what to do. It's the middle of the night. They didn't know if Lucas was there. Manuel knew he left town a lot from rumors in town. He had no way of knowing if he was home now. William seemed to have his wits about him much better in that moment. He turned to Manuel, "look we need to be patient we sit and wait. Even if we have to sleep here and see who comes out in the morning we wait." Manuel agreed so thay both sat back against a bush. They could see the front door of the house as they kneeled down. Many hours had passed and the sun was rising. Manuel had dosed off for a while, but then they could hear men on the opposite side of the house. They seemed to be waiting for Lucas. They came from the other side of the property. The noice woke Manuel and William quickly motioned to him... "shhh" as he put his finger across his lips... "shh." They watched Lucas finally come out the back door. Then the maid opened up the front door. She was sweeping the porch out. Eventually they could smell food coming from the kitchen of the house. Manuel quietly reminded William that might be Annabelle cooking that food right now. William knew the only way they could safely get her out of there. It would have to be at night, but he hadn't figured out how to pull it off yet. The day was long and hot especially sitting in bushes on the ground. William had a cantene on his hips of his pants. It was buckled on him. He pulled it out periodically and took a swig then shared with Manuel. William was suprised that Annabelle still has not even stepped outside one time and it was nearing late afternoon. Then she finally appears. William was determined to get a closer look so he gets down on his hands and knees. He proceeds to crawl through the bushes towards the back of the house. Manuel was getting nervous that he was getting too close. He kept motioning to him to stop. He whispers "come back," but William wasn't having it. He wanted and desperately needed to see her even if it was only through the bushes.

He had waited for so long he couldn't wait any longer knowing she was only about fifteen feet away from him. He couldn't even hold her. He had to see her so he slowly pulled his body closer and closer then abruptly stopped. He heard a mans voice. It was Lucas. He was heading back towards the rear door of the house. Just as Annabelle exits the back door. She had a large bowl in her hands. It looked full of scrap. It was food for the chickens. As she first stepped outside the bowl was so large she could barely seem to carry it. William saw her face and he felt butterflies in his stomach immediately. With all the love in his heart in that very moment he saw the nightmare before him. Lucas stepped up to the rear patio where Annabelle had just arrived. He could see Lucas yelling in Belles face. Then Lucas grabbed a hold of one of her wrists and pushed her into the rear door. It took everything for William to control himself from jumping out of the bushes and killing this man for hurting her in this way. He felt himself sweating perfusley and clenching his hands together ready for a fight in his loves honor. William started breathing heavier and winced his eyes with an intence glare while his slanted eye was almost closed shut. His jaw tightening as every moment passed that seemed like an eternity. William could not make out what he was saying to Annabelle, but it was terribly obvious that he was being abusive once more. What bothered William more then anything was seeing her expression as Lucas was pushing her around. She seemed like a rag doll. There was no reaction by her to him. No fight at all. She just complied with him as if she were a slave. Lucas pushed her aside and went into the house. Then Annabelle proceeded out to the back property towards the chickens. William made his way as close as he could possibly get without anyone knowing he was there. By this point Manuel was in a panic, but he couldn't get William to come back. He just remained where he was waiting and hoping they didn't get caught.

William started to feel guilty that he couldn't tell Annabelle he was there. Watching her, but he just couldn't risk her reaction getting the attention of Lucas or his workers. She quietly tossed the food in to the chickens and went back to the house. William was so broken hearted to see the love of his life so completely broken. A tear rolled down his face. He put his head down and prayed. "Dear god please help me help her." Manuel could see that William was so distraught. He completely understood how he was feeling because he felt so much the same. So there sat two men in Annabelles life who truly loved her and wanted to protect her. Both sitting just outside the house and Annabelle felt more alone then she had ever felt in her entire life. By early evening the men started heading back to the house to finish up the days work. Lucas not far behind. William and Manuel sat patiently waiting and watching hoping Lucas would be leaving the house. It started getting late and William grew concerned that they may not be able to get her out tonight. Then suddenly they could hear the front screen door open. Willam and Manuel slithered towards the front of the house to see who it was. Fortunately it was Lucas. He got in his vehicle and drove away. As soon as William could see he was far enough down the road he turned to Manuel. "Ok Manuel how do we want to execute this plan." As far as they knew the only people in the house would be Annabelle and the maid they saw sweeping the porch earlier in the morning. "We just go in that house and get her that's it" William started rubbing his chin in thought. "Do you think the maid will say anything?" Manuel shakes his head not sure of her reaction. "Well I guess were just gonna have to take our chances." William stands up in confidence. Manuel was so impressed with William. This was a man who stood like a true cowboy. His blue jeans and button up shirt the boots well worn from a hard working man. Manuel was proud that his little sister would have someone to protect her in the way he knew William would.

They both quietly approach the front of the house as they knew there were some small shacks in the back of the house. They held a few of the working men on the property. They couldn't take a chance in them hearing them. The front door wasn't locked. Those were the days when people lived with more trust and less security so most homes weren't locked. As William entered first he crept in and saw stairs just in front of him. He assumed the bedrooms would be up the stairs. That's where he headed first. Manuel motioned to him that he would stay at the bottom in case anyone came. Annabelle was lying on the bed in her room holding her doll once more. She had no inclination of anyone coming in the home. She had on a long nightgown that covered her entire body with long ruffled sleeves. Her hair was out and loosely draping over the side of the bed. She had dark circles under her eyes and was so pale. She had lost a lot of weight since living in this house. Depression made her stomach queezy. She just had such a little appetite. She even sometimes would throw up trying to rid of the stomach aches. William could see a door way cracked open as he approached quietly. He could see Annabelles feet. He crept in and started to whisper.."Belle, Belle is that you Belle?" Just as he said it Annabelle jumped up scared thinking it was Lucas. She curled up in a ball and squeezed her doll close to her in fear he had returned to hurt her. Then William approached to the entrance of the door and could see Annabelle shaking. Just as she looked up and saw it was William her mouth opened in awe and complete shock. She didn't react at first. It was like she was in a dream. Never did she ever believe she would see William again. William approached her slowly. He could see that she was so thin and so scared. He knew to move slowly and gently towards her. He whispers once more, "my sweet Annabelle it's ok menina." He reaches his hand out for hers. Belle stares at his hand for just a moment in complete disbelief. Then she realizes this is real. He is really standing before her. She reaches her hand out to him and suddenly rushes forward dropping her doll to the ground. She clenches her arms around his neck as if she was holding on for her dear life. She starts to cry almost to the point of a loud whale sound. You could hear her desperation in the cries. It was so heart wrenching for William to hear it. Tears started rolling down his face as he held on to her as tight as he could. He wanted to make her feel safe again. Suddenly William realizes they have to get out of there before Lucas comes back. William wipes his face so Annabelle can't see he was crying with her. He gently pulls her away, "Annabelle I have to get you out of here. We have to go now." Belle suddenly feels the fear rushing back through her. She quickly grabs the doll. For a moment starts to think to grab something else. She then realizes there is nothing in this home that even belongs to her, other then her doll. William reaches for her hand and they quickly rush down the stairs. Annabelle could see Manuel at the bottom of the stairs. She puts her hand over her mouth in astonishment as she runs with William. They get to the door and rush out quickly, but quietly. Just then you could hear a voice from the house. It was a quiet voice of a woman. "Goodbye...... Annabelle," Belle turns to look as she is rushing out and can see Martha peeking out the door. She was waving goodbye, but smiling for Annabelle. Martha had seen the entrance of the men as they were rushing down the stairwell. When she saw Belle holding one of the mens hands, she knew it was someone coming to help Annabelle. Martha was happy and relieved for Belles sake. Belle waved goodbye to Martha and blew her a kiss. William and Manuel didn't say much they just kept running. They wanted to get Annabelle as far away as possible. As quickly as possible. Martha had decided it was time for her to leave this house as well. She knew as soon as Lucas returned and saw that Belle was gone he would be irate. She didn't want to be a part of such an abusive situation anymore. She went into her room and packed up her clothes and left the house for good. As she closes the door behind her she muttles out the words, "good riddance." She smiles to herself and thought, "as it should be." William finally got them all to the horses.

He quickly strattles himself up and reaches down and pulls Annabelle up. He slings her on the seat with him. He grabs both her hands behind and pulls her hands and arms around his waste. The moment was so serene for Annabelle. She felt like her prince charming rescued her. It was like a dream. She could hardly grasp and never believed could ever happen. Yet here it is happening before her eyes. Holding his waist and clenching her body close to his. She never wanted to let go. She didn't even care where they were headed, or where her future was going. She just cared about that very moment holding him close to her and feeling so safe. As they all rode away into the sunset you could see Annabelle's long hair flowing behind them.

Chapter 18

It was to be a long ride where they were going and absolutely nobody knew there destination except William. William held on the reins with one hand and held onto Annabelles arms with the other. Her arms were so tiny. She had lost so much weight. It felt like nothing but bones. He wrapped his fingers around her wrists and hands holding on so she could sleep. She drifted into a deep sleep. Belle was so exhausted she hasn't slept in a very long time. Every once in a while she would wake up and realize where she was and start to cry. As she cried she held on to William tighter and tighter. It broke Williams heart to hear so much pain coming from the love of his life. It was like she had so much emotions and couldn't release them for so long that now it was a waterfall that just couldn't shut off. She would drift away and sleep, then wake and cry. Manuel could even hear her as he rode ahead of them. Finally they were far enough away they could stop in a field and rest for a while. William pulled Annabelle down from the horse.

She was asleep. He carefully pulled her down and Manuel laid down some blankets on the ground under a tree. William placed her down gently. He covered her up. He so desperately wanted to kiss her, but he didn't for fear that it would startle her. He just caressed her head and hair for a moment so tenderly. Manuel started grabbing sticks and timber to build a fire. They were both very quiet. It was such a dramatic time for them hearing the terrible cries for so long out of Annabelle. Their minds both wondered for a very long time. *How truly bad was this situation for her?* Finally William puts his head down. He couldn't hold back anymore. He was so emotionally broken down. He just begins to sob uncontrollably. Manuel didn't think any less of him as a man. He completely understood. He felt like doing the same thing. It broke their hearts, but then Manuel pats William on the back. "I understand, but brother we have her now. She is safe. It's going to be a long journey to bring her peace again, but I'm sure thankful to god it's you who is going to do that for her." William nods his head as he stares up to the skies in thought. He lays back on the ground with his arm extended out holding on to Annabelles hand. Manuel Leans back against the tree. "William try to get some sleep, I will stay awake and keep watch." William could't sleep. He just stared into the skies and prayed that he can help his Annabelle heal through this. His mind was just racing the entire night.

After a good rest Manuel kicks at Williams feet, "hey William we should get going again." Annabelle heard him and opened her eyes. She sat up and looked at Manuel. She reached her arms out to him. "Manuel my brother thank you so much." Manuel goes over to her and she stands to her feet and hugs him. Manuel quickly composes himself as he pulls her away. "Now sis this is where we have to seperate. I have to go back, while William takes you to the destination." Suddenly Belle becomes concerned, "wait, why? I don't understand?" "Lucas will be suspecting me as the one who took you. As long as he wastes his time on me he will never find you. I won't even know where you are. Do you understand?" Annabelle becomes upset, "oh no... no wait Manuel no.... something bad could happen. You can't go back please no." She shakes her head adamantly. Manuel immediately takes control of her emotional out poor. "Sis please don't get upset. Everything will be ok. We just have to make sure he doesn't find you. It will just be a glimpse in time and you will see me again. I promise you that, but we have to do this right." William wakes and hears the conversation. He jumps up and strokes Annabelle's back trying to calm her. Annabelle looks down to the ground feeling so much fear as William whispers to her, "you have to trust us Belle." She nods and clenches her hands together looking up again at her brother. Manuel reaches over and holds her hands, "everything will be ok sis." He turns back and starts readying the horses for their journey. Manuel gives Annabelle one last hug goodbye and gives her words of encouragement. He then turns to William and extends his hand to him. William was about to extend his hand and realizes "no.. no your my brother," he reaches over and gives him a hug while patting on his back and pulls away. "Be safe brother. When the time is right we will find you." Manuel nods his head, "no worries, I trust that we will find each other some day. I will make sure to leave a trail so you can find me." Manuel jumps on the horse and slowly trots away. He yells back to Annabelle, "Te amo irmã." Annabelle clenches on to Williams hand and yells back to Manuel, "Te amo irmão." William knew they were telling each other they loved each other. William gets up on the horse and pulls Annabelle up seating her behind him once more. Belle held on to him for dear life. She was still so very afraid that Lucas might find her. They rode for many hours farther and farther away. Belle had no idea where they were going. She just knew it was far away from Lucas. They stopped periodically to rest. Then would head out again. The trip took many days. Annabelle still tended to curl up in a ball afraid to be physically close to William. She had been through so much abuse. It was hard for her to give herself to anyone even though she loved William with all her heart. She felt dirty and used up. She felt unworthy of any mans love. William could see that she had many bruises on her. Some scars on her face and arms. He could only imagine how the rest of her body must be with scars. He was compassionate enough to understand that the trauma she had to have gone through will effect her for a very long time. He always approached her slowly and gently. He would only ever extend his hand for her to hold. He would stay close enough to her so she would feel safe. It was a very long journey and Annabelle didn't talk much. It would be a while before she could bring herself to speak. Sometimes if she did speak it would only be to ask permission to eat, or something to drink. This bothered William greatly because she was so affected that she was afraid to even make decisions. She felt the need to ask permission. William would continue consoling her that she is free. She doesn't have to ask anymore. She is free. But truly Annabelle didn't understand that concept yet.

It would be a while for her to heal and become confident again.

Finally they reached a ranch with a very large house. William didn't even approach the house, which then confused Annabelle. He went past it and started riding through the back woods. Behind this home he rode for quite a while. They eventually reached a caboose sitting out in the middle of nowhere. William stopped and got off the horse. He tied him to the tree. He pulled Belle down from the horse. "This is where we are going to stay for a while. At least until we know it's safe. This is my Aunt and Uncles property. They know were here, but nobody can see you. We have to be sure we leave no clues that you are here. You will meet my family eventually, but for now we will maintain our life here. I will make sure we have supplies. We can make this work for now ok Belle?" Belle looks over at this caboose. It was a real caboose. A piece of a train. Annabelle touched the stairs on the caboose and slowly walked up them to this narrow door. She walked through. It was basically a square box. Just enough room for a bed and maybe a few personal things. She sighed for a moment and looked over at William, "this will be just fine." She didn't smile, but she seemed content. In her mind it didn't matter. If she slept in the woods, or in a caboose as long as she wasn't in Lucas's house. William went outside and started digging an area for a fire pit and collecting wood. Since William's Uncle knew the plan he had already dug up a water source with a pump for them to have easy access to water. His aunt left things in the caboose for them. She left some blankets, bowls and cups. She also left some fresh bread, green beans and other beans as well. She left a small bowl of oranges on the counter. The uncle had built a counter inside the caboose for them. He also made a small table with two chairs and managed to fit that in for them. The bed was simply a small mattress on the floor with a few blankets. Annabelle sat down on one of the chairs and just looked around for a while. She was still very numb. That person she once was has been lost for a very long time. She's not sure how to find herself in there again. She watched out the window of the caboose as William was getting a fire going for them. Once he was done, he decided to go in to the caboose and try to get Annabelle to come out by the fire. He stood at the entrance. "Annabelle will you come out and sit with me." He extends his hand to her. She flinches for a moment and William pulls his hand away. "I'm sorry... I'm sorry... I won't make you. I guess I will just sit out there and whatever you want to do is fine with me ok?" He walks back out and sits. She finally gets up enough bravery to walk out. She slowly goes back down the stairs and places herself on the opposite side of William by the fire. He gulps he is so nervous and wants so much to help her, but he isn't sure how. He fumbles around with a stick then decides to go get the beans with a bowl and comes back out. He starts breaking the green beans up to keep his hands busy. Annabelle wasn't sure what to say or do. She was use to doing a ton of house work. She decides to grab a bucket and get some water for his beans. She could help him. He watches her closely. He still see's her as the most beautiful woman in the world. He wants so badly to hold her again. He knows he can't. Not yet. She brings back some water and sets it down by him. William was so nervous he gets up thinking.... *get her a cup so she can drink some water..* not even thinking about having the bowl of green beans on his lap. As he stands. He accidentally drops all the green beans on the ground. William quickly fumbling around, Annabelle manages to giggle at him. He looks up in complete embarassement and grins. He was glad it made her laugh. It made him happy that she still had a glimpse of joy in her to giggle for him like that. William joins in and laughs with her.

As nightfall comes and they both had some food and water it came time for rest. William knew this would be awkward and difficult. He immediately suggests to her that she sleep in the caboose and he will stay outside. Annabelle was relieved she wasn't ready to be close to anyone. Many weeks passed and gradually William could get Belle to talk with him. He would talk about his experiences in Arizona with his family. He told her about his aunt and uncle on this property. She never talked much about her life and what had gone on. She would start to express interest in his stories. The awkwardness grew less and less as time went on. William continued to sleep outside. Eventually Williams Uncle and Aunt came out to meet Annabelle and bring them supplies. The aunt was very sweet and she knew Belle was having troubles. She made every attempt to be-friend Annabelle and help her through whatever she could. The aunt also brought her clothes since the only clothing Belle had was the nightgown. Annabelle loved the clothes she brought. She was so grateful. She was able to give more trust to the aunt at this point it was easier for Belle with woman. William called his uncle tio and his aunt tia they were both very kind people. They would do anything to help William. William was always helping them through the years with work they needed done. William was very close to both of them. tia brought two very beautiful dresses for Belle. They were made out of cotton and so soft. Belle had never had any dress made out of cotton. One was green with a satin ribbon around the waist and little tiny buttons in the front. Short sleeves and a beautiful V shape neck line. The dress was long and flowed so nicely. When Belle tried it on and came out to show tia. The men where astonished. The dress fit her shapely body like a glove. The green color made her brown eyes shine. tia had even brought her a brush and helped her brush out her beautiful dark brown thick long hair and put it up in a loose bun. Some of the hair still hung down on the side of her face all wavy and loose. She had even gained a little weight since being with them. William was in awe. He just stood there and looked at her. Annabelle started to become uncomfortable and became figgity looking down and blushing. William walks up to her in a daze and touches her cheeks like he once did when they were younger. She looks up at him and almost smiles. William knew in that moment that she was gonna come out of this dark hole. He could see in her eyes. She was still in there and he couldn't wait for her to come back to him. He whispers, "you are truly the most beautiful woman I have ever seen." She blushes more and looks down. She reaches up and grabs his hand from her face. She pulls his hand back down nervously saying thank you and you could almost hear a giggle. There was hope in both of their hearts. With time it did become easier. Annabelle was searching for herself again. William still continued to sleep outside until one day he could hear Belle in the caboose calling for him. He carefully entered she was sitting at the table. He sat down very cautiously. She reached her hand out to him on the table. He didn't hesitate to give her his hand. "William I need you to lay next to me and just hold me. Can you do that for me?" In that moment William knew she finally felt she could trust him. He was so happy in his heart. He waited for so long for this time with her. Just to hold her close. They both layed down. He slowly reached his arm around her and held her close to him. They both slept that night together and just held each other. William was so grateful. She never talked about her experience with Lucas. William never would ask. Out of respect. He wanted to just move forward. He was willing to do anything to help her be ok again.

Chapter 19

Tia strolled over to see Annabelle one day and told her all about her Singer Machine and how she makes these clothes. Belle wanted so badly to see this machine, but she wasn't sure if it was yet safe for her to go to the house. William and tio discussed it and from what tio explained Lucas had made every attempt to find her. He even tried throwing Manuel in jail acusing him of taking her. After a while he realized he wasn't finding her through Manuel. He still had no inclination that she was with Williams family. It was far enough away and there has been no reason to believe he would suspect she was there. Salvador was extremely concerned and still had no idea what had been going on. He also did not know who was involved. The rumor was that Lucas finally gave up and filed for divorce. He had apparently another woman he was interested in and grew tired of trying to find Annabelle. So William and tio decided it would be ok for her to come to the house once in a while. She was so anxious and happy to leave the caboose for a while. She headed back with tia while talking about all her great fabrics. Annabelle had developed trust in tia. She was such a sweet woman. She had mostly gray hair always in a bun. A very natural beige skin tone and pretty little brown eyes. You could tell she was a hard working woman. She helped tio a lot with their ranch. Sometimes tia would ask questions about Annabelle's experience in hopes that she could help her release her pain. Annabelle would share some things with her. It was hard, but Belle was so relieved to have a woman friend. Tia would constantly try giving Belle affirmations to build up Belles self esteem. She brought Belle into the house and in to see the sewing machine. Annabelle loved this house. It was so beautful. Tia decorated so well. Tia made curtains white, with red roses on all her windows. She had a table cloth on their dining table that matched the curtains. Annabelle became excited. "Could I make curtains also?" Tia loved her excitement. This gave her an idea. "Annabelle we could dress up your little caboose. Make it more like a home. Let's make some pretty curtains for you and a table cloth." Annabelle was excited and loved her idea. In that moment the sweet Annabelle, the one who dreamed. The one who did beautiful things and loved life. She was starting to shine through. Tia brought together some fabrics and let Annabelle pick whatever she wanted. She was drawn to the yellow daisies it made her think of sunshine. The fabric was perfect. It had tons and tons of yellow daisies all throughout. Tia worked with Annabelle and showed her how to use the machine. Belle had so much fun. She enjoyed her friendship with tia.

As the day went on and they finished the project. Tia held up the curtains and the table cloth to show her the finished product. They were so great. They had sewn a white lace around the edges of the fabric. It turned the curtains into a ruffly fancy design. Then tia had an idea to do one last little thing. That was to make a new dress for her doll. The very doll Maria gave Annabelle that she still has. Tia had no idea it would upset Belle, but when she held up the dress for Annabelle as soon as Belle saw it she began to cry. Tia felt so bad. "Oh my goodness Belle. I'm so sorry I didn't mean to hurt you. I'm so sorry." Belle just sat at the table holding her face in her hands. She started to wave at tia, "no it's not your fault tia." So tia sat next to Belle and extended her arm around her rubbing her back. Belle started to talk to her about some of her nightmares. Tia just listened in absolute shock of the horror she went through. Then Annabelle admits to her, "I'm so afraid that William and I will never be together intimately. I don't know if I can do it." Tia looks directly at Annabelle "love finds it's way, but you have to trust. You have to be ready and love will find it's way." They spent that afternoon bonding and sharing. Tia knew it will take time for Annabelle to heal but their is hope. She prayed for Annabelle daily. They finally went back to the caboose and tia helped her make the finishing touches of her curtains. She laid out the table cloth. Then Annabelle went outside and picked some wild flowers. She brought them in. They placed them in an old soup can with water putting that on the table. They both stood back and admired their work. Belle and tia smiled, "luce estupendo annabelle." (it looks great Annabelle) Tia spoke her native language spanish. Belle smiled, "yes it does. Do you think William will like it?" Tia smiled, "well he is a man, but I think so." They giggled. Tia headed out while Annabelle started to peel some potatoes for dinner. She was anxious for William to see what she did.

When he walked in he noticed it immediately. He looked around. Then looked at Belle and he could see a smile. He was so pleased to see that. "Did you make this Annabelle?" She smiled, "yes... yes.. me and tia." He nods his head and closes his slanted eye as if to be examining her work. She giggles again. She finally starts to see William the way she once did so long ago. She realizes once again how very handsome he is. She starts to examine his movements in admiration. He turns towards her and touches her hand on the table. She puts her potatoes down and stands. They approach each other slowly. Their eyes are locked on each other. They have been here for over a year and just now they are about to kiss. That moment is now for both of them. They continue to hold each others hand and pull themselves together. William leans forward and gently touches her lips with his. Annabelle held on to his hand tight. She was still feeling some of her fears. In her heart she knows, if she holds his hand she will be ok. He gently kisses her. Touching her lips as long as he can. They both slowly pull back looking in each others eyes. It's like all the love they have carried for so many years was there. Right in front of them. And finally Willaim sais it, "Annabelle I am madly in love with you." Belle feels the rush of love in her gut and a tear rolls down her face as she speaks. "I am also so very in love with you William." Willaim knows they cannot go any further then that. He wants to give her the honor she deserves and that's by marrying her before they are intimate. He smiles at her and holds her face again. "You did a beautiful job on the fabrics my sweet Annabelle." He gently walks out to start the fire for dinner. She just stands there in awe thinking to herself... *Is it possible? Is it really possible that I could be ok?"* She asks herself honestly not knowing for sure. *But I want to be ok.* She stares out the window at him for a while and goes back to peeling.

As time passes William decided it's time for him to make some money. He wants to provide a home for Belle and him. He wants to marry her and start a family. He ventures out and manages to do some work on other farms. Belle continues to make the caboose more like a home for them. Annabelle begins to think more about what her sister had told her about her having a twin. She couldn't help but wonder what the story is behind that. And where this twin sister could be. Why she wasn't in her life? She talks about it periodically to tia and to William. So many questions in her mind she wants answers to. William decided to make an effort to contact Maria and suprise Annabelle with a visit. Maria finally shows up and tia guides her out to the back property. As Maria approached the caboose there sat Annabelle by the fire cutting some vegetables into a bowl. Maria shouts out in excitement, "Annabelle!" Belle looks up and just screams in absolute joy. She went running to her sister Maria. Belle dropped everything in her lap and didn't care. She ran right into Maria's arms. They hugged forever it seemed. William was so pleased to see how happy this made her. As they settled down the two of them went for a walk into the woods. Maria shared with her about how her life has been. After a while Annabelle decides to bring up the subject of the twin. "You weren't able to tell me the whole story. I want to know about this twin? please tell me?" Maria shares with her everything she knew. It wasn't much, but enough to spark more curiosities in Annabelles mind. She tells her about the affair their father had and thus created twin babies. Annabelle finally begun to understand why the mother she called mother would not be close to her. "So my mother is not who I thought she was?" Annabelle was sad for a moment, but then realized for so many years she just thought her mother didn't love her. When in all reality she just wasn't her mother. This woman tried, but obviously struggled. "I only remember this nun brought you to pappa. Before she drove away she told pappa there was a twin. She also said her name was Serena." Annabelle was so frustrated, she wanted to know more. Maria didn't know anymore then that. "None of us know for sure there were rumors that your twin died at birth." Annabelle shook her head, "no she didn't." Maria looked at her sister with curiousity. "Why do you say that? How do you know?" Annabelle had this confused look on her face. "I don't know how I know. For some reason I just know she's not dead." Annabelle didn't share her horrible past with Maria. She never even mentioned that time. Maria knew enough in Annabelle's mind.

Manuel also visited Annabelle there once as well. They remained very close. Manuel told her always know I will never be too far. Both Manuel and Maria were pleased that Annabelle was finally safe and being taken care. Manuel did share with Maria what happened and what Annabelle looked like when him and William got her out. So she had a heavy heart until she could see Annabelle for herself. Maria was so happy she was doing well. Just as things were moving along a letter came in the mail to William.

Tia came rushing down the field, "William!!! William!!!" She yelled as he came out of the caboose and ran to her. He opened the letter and they both stood there looking concerned. Belle stepped out and watched them. She could tell something was not right. She slowly walked towards them as they both turned and looked directly at her. "What's wrong? Whats going on?" William had such a strained look on his face. Annabelle became scared. "Tell me please. What is it?" Annabelle looks down at the paper William was holding. They were draft papers. William was very concerned. He sighs and reaches out for her. Tia covers her mouth in astonishement. Annabelle becomes impatient. "For peets sake what is it?" William grabs her hand, "Belle I'm being drafted." Belle still didn't understand, "what does that mean?" William explains, I have to join the military. They are drafting me. She becomes upset and immediately her legs go numb and she almost drops to the ground. William catches her and brings her back to her feet. "No... no.. they can't take you away... no please." Tia rushes to Belles aid and holds one of her arms, helping William to steady her to her feet. Once again William remains strong and convinces Annabelle everything will be ok. While in his mind he was just as concerned as her. He was sent off to a base for Army military training and was expected to be back in a few months. Tia and tio took good care of Annabelle while he was away. This time away from William made Annabelle realize that she never wants to go without him ever again. She felt ready to be the wife he wants. The wife she desperately wants to be. So when he returned and proposed to her. She would be ready. He had managed to save enough money from his off jobs prior to the draft that while he was gone he purchased a ring.

He had gone through a very long vigorous training. The military mission for all the basic training was set up to break you. Then build you back up. The Sergeants would yell in your face and William would have to simply stand there and take it. They had the men doing intense physical training. Climbing up ropes and through mud. Running and carrying heavy equipment. William was an exemplary soldier. He impressed the Sergeants with his leadership abilities. He took on every challenge and exceeded all their expectations. When he finally completed the training he was given his orders to report in Florida within a few months. This allowed him some time to go home to see Annabelle and set up plans to get her on the base with him eventually. He was anxious and ready to go back to his Annabelle. He took a long bus ride home in his uniform. He had his large green Army pack in his lap. He stood with so much pride with his accomplishments in the military. He was ready to take on any army mission in his mind. It was a long ride home. The bus dropped him off to the nearest town of his destination. He walked the remainder of the way to the ranch. He didn't even stop to say hello to his uncle and aunt. He was so desperate to see Annabelle again. As soon as he walked up to the caboose in his uniform Belle could hear someone approaching. She stepped out of the caboose and there he stood before her. He was so handsome. He was slender, but muscular with his perfectly ironed uniform and soldier hat. His hair was very short and in perfect placement. His shoes shined bright. Every button on his uniform was perfect. There was no dirt in his nails as was before when he was working the fields. His nails were clean and cut short very manicured. He stood there with so much pride she almost didn't recognize it was him. His slanted eye shined through under the soldier hat. Everything about him she loved. She ran to him and hugged him so tight. He was so happy to see her. He then grabbed a hold of one of her hands, her left hand. William knelt down on one knee. He reached into his pocket and pulled out a little black box. Annabelle was speechless. "My sweet Annabelle, how much I love you. Will you honor me and be my wife?" Annabelle watched as he opened the box and pulled out this shiny gold ring with four little roses. It was so beautiful. The most beautiful piece of jewelery she had ever seen. She gasped for a moment and smiled. She almost was so taken back she forgot to answer him. She just stared at this ring in astonishment. "Belle..? Belle..?" Annabelle started to giggle realizing he was waiting for an answer. "Yes, yes of course I will. I will marry you." He jumps to his feet excited picking her up high off the ground. He begins swirling her around. She just smiles and laughs.

Tia and tio join them at the campfire later that evening to celebrate. William had arranged for a priest to meet them at the property that evening. He explained to Annabelle that they couldn't wait to do a large wedding. Since he already had orders to go to Florida. There was little time. Tia had brought a special gift for Belle in a box. It was a little pin that pins to your clothing. It was a pin of a little tiny clock all in silver and so petite. Annabelle absolutely loved it. Tia put together a lacy baby blue dress. She even made a small white lacy trane of fabric to hang down from the middle of her back. The dress would drape to the ground. She put together a lacy vail to pin to the back of her hair it only laid down to the middle of her back. It was very tastefully done. Annabelles hair was set in large rollers. Tia dropped the rollers out of her hair and the curls flowed loosely around her head. Tia pinned some of the strands of hair up and around the top of her head. She then put little white flowers throughout her curls. They did a very quick ceremony. Just the four of them. That evening Annabelle was preparing herself for their very first night as husband and wife. She was still very scared, but she wanted so desperately to try. She hoped in her heart that somehow she could push through this and still be ok. She trusted William with all her heart, but the fears of her horrible past haunted her. Once tia and tio left Annabelle went into the caboose and changed into her nighty. She was so scared, but she finally peeked out the door and let William know he could come in. She was ready for him.

William approached her standing before him in her night clothes. He remained the same perfect gentleman as he always had done. He carefully walked towards her admiring her beauty. He held her close to him and picked her up. He then carried her to the bed. He kissed her lips for a very long time holding her body close to his. He gently unbuttoned her gown in front and started to pull the nighty down. He caressed her bare skin slowly and carefully. Belle started to shake and he could feel her shaking. So he stopped for a moment and whispered. "Sweet Belle are you ok? Is this ok?" He was so worried she wasn't ready. He didn't want to force her on anything. She looked up into his eyes. "I want this, but I am scared." He slightly grinned at her. "My sweet Annabelle. I promise I will be most gentle. Do you trust me?" She sighed and nodded to him. He pulled her face close to his again and kissed her lips more and more. Then kissed her neck. It was the most gentle love Annabelle ever could have dreamed. She hadn't realized how special this would be until this night. He made her feel like this was the very first time for her. He gave that back to her. She never thought it possible, but he did it. It was the most amazing night. They remained close making love throughout the entire evening. As the night went on Annabelle started to reminisce when they were just children. When they had their first kiss. She thought about all the letters and all the time they had together. She prayed and thanked god for letting him be in her life. She finally could see that maybe she can be happy again. As she watched William sleep. She caressed his hair and face realizing what tia had said to her was so true. Love did find it's way. William opened his eyes and saw how Annabelle was watching him. He smiled at her and immediately reached for her lips once more. They had so much passion for each other that nothing outside seemed to matter anymore. They were madly in love and continued to show each other all the passion they could.

William was only able to spend a few short weeks with Annabelle before he had to report back in Florida with the military. With full intention of sending for her. They spent every moment together and finally William was seeing Annabelle smile. He even started to see the Annabelle that he remembered long before. She was hanging some laundry and started to hum and even sing a few words. William watched her and listened to her effortless voice. It was like it was so easy for her to create this sound. She would sing a few words and the chime of her voice was gliding through the wind. He was so happy inside knowing she was finally seemingly ok from it all. He walked up behind her as she was hanging the clothes and started to tickle her waist. She turned and giggled grabbing his hands away, then persuing his waist. She chased him out towards the woods as they laughed. When the time finally came that he had to go Annabelle dreaded him leaving. William kept reassuring her, "it will only be for a short time. I will be sending for you. I promise my sweet love." They were so happy together. It was so hard to say goodbye. Belle cried and hugged him. She just didn't want to let him go. He caressed her hair and face. Then kept telling her it would be ok. They kissed and he wiped the tears from her face. Kissing her face once more. Tia stood close by as William walked away and headed back to his destination. He yelled out, "I will be sending for you soon. Watch for the letter." Annabelle waves, "I will… I will be watching." Tia quickly steps to Belles side, "cmon now… we have some planning to do Belle. You will be taking a trip in no time at all." Tia always attempting to make everything easier on Belle. She defnitely kept her busy. She didn't have too much time to think about missing William.

A few months passed and still they had not recieved a letter. Annabelle was getting impatient and concerned. Tia kept telling her, "no worries it's fine. I'm sure everything is fine." One day tia was having Belle help her with a quilt she was making. Belle stood up to go get more thread and suddenly falls to the floor. Tia was so alarmed she runs to the floor, "Belle, oh my goodness Belle. Are you ok?" She pats Belles face trying to get her to wake. Tia noticed she was a little pale and her face was a little plump. After a few moments of tia shaking Belles head Annabelle finally opens her eyes. "Whaa.... wha..at happened?" She sits up composing herself. Then looking around seemingly confused. Tia chuckles at her. "What is going on with you? Did you not eat today?" She was very concerned. "Should we take you to the doctor?" Annabelle shakes it off, "no of course not. I'm fine. I'm sure I just got a little dizzy, that's all." Then suddenly it dawns on Tia, "wait a minute Annabelle. Have you been feeling nauseous at all?" Belle thinks for a moment, "hmm well yes, I guess. I have been the last month or so. I've been throwing up... why?" Tia becomes instantly excited. "Oh my dear goodness... ohhhh... estoy muy entusiasmada que tiene un bebé." She just continues rambling on. Annabelle becomes confused. "What.. what are you saying?" Tia waving her hands. "Oh little miss Annabelle Oros the wife of William Oros. You are having a baby." She jumps up for joy. "Un pequeño bebé oros. A little baby oros." Then suddenly Annabelle realizes. "Oh my.... I am.... I am pregnant with Williams baby. We are having a baby." As it dawns on her she just smiles and jumps to her feet hugging tia. Then Belle realizes, "I have to tell William. Oh my... what if it takes forever for him to send for me? I want him to know?" Tio comes in the room hearing all the noice becoming curious as to what it is about. "What are you ladies up to in here?" Tia couldn't help but say it while rubbing Annabelles belly. "Oh just Williams baby that's all." Tio gets excited, "oh that's great! Oh William will be delighted!"

They finally recieved word in the mail about two months later. By now Annabelle is four months along. The letter was short, but he told Annabelle he couldn't send for her for at least another two or three months. He will be getting some leave time and coming back for a visit as soon as he can. Annabelle was so sad. She wanted William to be a part of the pregnancy. Tia was a great help to Annabelle. She even moved her in to their home. They worried about her being so far out back and being pregnant. They wanted to watch over her. As the time neared her seventh month William was finally on his way back to Annabelle. He still had no idea about the pregnancy. When he walked in to his Uncles house there sat Annabelle very pregnant. She saw William and jumped up and ran to hug him. He was shocked. He immediately pulled her back and looked her over and saw this enormous belly. "Oh look at you, oh my... is this... is this.. am I?" He could barely get the words out when Belle jumped in. "Your a pappa!" William smiled so wide he immediately started to rub her belly, "a baby, we have a baby." He was so happy as was Annabelle. Fortunately he had a few months leave before they had to go back together. It would give time for the baby to be born. The time flew quickly as Annabelle seemed as big as a boat. Carrying Williams baby. He was enjoying every moment with so much pride. Tia had a mid-wife who would be assisting with the delivery when the time came. William was so careful with Annabelle. He wouldn't let her do much of anything. Always worrying she would strain herself. He coddled her the entire time. He loved feeling her tummy and feeling the baby kicking. They talked about baby names all the time. Teasing each other constantly. Of course Annabelle insisted if it were a boy, it will have Williams name. Annabelle felt that tia was her first friend who made her feel confidence within herself. She felt she wanted to honor tia thinking back about the beautiful rose curtains they made together. That's when the name

Rose came to Annabelle. It was a happy memory when tia became her closest confidant and friend. And Annabelle loved roses so very much. Also Belle's sisters name was Rose. William thought that was a very nice name. So it was decided. If it's a girl her name will be Rozanne. If it's a boy, it will be William.

Chapter 20

William was out in the field with his uncle when Annabelle let out a sudden loud scream. Tia ran to her side. Annabelle had been sitting out back watching the men. She stood up to walk inside when her water broke. Tia came running, "what is it Belle?" Tia looks down and can see Belle was wet and some water on the ground. She grabs a hold of Annabelle and walks her into the house gently. She yells for William and tio. "Quickly, come quickly!" She manages to get Belle in the house and lays her down on the bed. William was there so quickly. He was frightened Belle was hurt, or something was wrong. Tia sends William out of the room and walks him out. "Everything is fine William. You must get tio to go get the mid-wife and tell her it's time. I need towels and water. Lots of towels and water. Can you handle that?" William shakes his head vigorously. He could hear Annabelle screaming. He reacts by wanting in the room. Tia stops him, "now William you get going...go on." He was so frantic, but he listens to his aunt. He runs off and does as he was told. The delivery took many hours and William paced constantly. Every time he heard her cry out, he would feel the panic. Tio laughed as he watched him. Every once in a while he would go over and pat him on the back, "no worries pappa." It didn't calm William much. He was just too focused pacing. Finally they heard it. The noice they all waited for. The cries of a baby. William stopped in his tracks as soon as he heard it. Suddenly out came tia with a bundle in her hand. William stood there in awe. Tia quickly washed the baby in a wash tub then instructed William to come inside. She opens the door and William enters. He looks at his bride laying in the bed. She was sweaty and tired, but she had the most fantastic glow. He rushed to her side and kissed her forehead. She smiles up at him, "we have a baby girl William." William stands straight with so much pride as tia hands the baby to him. He opens up the blanket around the babies face and looks inside. He could see this precious bundle of joy in front of him. He smiles wide and looks over at Annabelle. "She is so beautiful. She is a perfect rose." Annabelle smiles back. Then announces the babies name. "Rozanne Darlene Oros," then reaching her arms out to hold the baby. William carefully hands her over to her. Then kneels down by her bedside to watch them bond. Tio kept peeking through the door. The midwife finally lets him in to see. He smiles as he watches the young couple together with their new family.

They were able to spend just a few weeks together after the baby was born and William had to report back. As soon as he reached his destination he was given permission to send for his wife and child. Annabelle recieved the tickets to take a train to Florida. Where William was stationed. This was the first time Annabelle would be stepping outside of the shelter she has been a part of for over two years. She's been on William's uncles property for so long and now she will finally be free to live her life. She found peace in her heart and healed from her past in that time with William's uncle and aunt. And she felt ready to face the world again. Annabelle was very anxious to be with William. It was a scary trip being alone with a baby. She was ready for the challenge. When she finally reached her destination, William was waiting at the station for her. He had his uniform on and as always was so very handsome. She could see him standing there waiting for her. She carefully carried her baby and her one bag off the train. William rushed over and grabbed the bag for her. He then carefully helped her down the steps. He hugged her and the baby. Then reached for little Rose. He wanted to hold her for a moment. Annabelle smiled she was so happy they can now live their lives together. The only fear Annabelle had was knowing this war has been going on and there is always this chance he could be deployed. She would constantly pray that he wouldn't be taken away from her. They lived in Florida in a small home near the base. It didn't take long for Annabelle to get pregnant once more. She was delighted that William would be a part of this pregnancy. They were very happy together. In time she had a son and she honored William like she promised she would. She named him William David Oros. They spent over a year there when William's time finally came to an end in the military. He was very fortunate he had not been deployed into the war. He had a few close calls, but Annabelle kept telling him her prayers to god kept him with her. They moved to California on a street called, "The Old Dusty Road" (written by: Shirley Francis Oros). Once again within a short time she became pregnant and had another daughter. They named her Shirley Francis Oros. She was born May 5, 1946.

Annabelle felt life had been everything she could ever ask for. Except the one thing she could not get all the answers too. That was the twin. It bothered her and she really wanted to know more somehow. Annabelle decided it was time to get more answers so she confided in William. She wanted to go back and speak to her father. William was very concerned it was just too close to Lucas. He didn't want Annabelle to have to deal with anything bad. So he offered to go speak to Salvador for her. She finally agreed to step back and allow him to go see her father. She waited patiently praying she would get more answers. Just to see her sister would complete her life in her mind. When he arrived Salvador was still in the same house. He went to the front door. He fumbled a little nervous since he would be telling Salvador where Annabelle was. He worried if he could trust him. Salvador answered the door. When he opened it, he didn't hardly recognize William. "Can I help you?" Salvador still did not know who was standing before him. "Well yes sir you can. You don't remember me, but it's me William." Salvador thought for a moment, "William hmm." He still couldn't recollect. William elaborated, "you know Salvador. I was the one who came here for Annabelle not too long after you sold her!" William stated in a very irritated tone. Suddenly William realized he was still feeling anger towards Salvador for that day. He thought to himself, *maybe this was a bad idea.* Salvador then knew exactly who he was. He widened his eyes and almost began to glare at William. He stepped out to the front porch closing the door behind him. He didn't want Jessica Amelia to hear what was going on. "What do you want now? I told you then." William interrupts him, "yeah you told me then... that she married a man. You were insinuating she wanted to marry this man. When in fact. You sold her!! William begins to sweat and clench his fists feeling the anger rising within him. "That bastard hurt her in ways you can never imagine." Salvador steps back. He could see that William was becoming angry. "What... what are you saying? How do you know?" He then gives William a suspicious look and glare in his eyes. "Look Salvador, if you loved your daughter at all there is only one thing she needs today. That's information. I'm not leaving until I have it."

Salvador becomes angry and throws a punch at William, but now that William is older and stronger he can handle this old man today. He grabs his fist stopping the punch from hitting him in the face. "That man abused her. She was your daughter. He hurt her bad. Do you understand?" Suddenly Salvador pulls away his fist. He realized he needed to hear what William had to say. "What are you saying to me. How do you know this? Is she ok?" Finally he shows remorse. That was what William was looking for. Salvador never intended for her to be in a bad situation. He never dreamed it would be as bad as William was saying to him. He allowed William in the house. He then explained to Jessica that they needed to hear him out. William spent several hours telling them both what had happened. The story was so terrible even Jessica Amelia sobbed. She never intended for this to have happened. Even knowing she wasn't her mother. She wasn't cold hearted and felt terrible. "May I see her William?" Salvador felt desperate, but William wasn't about to open that door to him just yet. "Annabelle needs to know where she came from. She needs to know the truth about her twin sister. You are the only person who can tell her this." Salvador becomes deflated realizing he won't be seeing her. He understood. *He probably didn't deserve to see her,* he thought in his mind. He concedes to write down everything he knows that could help Annabelle find out what she's looking for. William leaves with the letter in hand. He didn't give any goodbye greetings. He just simply leaves. It would take a lot for William to ever forgive what Belles father did to his sweet Annabelle. As he was walking out the door Salvador attempts to stop him grabbing hold of his shoulder. "William can you please tell her? We do love her. Please, if she is ever ready to give us a second chance?" William stops in thought looking in Salvadors eyes, then glancing over at Jessica Amelia. He could see remorse in their eyes, so for a moment he considered. He nodded at Salvador with some hesitation. He then turns and walks out the door. Salvador watches him go. He places his hand on the wall pressing his face against it. He began clenching his upper lip with his teeth. He wanted to cry, but wouldn't allow himself. He drew into such deep thought of the terrible mistake he had made with Annabelle. Jessica Amelia walked up behind him. She knew she was the reason he did what he did. She felt guilty for it. Their were no words that could be spoken to lesson the pain in that moment.

William brings Belle the letter telling her how everything played out at her fathers house. She then begins to wonder if she should give them another chance. Her focus is on the information she wants first. She opens the letter. William didn't know what Salvador had written. He felt Annabelle should be the one to tell him. If she wants him to know. The letter was kind from her father. He adamantly apologizes to Annabelle then proceeds with the information she was longing for. Unfortunately it wasn't as much as she hoped for. Her father didn't even know where the sister was, or if she lived. He repeated that he was told there was a twin. That he believed she was alive possibly at the convent. Since the nun was who brought Annabelle to him. He explained the entire story of how and who was part of her life. Who her real mother was. That she committed suicide. He also told her about the button. This was the one piece of information that Belle did not know. She still had her doll with the button sewn inside. As soon as she saw that in the letter she began to cry. All those years she held this doll. Through all her hell she held that doll with that button. Belle was glad to finally have a better understanding of what took place and why. She wanted desperately to find her sister if she was still alive. She shared everything with William. He was always so supportive and did everything he could to help her through. William did have an idea. He thought it might help to give them more answers about this twin. He suggested to Belle to write a letter to the convent. Asking if any of the nuns were there? Explaining as much as you can. "Maybe someone will know something?" he explained. Annabelle decided to do just that. She composed a letter with as much information as she could think of and quickly sent it out. She was hoping something may come of it. Annabelle still had a family and a life to live. She moved forward in hopes that if more answers came she would find them. In the mean time she would continue to care for her children and show them love.

William had a distant cousin who was celebrating their daughters fifteenth birthday. The spanish and mexican tradition was a party called a quinceneta. This was how they celebrated the turning of fifteen from a child to a woman. It was a fabulous event. The fifteen year old would have several young girls in the party. They all dressed in beautiful fancy dresses. While the one turning fifteen wore a white dress that resembled a wedding dress. Then all the girls would also have a gentleman in the party with them. They dressed in tuxedos. It was like a big wedding almost, but the celebration was of that birthday. They always had a lot of food and a big cake. The decorations resembled a reception. All the colors would match the dresses of the girls. Lots of family attended. They danced and sang throughout the night. It was very fancy and elaborate. Annabelle had a great time. William had been so kind and bought Belle a pair of alligator heels as a gift. He wanted her to have something pretty to wear to the party. She absolutely adored them. Belle loved how the girls were dressed. Her daughter Rozanne was so little, but such a joy. She would giggle and dance. This would be the first time William had an opportunity to take Annabelle on a dance floor since they were children. As soon as the music slowed down he brought her out on the floor. Always such a gentleman he was. He glided her around the floor. Annabelle felt like a queen. She was still very much in love with William. As he was with her. This big family of his was so great for Annabelle. It filled so many of her lonely places in her heart. They had a great evening and so did the children. Baby Shirley was still far too young. She stayed in her little basket covered up and sleeping most the evening.

The next morning Annabelle needed to go to the market as William left early to work. They lived close to town. She could walk with the children. She had a small bag in her hand to fill her groceries in and started rustling through the vegetables. She was deep in thought figuring out what she needed for her recipe. Suddenly a woman approaches Belle and begun to stare at her. Belle hadn't noticed. She just continued putting some vegetables aside and looking for other things she needed. Little Rozanne starts tugging at Belles dress, "mama, mama." Belle looks down, "yes menina what is it?" Rozanne points at the woman looking at Belle. Belle looks up and sees her, "hello" Belle sais politely. The woman steps back for a moment, "is it really you Serena?" Annabelle turns her head in confusion squinting her eyes. "Serena, who is Serena?" The woman then realizes she may have mistaken, or maybe said something she should not have said. She becomes fearful and starts to turn and leave. "I'm sorry...I must have mistaken...I'm truly sorry." As she continues stepping away. Belle then realizes, *wait she might know my twin sister. She said Serena..*"Wait please...wait. Do you know my sister?" The woman continues to run away. Annabelle tries to catch up with her, but she couldn't leave the children. She stops and just watches the woman leave. Then at that moment Annabelle realizes, *I was right she is still alive. She has to be.* Later that evening she tells William what had happened. He continues to console her as they cannot seem to find any new information. William's job was nearing to an end. He was offered an opportunity to work in Mexico for some fairly good money. Annabelle was not happy that he would be leaving them for long periods of time, unfortunately it just couldn't be helped. Annabelle was especially concerned about him leaving. She has once again discovered she is pregnant. William was frustrated, but he had to take this job. They needed the money. He was happy to have another child, but sad he would not be there for most of the pregnancy. He didn't want to do that to Annabelle, but they had very few choices.

It was a small town on this old dusty road, but lots of children for the kids to play with. They also had a creek close by the houses. There was a small store down the road. Where a very kind couple lived and ran the store. The neighbors were kind. Many of the woman shared pie recipes. They all watched over all the kids on the block. This was a lower income neighborhood. Many of the neighbors did not have most of the modern convienences. They used large wash tubs for baths. Hand washed most of the clothes. Some of the wealthier people in other areas had wash machines and ice boxes to keep food cold. Not here, it was a simple life. The woman worked hard to make food stretch. The children generally had to use their imaginations. Toys were expensive and not a common luxury for the families in this neighborhood. You could see children climbing trees and playing in the dirt. Believe me they still found ways to get into trouble. Annabelle was always checking on the children. You could here her sometimes in her frustrations using her native portugese language. She would clap her hands together trying to get the childrens attention at dinner time. "Crianças pagam atenção", (children pay attention) ,or "ser bom" (be good). Annabelle was a good mother. She taught her children about god and morals. She also taught them about their family history. She always told them to be proud where they come from. All the children were blessed with so many of the perfect features of Annabelle. With William they were blessed with beautiful eyes, thick hair and pleasant smiles. Belle was many months pregnant and William had been gone for so long in Mexico. She desperately missed him. He had finally sent a letter with a picture for her and the children. It was a picture of William on a horse with his cowboy boots and spurs. He had a cowboy hat on and a big white rope he used to lasso the cows. The rope was wrapped up in a coil hanging on the saddle by where he sat. He sat up looking so proud on this horse. Annabelle admired the picture for a very long time. She was so proud of him. To her he was a perfect man for her and her family. She showed the children the picture and they were all so happy to see it. Little Shirley started calling her pappa a cowboy after seeing that picture from that day forward.

Chapter 21

While life continued with Annabelle and her children the letter that she had sent finally made it's way to the convent where she was born. Belle had no idea the nun named sister Abbey was still there. The very nun responsible for her sister's adoption. The very nun responsible for Belle's life with Salvador, her father. Sister Abbey is much older now so she does very light work at the convent. She does some book keeping and watching over the church fundraisers. When the letter arrived one of the other nuns opened it and read very carefully the information Belle had given. This nun sister Ruth, had known from the dates and times Annabelle provided that sister Abbey would have been the one who was a part of this childs birth and life. So she took it over to sister Abbey. While handing it to her she explained, "it seems this woman is trying to find a twin sister that may, or may not have survived?" As soon as sister Abbey began to read she saw the name Salvador and knew immediately who this Annabelle was.

She remembered this birth very vividly as it was such a sad time. She recalled poor Jenine and her suicide. Sister Abbey read the letter quietly. It took her into deep thought of that time. She remembered how sweet the twins were as they layed in the crib together. She hated having to seperate them like she did.

As the other sister stood waiting and watching patiently for sister Abbey to finish reading she made sure to mention, "now sister Abbey you know we cannot divulge any confidential adoptions. Nor any information regarding them to anyone." As she states sternly in Abbey's direction. "That has always been the rules here." She glared at sister Abbey almost rudely. This particular sister has been the head nun for some time now. She took rules very seriously. As sister Abbey completed the letter she sat down next to the window in deep thought. She clenches her upper teeth over her bottom lip concentrating for a moment. The head nun looks over at her curiously, "sister Abbey what are you thinking?" She states in a condescending tone. Suddenly Abbey looks over at her, "well now there wouldn't be anything wrong with simply forwarding this letter to the adoptive parents of the twin. Then we would simply be giving them the opportunity to decide for themselves. If they want their daughter to know her sister." Sister Abbey said it in such a way that she wasn't asking permission. She was simply stating a fact. Even with this nun being the head nun, sister Abbey has been a part of this convent for so many years that all the nuns were to respect her at the highest level. This head nun sister Ruth always showed true irritation of sister Abbey, but always has had to watch her tone. Abbey stood up and glared back at the nun. "I will take care of this you just mind yourself. I have some files to look through." She walks away in confidence. The head nun becomes annoyed and walks huffing in the other direction.

It took sister Abbey many, many days to find the file. It was nearly over twenty years old, *maybe more* she thought. When she did find the file and looked through it, she read all the information she had put into this file. There was so much to consider. Such as the parent who adopted little Serena. They had put the address they had at the time of the adoption. So this could have all changed through the years. She at least had their last names and the occupation of the adopting father. *Maybe once I pulled everything I have together..... Maybe I could find them? Then get this letter to them*? She Pondered in thought. As she was thumbing through it she suddenly heard father Roberts. "Ah hem, Ah hem." Sister Abbey was startled, "Uh yes father Roberts, yes." The nuns always treated the priest of the church with highest regards. "Sister Ruth has informed me that a letter had arrived. It was a few weeks back regarding an adoption that occured here many years ago?" Sister Abbey cautiously places the file down as if to conceal it. Unfortunately father Roberts could already see that she had the file. Father Roberts looks at sister Abbey in a scolding manner. He reaches down for the file and pulls it out of her hands. He opens it and looks it over for a moment. He then peers over the file at her. "You do understand how we could have serious repercussions for our actions regarding old adoptions of any kind, don't you?" Sister Abbey looks down to the ground. Father Roberts turns and walks out of the room with the file. Sister Abbey was not about to give up so quickly. She followed father Roberts out of the room into the hall. "Wait please... father wait." He stops and turns to her. "This story of this adoption, it was very sad. The only request this young lady had was to know of her sister. If she lived. If she can some day know her. Is that really too much to ask? I was simply going to send the letter to the adoptive parents to inform them. Why not let them decide? Is that so wrong?" Father Roberts stood there in deep thought for a moment. "I will need some time to look this over. I should bring this to the attention of the pastoral leadership." Sister Abbey became nervous instantly. "Wait please father, if you do that there is no chance they will allow this. Please reconsider?" Father Roberts was getting frustrated with her, but held his patience as he shook his head. "Sister Abbey trust is a very important thing, you must go and pray. We will re-visit this matter." He turns and continues his walk down the hall with the file. Sister Abbey just watches him walking away and sighs in frustration.

Abbey waits patiently for several weeks. Then while she was praying one day in the church as she finished up her final words and stood, sister Ruth calls to her attention. "Father Roberts wants you. He is in the library." Sister Abbey becomes anxious and hopeful immediately. She rushes to the library. Father Roberts is seated and reading as he looks up and there stands sister Abbey. "Yes father you wanted to speak with me?" Father Roberts completes his sentence and closes the book. He carefully sets it down on the table next to him. "I haven't spoken to anyone regarding this file." He points to the file that was sitting just under the book. "You see something that had to be considered is... if you simply sent this letter off to the adoptive parents. Let's just say Serena accidentally comes upon this letter." He scratches his chin as he speaks in deep thought. "Before the adoptive parents. That could lead to a disaster," *hmm*...he muttles. "That would mean the adoptive parents were not given the opportunity to make that decision. If they wanted to share any information." Abbey begins feeling distressed and worried as to the fathers decision. "You also don't know if these parents told Serena she was adopted. I think that also could lead to a disaster." He then sits up in his chair more sternly. "Don't you agree sister Abbey?" Abbey hadn't considered all of that, thus making her sad. She was feeling defeated in this situation. She wanted so much to help Annabelle, but she realized she hadn't considered everything as father Roberts had explained. "Yes father I guess I do agree." In that moment she realized she was wrong in her thinking. Then suddenly father Roberts stands and reaches over grabbing the file handing it to sister Abbey. She became shocked and confused. "Well then", father exclaims, "I think the proper way to handle this would be for YOU, sister Abbey to take a trip. You will go to these parents. This will enable you to be sure they are the ones who recieve the letter. Then they are given the opportunity to make the decision. If they want to pass it along to Serena." Abbey reaches out for the file smiling ear to ear. "How do you feel about that?" Sister Abbey was so suprised by his suggestion. She stepped back for a moment holding her mouth open not sure what to say. It wasn't often that nuns were sent out into the world. They mostly would only go out to help with certain charities, or hospitals. Father Roberts had come to the conclusion that Abbey had committed her entire life at this convent. In some way this is the workings of gods will. He felt she earned the respect and admiration of many. So with that, he felt this was a god guiding moment. She needed to do his works for this family. He arranged for her to take a trip to the last known address of the adoptive parents. He patted her on the shoulder. Then while clasping his hands together in a prayer motion he nods his head and proclaims, "god be with you." Sister Abbey immediately clasped her hands together and quickly echoed back to him "and also with you. Bless you father", as she grins and closes her eyes.

Sister Abbey was given train tickets and scheduled to begin this journey first thing the very next morning. It was a bit of an adventure for her. She felt blessed in many ways. She was headed to Los Angeles. According to the file the adoptive father was very much a part of the banking industry. Sister Abbey had high hopes that he stayed in the area and was thriving in that business. As Abbey headed out to the train station she kept her rosary beads in hand. She continued to pray for this to be a blessed venture. In whatever manner Gods will would be. Everyone at the station was very polite to her. She entered the train when they helped her carry her bag up. They then guided her to her seat. Once she arrived to her destination she started to feel nervous. She knew she couldn't give in to her doubts. One of the men at the station offered to help her since she was a bit confused. Abbey hadn't been this far out in a very long time. She informed the man she needed a ride to an address. He immediately called out for a driver in the station to take her where she needed to go. She sat back in the vehicle and took a short nap. Her old bones were getting tired. She desperately needed a little rest. When they arrived to the address the man called back to her. "Miss.... miss we are here." Abbey opened her eyes and as she looked out the window she could see a lot of large buildings. Just in front was a nice size home. Her first thought was, *well if she lives here she was a fortunate child.* Sister Abbey grabs her things and works her way out of the car. She offers to pay the man and he declines, "no mam... it was my pleasure mam." He waves his hand at her. "Well thank you kindly sir. God bless you." She stands at the enterance of the door for a few moments as the man drives away. She's so unsure how to talk to these people, what to say. A woman inside the house could see that the car had drove up and dropped someone off. Nobody came knocking at the door. It made her curious.."Hmm..." She then proceeded to open her front door. There stood Sister Abbey. The woman in the house was a tall blonde haired woman dressed very fancy. Her hair was perfectly pinned in place. She even had a little red lip stick on her lips. Her dress looked very expensive, at least to sister Abbey. "Hello can I help you?" The woman asked in confusion. Sister Abbey wasn't sure where to begin, so she just begins. "Well um..., yes of course, of course, um..." Sister Abbey proceeds to clear her throat. "I needed to speak to Mr. and Mr's Rol--la-n--d-u-s." She had much difficulty pronouncing the last name. Abbey couldn't honestly remember what the couple looked like. It was just too long ago. The woman chuckles, "yes Rolandus, yes that would be me. My first name is Dixie." She extends her hand politely to shake Abbeys. "Oh good, oh my goodness, I'm so grateful it's you." Dixie crunches her eyes together in confusion. Wondering to herself, *should I know this woman?* Suddenly Abbey realizes she needs to introduce herself. "I'm so sorry. How rude of me. My name is sister Abbey. May I come in? I need to speak with you more in private, is that possible?"

Dixie felt it was harmless enough, "of course come in please." Dixie guides her into the sitting room in their home. It was quite a fancy home. Satin curtains on all the windows. Victorian furnishings throughout. Many bookshelves full of books in a library. They were just before the sitting room. It was quite impressive. "You like to read? That is wonderful. So many books my... my..." Dixie chuckles again, "yes well our daughter does. She is studying to become a teacher. She absolutely loves books." Abbey suddenly becomes excited to hear that. "Oh that is so wonderful to hear." Now Dixie is becoming more concerned of this visit and starting to question what this nun is here for. "Mam please explain what I can do for you?" Abbey suddenly realizes she better get to the point. She pulls the letter out. While holding it in her hand, she begins to explain. "I don't know if you remember me? It seems you may not, but well...., well...., you see, you adopted Serena from our convent many, many years past." Suddenly Dixie is remembering Abbey now. "Wait yes I remember you I think. Why on earth would you be here so many years later? I don't understand?" Abbey begins again to explain. "This is very difficult, but there is something you and your husband did not know." She goes on to explain about the twin and most of the story on how Annabelle ended up with her father Salvador. She could tell that Dixie was becoming slightly annoyed so she stopped her story and simply handed her the letter Annabelle had written. Abbey puts the letter into Dixies hands. "Just consider reading this please? Consider what this child is asking please?" Before Dixie could answer suddenly someone comes through the front door and walked into the sitting room. Abbey looks over at the entrance and there she stood. Right before Abbey.

Dixie quickly turns and faces her, "Serena!" Suddenly you could see Dixie was not comfortable at this point. She quickly starts to guide Abbey out the door. Abbey just couldn't help, but stare at Serena for a moment. She didn't even realize Dixie was attempting to push her out quickly. Serena was beautiful. Just as Abbey imagined she would be. Serena became curious quickly, "mother why are you being so rude? Offer this sister a glass of lemonade, or something?" Her hair was pinned up just as her mothers was. She had the same thick dark hair like Annabelle. She was holding many large books in her hands. They appreared to be college books. Abbey always knew both the girls would have the thick hair. They were both most certainly born with a lot of hair. She had a beautiful natural glow in her soft beige skin. Big brown eyes and a very pleasant personality, so it seemed so far to Abbey. Dixie continued walking sister Abbey out to the front. Dixie began whispering to Abbey. "Please... please... you have to give me the opportunity to speak with my husband. Now please you should go." Abbey abides by her wishes while handing her the letter. First before she leaves the home she sais in a very low voice, "twins must know each other, or they stay empty. Please just decide to give her this letter? Serena needs to know of her sister. Also Annabelle needs to know of Serena." Abbey looks deep into the eyes of Dixie in hopes to persuade her. "Do you understand?" Abbey tried her very best to stress how important this was. Dixie simply nods her head and takes the letter from her while she guides her the rest of the way out of the home. As soon as sister Abbey is outside Dixie closes the door and Serena is standing firmly behind her. "Mother what on earth was that all about? That was not very nice?" Serena was extremely disapointed and truly confused of her mothers actions. Dixie just stood behind the door leaning on it in frustration. She clenched the letter in her hands close to her body. Trying to conceal it from Serena. It was a lot for Dixie to take in. She really wanted to see what this letter said and speak to her husband about it. She quickly looked around the room to try and come up with an explanation for her actions. Dixie saw her mail on the table with a few stamps on top. She had set them there earlier in the day. This gave her an idea, "oh Serena no worries. The local catholic church was selling stamps to raise money for something. It was nothing important to worry yourself about." Serena shook her head at her in confusion. She did accept the explanation. She grabbed a pencil off the side desk near the library, "well then I guess I will get back to my studies." She turns away and walks up the stairs. Dixie was relieved.

That evening after dinner Dixie quickly finishes her food and tells her husband they need to talk. They spent the first part of the evening going over this letter together. They both decide to share it with Serena. They had told Serena from the time she was ten that they had adopted her. They were never able to have children. She was their only child. For so many years Serena always felt lonely for a sibling. She would cry as a young child always saying to her mother, "I need a sister mommy." It always made Dixie sad because she could not give her a sibling. Dixie's only fear about this letter is that Serena will think they took her away from her sister. They honestly had no knowledge she existed. Serena was busy studying in her fathers office. She had many college exams to prepare for. Both Dixie and Serena's father came in to the room. Dixie lightly knocked as they entered. Serena looks up at both of them. She could easily see that something was wrong. Dixie simply places the letter on top of her book and they both turn and walk away. Serena pierces her eyes at them. Then at the letter. Serena calls after them, "what is this? Wait, wha...t is this?" Both of them just continued out of the room and down the stairs. She opens the envelope curious as could be. As she unfolds the papers and begins to read, her eyes become wide. She looks closer at the paper as if the letters were becoming smaller. Her mouth drops open and she covers it with one hand. Both of her parents were readying themselves for her questions while they waited in the sitting room.

Chapter 22

Annabelle was making an afternoon snack for the children. They would be returning home from school soon. She cut up some apples and made a plate for each of the children. She was nine months pregnant and extremely tired. She walked out the front door to watch for them. Suddenly up came a cab in her driveway. Little Shirley plops out of the back seat. At first Annabelle was about to panic, "what on earth?" Shirley was only three, she had no business in a cab. Just as Annabelle spoke, out came William home from Mexico. Apparently he saw Shirley and stopped the cab just before the house picking her up on the way. She was so excited as he stepped out of the cab she dropped her apron and ran directly to him. He was so tan from working in the sun for so long. His skin looked so dried out. He also looked very happy. He was pleased he was able to come home before Annabelle had their baby. William started rubbing her belly. He glanced over at Shirley, "are we ready for the new little baby?"

He smiled and kissed Annabelles stomach. As the rest of the children came home they were all very happy their pappa was home. They planned a big luncheon get together with all the neighbors. In celebration of William's home coming. All the woman brought their special recipes of something. They brought pies, potatoe salads, canned fruits with sweet beets. Everyone was having a delightful time. Then suddenly as Belle was setting down a plate on the picnic table she let out a loud moan, "ooooh... ooooh my.... ooooh...." She grabbed her stomach wincing her eyes in pain. William heard her and immediately rushed to her aid. "Belle, Belle is it time Belle?" Everyone knew she was going into labor. One of the neighbor ladies jumped up from her seat and ran over. Her husband rushed over as well. He went into his pocket grabbing his keys to his car and handed them to William. "Here William, go get my car." William rushes to the vehicle and pulls it closer to the house. They all get the kids in. Then William jumps back into the driver seat. Their friends help Annabelle in as well. William took off quickly while trying to hold Belles hand and drive. "It's ok baby...it's ok... I will get you there, it's ok." He was trying his best not to panic, but it definitely was a difficult task for him. As soon as William drove up at the emergency entrance he rushed in yelling, "doctor, doctor, I need a doctor. My wife is in labor!!" A couple of the nurses run to help him. One grabs a wheelchair. They follow William out and manage to get Annabelle in the chair rushing her in. William seemed confused, *should I go, ooh gotta get the kids, oh yeah....* One of the nurses steady him, "everything will be fine, just fine. Go on now get your children, park your car." The children were just as anxious knowing a new brother, or sister was on it's way soon. He gets them up to the waiting room and begins pacing back and forth, back and forth. It was rather comical for the children to watch. To them he was always so strong and generally serious. They had never seen him fumbling so much as he was. It was a very long wait. Most of the children fell asleep in their chairs. William couldn't sit still much longer. He was growing impatient. He walked up to the desk were the nurses where sitting. "Is there an update yet regarding my wife please." The nurse smiled she always knew when a new father was waiting. It was so much the same...just different faces. All the men were always so frantic. "Yes sir, if you could give me a moment. What's your wifes name?" He quickly gives her the information she needs. She steps through the revolving doors and heads down to the delivery room. It didn't take long for her return. As soon as she came back out William was right there, "well, well anything?" He was sweating as he asked insistantly. "Yes well, she's almost there. Just a little more time." William became flustered again. He just turned away and continued pacing.

The doctor came through the revolving doors about an hour later. He had his white mask and gloves on. He was standing there pulling the string out from behind his head. He removed the face mask. "Mr. Oros, Uhhhh... Mr. Oros!!" William quickly strided to his side, "yes, yes doctor that's me." The doctor was pleasant and grinned at William. "Yes, well you have a healthy baby boy. Born just a few minutes ago." William clapped his hands together over joyed once more. "Can I see my wife please? I need to see my wife?" The doctor waved over to the nurses station. "Yes, yes of course. Nurse please show him back?" One of the nurses stood up as William was going to go get the other children. The nurse named Miss Emily stops him. "Why don't you let me care for the children for a bit. It will give you time to see your wife. They should be fine." She waves her hand at him casually. William complies and checks on the children before following the other nurse. She guides him in to Annabelles room. You could see Annabelle was exhausted holding a small bundle in a blanket. She smiled wide at William as he entered the room. He crept forward slowly and gently pulling the blanket away from the babies face to see. As soon as he peeked in Annabelle announces to him, "we have another boy William." William smiles wide he was so proud. He gently rubs the babies cheeks. The baby grabs hold of his finger holding tight. "Ahhhhh look at that strong boy." Annabelle laughs. They both decided on the name to be Gilbert Warren Oros. Miss Emily felt it was time to allow the other children in to see the baby for a short moment. She anounces to them to wake. Their new baby brother has arrived and it's time for a visit. The children peeled their eyes open rubbing them and yawning. Little Shirley asks the nurse, "Is Mr. Brown here?" She was referring to the new baby. Miss Emily became confused. She leans down closer to little Shirley. "Who is Mr. Brown my dear?" Shirley grins and blushes. "That's the new babies name of course." She giggles not realizing little Shirley was feeling a little threatened by the new baby. She was slightly jealous thinking she wouldn't be the baby anymore. So she decided to nickname him Mr. Brown. Miss Emily simply smiles at her reaching out her hand to take Shirleys. She then reaches out her other hand to Billy. The nurse instructs Rozy to hold her brothers hand. They all walk with the nurse down the hall. As soon as they enter William holds up the baby to show them. "This is your new baby brother," he states proudly. Little Gilbert was a sweet baby. He was born with a full head of hair just like the other children. It was dark brown and very wavy. He had very round dark brown eyes. He resembled his mother in so many ways. After about a week the hospital let Annabelle and her new baby go home.

One afternoon William was sitting on the front porch having a cigar. Little Shirley strolled up to him and sat next to her pappa. "What ya doin pappa?" She loved chatting with him. He would tell her stories about the good old days. When he was younger. He loved that she was always so interested in his stories. He chuckled watching Roz and Billy fighting over a stick they had. Shirley always had so many questions. Her great curiosity amused him. "Pappa, what was it like riding a horse? How did you cattle cows? What did that mean? What's a rr..rrrancher?" "William laughs, woooah, wooah, one question at a time little Shirley." Shirley went on with her questions. She didn't even hear her pappa telling her to slow down. "Pappa, what was Mexico like? Can we go there too Pappa? Is it hot like here pappa?" William chuckled again. He turned to Shirley with a smile. "You are so cute little Shirley. I am very proud of you. Shirley stopped for a moment when he said those words to her. She arched up her back. She looked at her pappa and said, "you are pappa?" She got a wide smile across her face. He placed his hand on her head and rustled her hair. Then patted her on her head. "Of course I am. Some day little Shirley you will have all the answers. For it is the one who keeps asking the questions that someday has all the answers." He winks at her with his slanted eye. Then he reaches down and kisses her cheek. "I love you Meha. Always know that."

It took several months for Annabelle to get back into her routine. She enjoyed caring for her newest addition to the family. Belle would just lay there rocking baby Gilbert and look at him. Admiring how handsome he was. Annabelle was getting clothes together and burpy cloths, throwing them in her basket. Little Shirley saw a doll under Annabelle's bed. She reached down and pulled it out and placed her own doll down on the floor. "Mama who's dolly?" Belle looked over and saw that Shirley had found Annabelle's doll. The one she had through all those years past. The very doll Maria had made her so long ago. It took her into deep thought for a moment. Then she simply patted Shirley on the head. "It was your mommys doll. You can play with it Shirley." The button still sewn deep inside the pocket. Belle decided that's where it would stay forever. It was quite chaotic after Gilbert was born. With now four children, Annabelle had her hands full. One being such a small baby. She had so many dirty clothes. She took her large basket out to the yard. She also grabbed a small basket carrying baby Gilbert while he napped. Little Shirley followed behind with the new dolly in her arms. Shirleys hair in little mini pig tails with ribbons. She had on a sleeveless sundress. Her little frilly white socks, with shiny white shoes. She had cute chubby cheeks and a bright smile. Her little tiny fingers wrapped around the dolls arm as she dragged her behind. She would play innocently making the doll dance as she watched her mama hanging the clothes. Once again Annabelle starts to feel cheery she begins to hum. William could hear her from the backyard. He simply stops what he is doing for just a moment to listen. It was such a peaceful sound she would make. He walks towards the yard where Annabelle is humming. He just stands there admiring how beautiful of a woman she is. He looks over at all of his children. Each of them so special in his heart. William leaned back on the house just admiring his family. Rozanne and Billy were busy playing in the dirt not too far. Billy looking deep in the hole for ants. Rozanne filling up a cup with dirt pretending it was tea. William could see his entire family together before him and was so proud. Never did he imagine that his life would be so blessed. Shirley continued playing with the doll at Annabelles feet. As Annabelle would take each piece of clothing and hang them in place on the line to dry. She began to sing her favorite song. William then sat on the front step drinking a beer watching and listening. Annabelle begins to sing in a low, but bird like sound in perfect harmony. Her voice glides the words...... "I come to the garden alonnnee....while the dew is still on the roses....and the voice I hearrr....falling on my earrrr...the sonnnn of god disclosesss..." What none of them realized at that very moment as she was singing away. They were all busy just doing life today.... there was a woman.... coming down... **The Old Dusty Road.** * It was hot outside and you could hear all the distant noices of children playing. You could smell the fresh pies being set in the window sills. Annabelle still singing her delightful song. Yet in that very moment,... there she was... the last

---

*   in connection to this Novel is the childrens book, **The Old Dusty Road** written by: Shirley Randol/Oros www.authorhouse.com, ISBN # 978-1-44908-946-7.

piece to Annabelles life....... The most important piece......
The one thing to make her complete..... The final step to fill
that gaping hole she carried her entire life....... The answer
to all of her questions....... Yes..... it was that moment there
she was.... walking..... closer...... closer, down that old
dusty road..... She now stands just behind Annabelle.......
Shirley dancing so innocently behind her mommy. She
walks behind her mommy and begins to tug at her dress.
"Mommy.... mommy..... mommy.... she looooks.......... liiikke
youuu. She...... loooks..... like you....." Shirley adomently
pointing. Annabelle hears what she is saying, but doesn't
yet understand. As she turns to see what Shirley is pointing
at, Belle drops the clothes from her hands and stares for
a moment in complete awe. William stands to see what
made Belle stop singing. The children, Rozanne and Billy
also look over with curiousity. Belle slowly creeps forward,
without saying so much as a word. Everything seemed
completely silent.... She puts up her hand to touch the hand
of her.. **TWIN SISTER...... SERENA.** Standing there
before her......as if it were a..... *MIRROR IMAGE. Inside
Annabelle's mind and heart. Her life is now complete..........*